"ICE IN THE VEINS"

"I think that's him," his stakeout partner whispered over the unit radio.

Detective Dino LaStanza held his breath and waited for the longest seconds of his life. Listening for footsteps, his heart pounding with anticipation of the bust, he held back and waited for the order to move.

A few seconds later. "Now!"

LaStanza moved quickly and silently. Before the man could close the door of his car, Dino was on him, jamming the muzzle of his service .357 magnum against the man's jugular vein.

"Freeze!" he barked, cocking his gun. "Hands against the windshield. Now!"

The man reached forward slowly and placed his palms against the windshield, his eyes riveted in fear to the tough cop's hard stare.

"You're busted, moron. Now spread 'em!"

HAUTALA'S HORROR—HOLD ON
TO YOUR HEAD!

MOONDEATH   (1844-4, $3.95/$4.95)
Cooper Falls is a small, quiet New Hampshire town, the
kind you'd miss if you blinked an eye. But when darkness
falls and the full moon rises, an uneasy feeling filters
through the air; an unnerving foreboding that causes the
skin to prickle and the body to tense.

NIGHT STONE   (3030-4, $4.50/$5.50)
Their new house was a place of darkness and shadows, but
with her secret doll, Beth was no longer afraid. For as she
stared into the eyes of the wooden doll, she heard it call to
her and felt the force of its evil power. And she knew it
would tell her what she had to do.

MOON WALKER   (2598-X, $4.50/$5.50)
No one in Dyer, Maine ever questioned the strange disap-
pearances that plagued their town. And they never dis-
cussed the eerie figures seen harvesting the potato fields by
day . . . the slow, lumbering hulks with expressionless features and a blood-chilling deadness behind their eyes.

LITTLE BROTHERS   (2276-X, $3.95/$4.95)
It has been five years since Kip saw his mother horribly
murdered by a blur of "little brown things." But the "little
brothers" are about to emerge once again from their under-
ground lair. Only this time there will be no escape for the
young boy who witnessed their last feast!

HALLAL'S HORROR—HOLD ON

CRESCENT CITY KILLS

O'NEIL DE NOUX

ZEBRA BOOKS
KENSINGTON PUBLISHING CORP.

For Vincent

ZEBRA BOOKS

are published by

Kensington Publishing Corp.
475 Park Avenue South
New York, NY 10016

First printing: May, 1992

Printed in the United States of America

New Orleans is an island. With Lake Pontchartrain to the north, the Mississippi River to the south, the Rigolets and Lake Borgne to the east and the Bonnet Carre Spillway to the west, it is completely surrounded by water. It is also the only major American city that is below sea level. Therefore, it is encircled by a system of levees. With seasonal rainfall affecting water levels, a portion of land usually exists between the levees and the water's edge. This land is called a batture. It is pronounced "bat-chur," with the emphasis on the first syllable. It is from the French word *"battre,"* which means "to beat," because women used to beat their laundry on the rocks on the water side of the levee.

One
Lower Coast

LaStanza watched his new partner's high heels sink into the mud on top of the levee.

"Welcome to Homicide," he told her before starting down toward the flashlights at the edge of the river. Searchlights from two nearby tugs helped illuminate the entire area, giving the crime scene an eerie, movie-set look. An occasional raindrop floated through the lights like a slice of silver falling from the black sky.

LaStanza almost slipped on the concrete apron along the base of the levee and cursed his luck. The driest spring in memory, first rain in a month and *he* catches an outdoor murder scene.

Taking an indirect route to the men standing next to the river, he stopped several feet behind the last patrolman. Beyond the line of policemen, he could see two bodies partially submerged in the muddy Mississippi water. One of the spotlights was trained on the bodies.

He could see they were women, lying facedown in the brown mud, feet in the water, their arms tied behind their backs. Both were clad in jeans. One had a white tee shirt, the other a red jersey.

A flash of light behind LaStanza caused him to turn

around. A crime lab technician was taking photos from atop the levee. His name was Sturtz. He was an old-timer, even had the horn-rimmed glasses to prove it. He needed no instructions.

LaStanza watched Sturtz work his way down to the river. When the man arrived, burdened with his 120mm camera, strobe unit and large crime scene kit, LaStanza pointed to the footprints in the mud.

"Gotcha," Sturtz said, immediately moving in to take photos.

"Anyone go near them?" LaStanza asked loudly.

"No, sir," answered the nearest patrolman. The uniforms edged back out of the way.

"Well," Sturtz said when he finished photographing and measuring the footprints, "all we gotta do is find someone with muddy socks."

Leaning close, LaStanza examined the three sets of footprints that led to the bodies. Only one came back from the water's edge, one without shoes. The clear imprint of socks was imbedded in the mud. He remained on his haunches for a minute, studying the mud, looking for anything else, but there was nothing.

A pair of stocking feet moved next to LaStanza. He gazed at his partner's shapely legs. Standing slowly, his eyes traced their way up to her knees. She was wearing a gray skirt with a wide black belt and a white blouse with ruffles in front and a large bow tied at the neck. Her blond hair was cut into a page boy. Her fair face looked . . . pale. She blinked her cat eyes at him. Jodie Kintyre had hazel eyes, a little too wide set for her small face, long feline eyes that for the moment appeared larger than usual.

Even in her stockings, she was taller than LaStanza. He looked up into her eyes and saw that worried, rookie-homicide look staring back at him. He knew that look well. He remembered his first murder scene, a street in the French Quarter and a victim lying on the sidewalk and how his eyes bulged at all the blood and at the knowledge that he was no longer a by-stander.

Jodie blinked again. He winked back at her and then led the way through the mud with his partner and Sturtz close behind. After close-up photos were taken, LaStanza knelt in the mud next to the first body and began to call out details to his partner.

"Victim number one . . . black female . . . positioned on her stomach . . . feet in water . . . wearing a pair of black boots . . . blue jeans . . . white tee shirt . . . wrists tied with some kind of cord . . . a thin cord . . . tied in several tight knots."

He reached over and felt the victim's arm.

"She's cool to the touch but no rigor."

Her face was tilted to one side. LaStanza pointed out the wound to Sturtz, then waited for more photos before continuing.

"Entry wound . . . right temple . . . contact wound or close range . . . stippling and powder marks . . . small-caliber weapon."

He looked back at Jodie. "See the outline of the muzzle?"

She leaned over and nodded.

LaStanza turned to Sturtz and asked for the bags to wrap the hands.

"I'll do it," Sturtz started to argue.

"I'm already here. Just pass 'em."

The technician passed four brown paper bags, one at a time, along with several large rubber bands. LaStanza bagged each hand and sealed it off at the wrist with a rubber band.

Sitting up, he caught sight of a figure lumbering down the levee. Even in the dark, there was no mistaking Sergeant Stephen Stritzinger of the Fourth District. At six and a half feet tall, weighing three hundred and fifty pounds, Stritzinger stood out in a crowd, even when there was no crowd.

"Hey! Candy-Ass!" Stritzinger yelled as he approached.

"What the fuck you got here?"

LaStanza was thinking of a smart reply as the sergeant stepped up and leaned his fat face over the bodies and belched. The huge face, pockmarked from childhood acne, was swollen from too much drink and sported a red drinker's nose. There was a wide, bleary smile on the face, a smile that ignored the hard look in LaStanza's eyes.

Stritzinger was not only a drunk; he was the ugliest man in uniform. So ugly, he was once called to Internal Affairs for scaring children on Halloween by wearing a Frankenstein mask while driving his police car. Only he never wore a mask. He was that ugly. He was also the nastiest, most degenerate policeman LaStanza had ever met. He was so gross, his nickname was Poo-Poo. And he *liked* it.

"Hey, Candy-Ass," Poo-Poo said as he looked around. "Who's the blonde?"

This caused the patrolmen to start snickering.

Focusing back on the body, LaStanza pointed to the wound again and told his partner, "See the way it's jagged, ripped like that? That's caused from gases exploding out from the skull when the pellet went in. That causes the skin to tear outward. But it's still an entry wound."

Jodie nodded as she jotted furiously in her notebook.

"She . . . your partner?" Poo-Poo asked.

Ignoring Poo-Poo never discouraged him. He belched again and said, "You fuckin' her?"

The patrolmen started easing away, unable to control their laughter.

LaStanza turned to the pink face and growled, "Why don't you just get the fuck outta here?"

Poo-Poo began to chuckle.

LaStanza stood up slowly and spoke to his partner. "We'll wait for the coroner to see if it's a perforated wound."

He could see a hint of confusion on her face.

"A perforated wound means through and through. A penetrating wound means entry and no exit."

10

"Right," Jodie agreed.

Chances were it was not through and through. Small calibers rarely came out the other side. They just bounced around inside. LaStanza remembered a murder where a man was shot in the shoulder with a .22, and the bullet ran brokenfield through the body, nipping the aorta, puncturing the vena cava, and perforating a lung before ending up in the heart muscle.

"Didn't you used to work in Auto Theft, little lady?" Poo-Poo had taken a step toward Jodie.

"No." She started to back away from the large man. "I was in Juvenile."

"Jodie," LaStanza said quietly, "don't answer him."

Poo-Poo nodded toward LaStanza. "He fuckin' you yet?"

Jodie didn't even blink. She may have been a homicide rookie, but she'd been a cop for five years.

LaStanza rose, stepped on the instep of Poo-Poo's right foot, and gave the big belly a gentle shove. Stritzinger stumbled back and fell on his ass in the mud.

The patrolmen scattered, some bellowing at the sight of the fat sergeant in the mud.

Narrowing his Sicilian eyes, LaStanza leaned toward Poo-Poo and snarled in a low, mean voice, "Get the fuck off my scene!"

He watched Stritzinger struggle to stand and wipe the mud from his ass before waddling back toward the levee. The obesity was actually laughing.

Two cadaverous coroner's attendants arrived as Poo-Poo reached the top of the levee. They came down to prepare the bodies and haul them out. As usual, no doctor came to declare death or perform even the most elementary examination of the corpses.

Before the victims were bagged, Sturtz took more close-up photos. Then LaStanza examined them more carefully. The second body was tied in the same manner as the first. She also wore black boots, except hers had no boot laces. Her laces had

11

been used to tie both victims' hands. The wound to her left temple was also a contact wound. There was no exit wound on either body as well as no identification.

"Well, at least we got pellets," Sturtz said.

Rolling the second victim over, LaStanza pulled her shirt up and examined her belly. There was no purplish lividity present. That and the lack of rigor told him that they had been killed not more than a few hours earlier, three or four hours at the most. He checked the victim's back and arms carefully in the unlikely event the bodies had been moved and the blood had already settled in another part of the body.

Sitting up, he turned to his partner and said, "You know the worst part?"

Jodie shrugged.

"One had to get it first."

"Oh," she said in a whisper, "yeah."

"Can you imagine knowing you're next," Sturtz added.

The attendants zipped the bodies into large black plastic bags before dragging them up the levee to the meat wagon. Sturtz began a deliberate search of the area, starting at the mud, in ever-widening circles, taking soil samples of the mud and then from the levee.

Jodie secured a statement from the tugboat captain who had found the bodies. LaStanza took the names of everyone else at the scene. He made sure no one escaped. It must have been a slow night. Besides Stritzinger, there were two other sergeants, three Fourth District patrolmen, a lieutenant, a state trooper, two Orleans Levee Board patrolmen, a Mississippi River Bridge cop, along with a pair of EMTs who never made it beyond the top of the levee. Two Plaquemines Parish deputies had come up from Belle Chasse because it was a *real* slow night in Plaquemines. And of course, there were the mandatory two Harbor policemen. LaStanza had been a cop for eight years and still had no idea what Harbor policemen were supposed to do, except fuck up crime scenes.

One of the patrolmen, a rookie fresh out of the academy, a

12

Dudley Doright-looking kid named Kelly, had been the first cop at the scene. LaStanza spoke to him at the top of the levee.

"I didn't pass any cars on the way here" — he pointed to the River Road — "and I watched the houses and didn't see any lights on either."

"Good."

"I'll check for any tickets or suspicious-person calls back at the district when I get back, okay?"

"You get anything, call me."

Kelly nodded and started down the levee toward River Road.

"You think of anything else," LaStanza said, "go ahead and do it."

"Thanks."

At least he was eager. He was all of twenty and looked it. He was not much younger than Jodie Kintyre, LaStanza reminded himself.

At the bottom of the levee, Kelly called back, "Stritzinger's a big asshole, ain't he?"

"Biggest douche-bag I ever saw!"

Kelly got a hard laugh out of that.

LaStanza turned back to the crime scene. He noticed, for the first time, the tall trees standing over the water. In a few weeks the entire area would be gone. The water would rise and erase the batture until the following autumn.

Across the river, the city lights blazed like some faraway Disneyland. Exactly seventeen miles from Headquarters, thirty minutes by car, Detective Dino LaStanza stood at the edge of Orleans Parish. It was called the Lower Coast of Algiers. It had as much in common with the rest of New Orleans as it had with its North African namesake.

He turned the other way and looked down at the River Road and the line of police cars parked along the narrow street. One by one, they were beginning to leave, the meat wagon leading the way back up the road that followed the river's winding path to New Orleans and points beyond.

It was even darker on the other side of River Road. Between the sporadic country houses, the Lower Coast consisted of thick woodland. There wasn't a house within a quarter mile of the scene. The killer had picked a good spot.

Turning again to the crime scene, he watched his partner. Still in her stockings, standing in the mud at the river's edge, she was finishing the tug captain's statement. LaStanza sucked in a deep breath of moist, sticky air. He had his work cut out for him. He was the case officer.

He used to get a knot in his stomach at the idea of it. He used to worry that he wouldn't solve it. Now he felt confident. Without a hint of arrogance, he knew he would find the killer. It was just a matter of time. The thought almost caused him to smile. He relished it so, the thrill of the chase. The long hours would take their toll. But in the end, he knew, he'd get the son-of-a-bitch. He always did.

The air was misty now, as if the rain might start up again at any second. LaStanza was thinking of the steps to take. First, he must find out who the victims were and everything else he could learn about them; only then could he find who did this to them.

When Jodie finished her statement, she joined her partner atop the levee and walked down with him to their car. LaStanza popped the trunk of their unmarked Chevy, took off his shoes and tossed them inside.

"Damn!" Jodie snapped and started back up the levee for her heels.

He pulled off his socks and threw them in with his shoes, watching as his partner crested the levee, bent over and yanked her heels out of the mud. She cut a nice figure, a little on the thin side, which made her look almost fragile. But *any* woman who would leave her high heels behind had the makings of a homicide man. At least he hoped so, for his sake. No, for her sake.

Jodie's heels joined his shoes in the trunk.

LaStanza climbed into the car. "Okay, let's canvass."

14

"Canvass what?" Jodie held her arms outspread.

LaStanza looked up the River Road and then down and realized that he could not see one hundred feet in either direction. From atop the levee a couple houses had been visible, but at ground level, along the twisting road, he could see nothing. The killer had indeed picked his spot well.

"Ammo dump?" Jodie said. She was pointing her flashlight a few feet away at the two yellow railroad rails sticking out of the ground in front of what once had been a ramp up the levee. Atop one of the rails was a small white sign with black stenciling that read: "Ammo Dump Ramp #2." A smaller "No Trespassing" sign dangled on a steel cable between the rails.

"You got me!" LaStanza finally answered.

He cranked up the Chevy and waited for Jodie to get in, then hit the brights and started slowly down the road. He stopped next to the first telephone pole and asked his partner to use her flashlight to read the sign nailed there.

"It says 'No discharging firearms.'"

"Sumbitch can't fuckin' read!" LaStanza glanced back at the yellow rails. "Ammo dump ramp number two. You gotta admit, our boy's got a flare for the dramatic."

There was one residence between the crime scene and the dead end of River Road at the Plaquemines Parish line, a two-story English manor house with a double garage and a white-haired owner named Clark.

When LaStanza asked if Clark had heard anything that evening, the man growled, "Do you know what time it is?"

"About two."

"I've been asleep since eleven!"

"Well, did you hear any gunfire?"

"You kiddin'? I hear shots all the time. This is the *country!*"

LaStanza told him about the double murder.

"Damn," the old man's voice rasped, "we live over here to get away from your crime!"

Their crime? LaStanza tightened his jaw and made note of the man's name, address and the time of the interview

15

in his own notebook.

Jodie broke the silence with, "There's a sign back there that says 'Ammo Dump Ramp'; do you know what it means?"

"Sure." The man's voice softened when addressing Jodie. "Used to be a World War Two armory at the parish line." He pointed toward the dead end of River Road. "The dump ramps were for the ammo barges."

"Oh."

Jodie thanked him as LaStanza turned to leave.

Clark added, "It's been closed a long time now."

"Thanks," she called back.

Continuing their investigation, they woke another country dweller a quarter mile on the New Orleans side of the crime scene. This one was an albino who *never* heard gunfire, even in the country.

Ten minutes later and ten miles up the twisting road, Jodie asked, "So what do we do now?"

"Too late for the news and even the *Picayune*. So we can take our time writing up scripts of the victims for the morning news. Then we get a couple hours' rest before the autopsies."

"Oh, yeah."

A minute later, he added, "When we get back to the Bureau, you call Headquarters in case the girls were reported missing this evening."

"Want me to check Missing Persons?"

"Why not? But I doubt they've been missing that long."

"Yeah."

He could see her watching him. "What is it?" he asked.

"Who was that fat sergeant?"

He told her about Poo-Poo, about the Frankenstein mask, about his using obscenities on the police radio, as well as the words "niggers," "spicks," "bone heads" and "porch monkeys," about asking if he could take "greasy dumps" while on duty, and about his penchant for going to bed with retarded women . . . no . . . "watermelon heads."

"Wanna hear any more?"

16

"Nope."

Approaching the Mississippi River Bridge, their sergeant called them on the radio. LaStanza nodded for Jodie to answer.

"Need any help?" Sergeant Mark Land asked.

Jodie told him it was under control and they were headed for the office.

"So am I," Mark said. He had just finished helping at another homicide scene.

"You shoulda seen this one," Mark said, "30 . . . 29S . . . with a butcher knife. Reminded me of the Unicorn. Except in the temples instead of the forehead."

LaStanza had to smile. He shook his head and told Jodie about the Unicorn Murder, about a large black man named Richard Lionel whose girlfriend implanted a butcher knife in his forehead, all the way to the hilt.

"Son-of-a-bitch was still alive at the hospital. He was blinking. So we asked the doctor to make sure he saved the knife for us. The doc said we could get it at the autopsy. Then Lionel stopped blinking. Goddam doctor killed him."

Jodie shuddered.

"Jesus," he added a moment later, "in the temples. That must have been a sight."

"He did say a suicide-murder, didn't he?" Jodie asked.

"Yeah."

"Suicide by butcher knife?"

"Hell, I've seen suicide by electrocution, by Drano, by light bulbs up the anus, by Pam, by train. Asshole put his head across the tracks and waited for the train."

"By Pam?"

"Yeah, the grease-spray. It gets them high; only it coats the lungs and they die."

"Light bulbs up the anus?"

He shrugged. "Welcome to Homicide."

* * *

17

The decor of the Homicide Office was apropos to its use. The walls were gray, the desks were gray, the chairs were gray, even the coffeepot was gray. The clock above the coffeepot, also gray, always ran ten minutes late. Just below the clock hung the unofficial logo of the New Orleans Homicide Division, a drawing of a vulture perched atop an N.O.P.D. star-and-crescent badge.

The clock read 2:45 A.M. when LaStanza and his partner waltzed in. Mark Land was fixing a fresh pot of coffee-and-chicory. Needing a haircut and a trim on his Pancho Villa moustache, Mark looked more bearlike than usual, especially hovering over the small coffee table just outside his office.

LaStanza stopped by his desk, dug out his coffee mug and joined his sergeant. Jodie was right behind, carrying her pink mug with small red hearts on it. LaStanza's mug was black with red printing on the side that read: FUCK THIS SHIT.

"Where's Country-Ass?" LaStanza asked.

"Dino, my boy, he took his new partner home. Seems Keith what's-his-name got a little squeamish at the scene."

LaStanza started to laugh, caught sight of his partner's nervous face, and let it lie.

Mark laughed. "Sumbitch turned green when he saw that knife sticking out of that temple." Then he told Jodie the story of the Unicorn Murder. She kept her face as still as possible.

When the strong coffee was ready, LaStanza grabbed the pot and filled all three cups, adding cream and two sugars to his own before returning to his desk.

"Pull up a chair," he told his partner. He grabbed a form, rolled it into the beat-up Smith-Corona typewriter on his desk, also gray, and began to type out the daily on the Batture Murders.

TO: Lieutenant R. Mason, Homicide
FROM: Detectives D. LaStanza and J. Kintyre, Homicide
DATE: Saturday, 20 March
ITEM: C1686

SIGNAL: 14:30 (First Degree Murder) 2 counts
VICTIM #1:

"Okay, give me the script on number one."

Jodie read from her notes the description of the girl with the white tee shirt, running a hand through her hair. Her notes were thorough. He liked that.

Between sips of coffee, LaStanza wrote his lieutenant all the data necessary for the early-morning news release. Somewhere, near the end of his report, he felt his stomach begin tightening up a little, just a little. He found himself tugging nervously at his moustache. He was beginning to feel it, he told himself, the homicide pressure cooker.

There were two bodies lying in the morgue without names, without identities, with nothing left . . . but him. He was the case officer. He was responsible.

"Hey," Mark called out from his cubicle, where he was typing the butcher knife murder-suicide daily. "Where are your shoes?"

On the way home, Jodie sat silently in the passenger seat, going over her notes again. She was thorough. On the only other case they'd worked together, an unclassified death that turned out to be a natural, her notes had been excellent.

"I just remembered another," LaStanza said a few minutes later.

"What?"

"Suicide by filet."

Jodie smiled.

"Guy in Broadmoor," he said. "A paranoid schizophrenic. He had an 'out of body' experience, wrote us a nice note and then fileted his left arm down to the bone in four long slices."

"Bled to death?"

" 'Exsanguination,' that's the scientific term for bleeding to death."

19

He saw her making note of it.

Turning off St. Charles Avenue on Calhoun Street, he slowed down, turned on Garfield and eased to the dead end along Exposition Boulevard. The Chevy's engine continued to sputter and spit after he turned it off.

Climbing out, he stretched and yawned and glanced at his watch. It was almost four. Jodie came around with her keys in hand.

He popped the trunk and grabbed his briefcase, muddy shoes and socks.

"I'll pick you up at seven sharp," he told her.

"Pick me up?"

"We're riding in style tomorrow."

He waited for her to pull away before walking down the wide sidewalk known as Exposition Boulevard. He looked out at the darkness of Audubon Park. The huge oaks, with their spanish moss, loomed over him like pitch-black giants with gray beards. Their leaves, brushed by the warm spring breeze, sounded like distant waves rolling to shore.

Reaching his house, he slipped open the wrought iron gate of his front yard and moved across the fine-trimmed lawn. He climbed the five steps to the front gallery and unlocked both locks of the cut glass front door. He reached in and punched his code into the alarm box to deactivate the system. After locking the door behind him, he reactivated the alarm, dropped his shoes and socks in the foyer next to his briefcase, along with his dirty pants, jacket, shirt and tie, then ascended the large spiral staircase in his Jockeys, his .357 magnum and ankle holster in hand.

He tried not to wake Lizette when he slipped into bed, but she rolled over and hugged him.

"What time is it?" she asked.

"Almost four," he whispered. "Go back to sleep."

It was so dark, he couldn't even see her, but she leaned over and found his lips and kissed him. Snuggling in his arms, she sighed and began to breath in regular rhythms that helped lull him into a fitful sleep.

He could feel his eyes moving beneath his eyelids. He could see . . . the levee again and the mud and the hands tied behind their backs and the look of death on their faces. But whose faces? Who were they?

He saw flashes of muddy stockings and horn-rimmed glasses and craggy entry wounds and boots without laces and trees looming . . . like ghosts. . . .

Two
Rosa Park

Just before waking, LaStanza dreamed of a girl in a tight red skirt. She was sitting at a desk. No, she was slumped over the desk, her white blouse covered with blood. Her face was to one side. He moved her long sandy hair and saw her blue eyes were open — and her lips were moving. He leaned over and she whispered, ". . . old . . . oldie . . ." He turned off her typewriter as the alarm clock rang.

He watched Lizette for a minute before getting up. Pressed up against him in a fetal position, she looked like a little girl, all snugly in her bed. He kissed her lips softly, and she sighed. His head ached, but he got up anyway and headed for the shower.

LaStanza's new, midnight blue Maserati started without any hesitation. He let it warm up a minute, and popped a tape into the cassette player, then turned up the volume. The tape hissed until guitar strains began a slow moan, followed by a snare drum and Marvin Gaye's voice smoothing in with his classic, "I Heard It Through the Grapevine."

Slipping the Maserati into drive, LaStanza pulled out on Garfield Street. The garage door closed automatically behind him. Tapping his fingers on the steering wheel, he rolled his shoulders to his favorite blues song. He touched the air-conditioner switch, putting it on low, and settled back in the deep, leather seat. Two songs later he pulled up in front of his partner's house and tapped the horn. It was 6:59 A.M.

Jodie lived in a tan, shotgun double on Milan Street. Her parents lived on the river side of the double, the two homes divided by a party wall. In the week they'd been partners, LaStanza hadn't seen her parents. He was beginning to wonder about them. Non-meddling parents were rarer than honest lawyers.

Jodie came out a minute later, carrying her briefcase and portable radio, a small purse slung over her shoulder. She took a moment locking the dead bolt before stepping down the small front stoop and crossing the tiny front yard.

She was wearing another conservative suit, a dark blue jacket and matching skirt, and a high-collar blouse, buttoned up and snug. There were buttons on the front of her skirt as well, which were also fastened snugly. She never missed a button. She also never seemed to need a lot of sleep.

"Get enough sleep?" he asked anyway.

"Nope." She grinned and climbed in. There wasn't a bag under either eye.

She pointed to his dark blue suit and said, "Wanna wear green tomorrow?"

"I never wear green."

"But you have green eyes."

Jesus, he thought, *not again.*

"I wore enough green in the army." Turning on Magazine Street, he added, "Did you practice this routine with my wife, or what?"

"Huh?"

"Never mind."

When Lizette had bought him a bunch of new suits, she had tried slipping a green one in on him. So he'd told her he never wore green. "Period." He also didn't like the idea of wearing the same color as his partner. He'd never had that problem with Snowood. LaStanza never wore rawhide.

Jodie leaned back, crossed her legs and said, "So, this is the hot rod, huh?"

"Hot rods don't have four doors."

"Oh," she said, her mouth fighting back a smile. "Is this a Spyder?"

"No," he answered slowly, "a Biturbo 425I." He narrowed his eyes at her, wondering what she was up to.

She ran her hand across the Swiss clock in the center of the rosewood dashboard and added the punchline, "Snowood says it must be nice to have a wife who buys you a bachelor car."

She chose the word "bachelor." Snowood called the Maserati a "pussy" car.

"My wife gave it to me *after* the honeymoon. I was that good."

Jodie snickered and settled back in her own leather seat.

She was being cute. He wondered how cute she was going to be when the scalpels hit the flesh at the autopsies. She didn't look nervous, yet.

Turning off Toledano on Broad Street, he remembered what Lizette had said when she bought both Maseratis, her burgundy and his midnight blue. "These are made for people named LaStanza."

At first he'd had a hard time getting used to it, especially the looks from people at stop lights. But he liked the sunroof and the easy way it handled and accelerated and especially the booming tape player when he cranked up the volume. He'd needed a new car anyway.

Dr. Turan "Goosey" Lucy was a creative pathologist. An ex-hippie, who was an FBI informer during the sixties, he used his liberal mind to come up with unique classifications of death. He invented the term "Death by Misadventure," which meant "I don't know how the fuck he died, so don't ask me again." This was used on corpses that had been dead too long to tell the cause of death. He also invented "A.P.D." or "Advanced Postmortem Decomposition." This was used on bums and derelicts who were "decaying before they died."

He wore thick black glasses and sported a thick moustache filled with the remnants of whatever he'd eaten in the last few days. He was bald-headed and fat, liked to smoke cigars during autopsies and usually spent the first autopsy each morning downing an egg salad sandwich or a tuna fish on rye.

He was munching a sandwich when LaStanza and his partner stepped into the Chamber of Horrors, which was the more common, more accurate, name for the New Orleans Coroner's Office Morgue. LaStanza couldn't tell what kind of sandwich it was because ketchup was dripping from Goosey's mouth.

The doctor nodded recognition at the detectives and ducked back into his office, like a hamster, protecting his munchies.

LaStanza grabbed one of the morgue attendants and asked if the Batture Murder victims could be first on the two tables in the cutting room. The attendant's large black face remained void of expression as the man nodded slowly and waved his co-worker over. These were men of few words. Silently, they located the two bodies from the pile of black bags in the hallway and hauled them onto the stainless steel tables.

A new crime lab technician showed up early, so LaStanza put him to work right away. He was tall, with hunched shoulders and the same disposition as the morgue attendants. He worked like a zombie. But at least he worked.

The bodies were photographed again, full lengths as well as close-ups of the faces for identification purposes. The bags were removed carefully from each hand and put into separate, larger paper bags, each marked accordingly: Victim #1 RH, Victim #1 LH, Victim #2 RH, Victim #2 LH. Then the hands were examined closely for any trace evidence, fibers or hairs. The technician collected the surface residue before scraping beneath the fingernails for additional evidence.

Before the victims were fingerprinted, LaStanza asked for a neutron activation test on the hands.

"What for?" the technician said.

LaStanza just stared at him.

"You think they shot each other?" The technician was getting hot.

LaStanza felt his temper rising.

"Look," he said in a strained voice, "if you don't want to do it, just leave and I'll call the lab for another tech." He felt more like yelling, "Just *fuckin'* do it!"

The technician did it. He huffed and slammed the lid of his crime kit a couple times, but he did it. LaStanza turned away but watched to make sure it was done right.

Jodie moved behind him and asked, "What kind of test is this?"

As the technician swabbed each hand, LaStanza took her aside and explained about antimony and barium and how these elements were rarely found together but were always in the primer caps of center-fire bullets. Then he told her how the residue would linger on the hands, but only if the weapon was not a closed-breech weapon like an automatic. It worked with revolvers.

"And," he added, "gather all the evidence available when you can. Cover *all* possibilities."

She nodded automatically.

LaStanza turned his attention to the boot laces as the technician cut them, careful not to disturb the knots. Then the victims were fingerprinted before the attendants removed the clothing, which the technician collected, putting each article in a separate paper bag for subsequent examination. Jodie took careful note of each garment as it was removed.

When the bodies lay naked on the tables, LaStanza pointed to Victim #2 and said, "Now, that's something you don't see every day." The girl had a shaved vagina. "Probably a whore. They do that in the Sixth District," he told his partner. The victim also had a gold front tooth with a five-point star cut out of its center.

Reaching over, he examined the victim's arms. Her needle marks looked like railroad tracks. "Okay, we got one black whore dope fiend here."

"Here, too." Jodie pointed to the telltale needle marks on the left arm of Victim #1.

"Good," LaStanza said, "at least they aren't nice college girls."

"How old do you think they were?" she asked.

"Nineteen or twenty."

"Awfully young."

"Not for a whore."

LaStanza turned to one of the attendants. "See any tattoos or scars?"

The man pointed a large finger at Victim #2's right elbow. There was a two-inch scar there. Dino signaled his partner to make note.

The technician began taking samples of head hair and pubic hair from Victim #1 as Paul Snowood and his new partner, Keith what's-his-name, strolled in.

"*Shit!*" Paul complained immediately.

LaStanza grinned at his old partner. "See what you get for being late?"

They would have to wait for LaStanza's autopsies before getting to the postmortems of their butcher knife victims.

"What the fuck time did you get here, anyway?" Snowood was wearing another Country-Ass outfit, this one somewhat toned down, for him. His suit only had moderate western piping. But the rope tie with the longhorn clip and the red cowboy boots gave him away. He must have left his Stetson in the car.

The morgue attendants began to measure the length of the victims. Jodie took notes. Cadavers on autopsy tables were measured in length, not height. Victim #2 was five feet even. The other was five feet two inches.

A high-strung voice broke the quiet with, "Why is it when you guys ride together, we only see one head?" It was Keith what's-his-name. Standing just inside the door of the cutting room, he tried to smile at his own joke but only succeeded in getting his lips to quiver. He was tall, balding and looked more fruity than usual, standing erect and trying to smile.

"If you don't know how to tell a joke," Jodie snapped back, "don't try."

"It's Paul's joke," Keith what's-his-name tried to explain. It sounded like a Snowood joke, without the country accent or the proper timing.

Snowood disgustedly tucked a wad of smokeless tobacco beneath his lip and plopped down in the only folding chair in the place.

Goosey Lucy picked that moment to enter, brushing past Keith what's-his-name and heading straight for the vagina of Victim #1. He had a swab in his right hand and stuck it into the vagina. Dropping the swab into a vial, he then took a sample from the anus with a new swab and likewise went after the throat. Then he moved to the second victim. The swabs would be checked for seminal fluid.

Gunpowder, soot and stippling were secured from each wound. Goosey's movements were like a well-choreographed dance of death. Floating back and forth between the autopsy tables, the pathologist began dictating his findings into the microphone dangling from the ceiling between the two tables.

Goosey and one attendant simultaneously produced scalpels and began the long "Y" incisions across the chests of the victims, above their breasts and then down the center of their bodies to the top of the vagina.

LaStanza was watching Jodie without her noticing. She was holding up well. Her nose crinkled when the bodies were opened and the initial stale smell filled the dense air of the small room. He remembered how he used to ease away when the bodies were opened. Now he didn't move away at all. Jodie eased back half a step, her eyes fixed on Goosey and his smooth-moving razor-knife.

Blood samples were taken. Then fluid was drawn from each eye. "That's where drugs and alcohol linger the longest," La-Stanza told his partner. Then he heard a loud crash behind them.

Keith what's-his-name was lying faceup in the doorway. LaStanza shot a quick look at Snowood, who was sitting with his mouth open. When their eyes met, LaStanza couldn't help but laugh.

"Splash some water on his face," Goosey said as he lit up a large cigar. "He'll recover. Eventually."

Jodie grabbed a paper towel, wetted it in the sink next to the door and knelt over Keith what's-his-name. She put the towel on his face.

Snowood looked away in disgust. *"Jesus.* A girl has to help him."

"Nice partner you got there," LaStanza said.

"If he dies," Snowood barked back, "shove him in a cooler."

Jodie helped Keith sit up and left him propped in the doorway.

"Put your head between your legs," Goosey told him.

"Yeah," Paul snarled, "you must be *used* to that!"

The autopsies produced the usual carnage. With the body cavities laid open, the organs were withdrawn and examined, measured and sliced like loaves of bread, before they were tossed back into the empty abdomen, like wet leftovers.

Then the faces were peeled away from the skull, and the shuddering cranial saws sent a fine mist of bone in the air until the cranium was ready to be lifted away from the brain.

Goosey paused over the head of Victim #1. He traced the path of the bullet through the brain, reached his gloved fingers next to the interior wall of the left side of the skull and withdrew a small-caliber, semi-jacketed pellet. It was in poor shape. He immediately withdrew a diamond scriber from the lapel pocket of his Morgus-the-Magnificent smock and inscribed his initials on the base of the bullet.

29

LaStanza made sure Jodie got the trajectory of the bullet correctly. It was right to left through the brain to the mid-lateral wall of the cranium where the pellet was found. Trajectory was fifteen degrees down and ten degrees back to front.

The same procedure produced a similar pellet from the brain of Victim #2. Except here, the trajectory of the bullet was left to right through the brain to the mid-lateral wall of the cranium where the pellet was found. Trajectory was fifteen degrees down and five degrees back to front.

"Probably kneeling when shot." Goosey stated the obvious conclusion.

After the technician put the pellets in separate envelopes, each clearly marked with the victim's number, LaStanza put the envelopes in his coat pocket.

Goosey added a postscript to the postmortems before LaStanza and his partner left. He was certain that Victim #2 breathed for a short time after she was shot.

"That's a cheerful thought," LaStanza said.

"Hey," Snowood called out as they were leaving, "why don't ya stay for the butcher knife twins?"

Jodie crinkled her nose again.

LaStanza looked over at Keith what's-his-name, who was sitting in the hall outside the autopsy room, his back up against the wall.

"I knew a guy named Keith in high school," Dino said. "He was an asshole."

Snowood said, "So fuckin' what?"

"So I never met a Keith who wasn't an asshole, that's all."

"You okay?" LaStanza asked Jodie as they crossed Gravier on their way up to the office.

"Finger's tired." She inhaled a deep gulp of fresh air and added, "Writer's cramp."

"Like I told you the first day. A pen's more important than a gun in Homicide."

"Then, why does Snowood call you Wyatt?" She was being cute again.

"Because he can't shoot worth shit."

LaStanza dropped off the pellets to Fat Frank Hammond in the crime lab. Slurping a Barq's creme soda, Frank belched in acknowledgement when asked for a quick examination of the pellets.

"I'll call ya upstairs in a few."

Jodie had already begun the daily report on the postmortems. He plopped at his desk, which faced hers, and said, "Think I'll follow up with missing persons." He reached for their communal phone.

"Already did that." She was typing at a furious pace. He hadn't realized how good a typist she was.

"Well, not much more to do until someone misses them," he said. He still had the phone in his hand, so he decided to call Lizette. The answering machine was on at their house, so he knew she was already at her parents' party. He smiled to himself. At least the Saturday autopsies produced one good result. He got out of the party.

When he put the receiver down, it rang immediately. It was Fat Frank. "It's a .22, all right," the man said. "Both pellets from the same gun. I'll hold 'em for the tech."

"Can you tell what model gun?"

"Not really. So many goddam .22's out there, it's fuckin' ridiculous."

"Thanks."

LaStanza called Lizette at her parents'. One of the maids answered, and he could hear muffled voices in the background when she put the receiver down to locate his wife.

"Good," Lizette said when she came on, "you're finished?"

"Yeah."

"Come on. It's lunch time and I need rescuing."

He hung up and told his partner, "Hey, padna. Lunch!"

Jodie crinkled her nose once again.

* * *

The Louviers had given the mansion on Exposition Boulevard to their daughter when Lizette married. Fulfilling Mrs. Louvier's life-long dream of living on St. Charles Avenue, they took their Greta Garbo sofa and Prince Murat campaign chair and the rest of their antiques and moved to an estate at the corner of St. Charles and Rosa Park.

LaStanza parked the Maserati on the avenue, directly in front of the estate, even though there were valets, two black guys in white tuxedo coats, standing at the entrance to Rosa Park next to the large signs that read: PRIVATE STREET—DO NOT ENTER. Louvier parties always provided valet parking.

Jodie shook her head. "Your in-laws live *here?*"

LaStanza nodded at the three-story, florescent white, Greek Revival estate. An even dozen large Greek columns ran along the front and uptown side of the gallery. Six smaller columns ran along the second-story veranda. Twenty wide marble stairs led up to the front gallery. Dino had counted them. There was a sheltered driveway on the Rosa Park side of the house with more Greek columns holding up the gingerbread overhang. The entire property was surrounded by a low, rock wall.

"Looks like a funeral home, doesn't it?"

Jodie agreed. She was still inside the car, so he told her to get out.

"They won't bite."

She hesitated.

He wanted to introduce his new partner to all the beautiful people in pastel colors, women in stockings of pale green and powder blue and especially off-white, with cute names like Muffin and Tweety.

"Come on. I want you to meet a couple full-grown men named Biff and Scooter."

The front door of the mansion opened, and Lizette came out. He had to smile. She was decked out in a black, double-

32

breasted jacket and a white, fitted miniskirt, gray stockings and black high heels. She had curled her long dark hair. Her lips looked extra pouty with the bright brown lipstick. Her nine-year-old brother followed her down the marble steps.

"Here comes my wife now."

Lizette descended the stairs, her hips moving smoothly beneath the skirt, the wind catching her hair as she smiled at him. He could see, out of the corner of his eye, the valets staring at her. Glancing back at his partner he saw the surprise on Jodie's face.

"Doesn't look like a frumpy wife, does she?"

Jodie looked at him as if he could read her mind.

Lizette breezed up and kissed him and remained pressed against him as he introduced the women. Pointing to the dark-haired nine-year-old still standing on the lawn, LaStanza said, "And that's Alex."

Alex was open-mouthed. "You got a *girl* partner?"

"Yep."

Lizette reached over and opened the back door and started to get in.

"I thought we were having lunch," LaStanza said.

"We are—"She climbed in and began to slide over—"Aunt Brulie fixed chicken salad for us at home." She turned to Jodie. "You like chicken salad?"

"Sure."

"Brulie's is the best. Her poppy seed dressing is even better than D.H. Holmes'."

He wasn't about to argue. He could already taste the tangy salad and sweet dressing and cool, iced tea.

"Well," Lizette asked as they pulled away, "how'd it go this morning?"

"The usual," LaStanza answered, "except when Snowood's new partner hit the deck."

"He hit something?" Alex was leaning over the bucket seat, still leering at Jodie.

"He passed out."

33

"What did he expect in Homicide?" Lizette said.

"Probably thought it was Homocide, the big fruit."

Alex fell back and laughed.

LaStanza turned to him and added, "Here's another lesson for you. You know anybody named Keith?"

"No." Alex leaned forward anxiously.

"Well, remember, anyone named Keith is an asshole. Bank on it."

Aunt Brulie was already gone, but lunch was laid out, four plates covered in plastic wrap sitting in the refrigerator. A pitcher of presweetened iced tea rested on the shelf above. LaStanza had long suspected Brulie was a witch. Not just because of the gris-gris dangling around her sinewy, black neck, but for knowing the phone was about to ring before it rang and knowing someone was about to ring the front doorbell before it rang and knowing they would have four for lunch.

Lizette served them at the kitchen counter. Alex sat next to Jodie and continued watching her. LaStanza tried helping his wife, but there was nothing to do really, except sit and eat.

Perched directly across from Jodie, his wife started up a conversation with his partner that continued throughout lunch. He never got a word in and didn't really care to. He felt a little relief, actually, that they hit it off so well. He knew he shouldn't have been surprised. Lizette made most people feel at ease.

He stole glances at her, watching her brush her hair back when she tilted her head in conversation, watching her gold-brown eyes light up when she grinned, listening to the deep sexy sound of her laughter.

The women talked about clothes at first but ended up talking about decorating. Lizette had a lot to say about this. After all, she had an entire Audubon Park mansion to refurnish.

He downed the last of his chicken salad sandwich and munched the tortilla chips, but he wasn't in the kitchen anymore; he was back at the morgue with the two bodies, with the

34

arms scarred from needle marks and the boot laces and the gold tooth with the five-point star. Who were they? He knew that answer. They were his.

He picked up the phone and dialed the Bureau and asked the duty sergeant if there were any messages for him. "Yeah," the desk man said, "call your sergeant. I think he's got something for you."

Mark was still at home. "I was just about to call you. A fella named Shelby thinks your girls worked for him. Got a pen? I'll give you his number."

"Worked for him?" LaStanza pulled a pen and small notepad from his coat pocket.

"They were waitresses."

When his sergeant gave him Shelby's phone number and address on Baronne Street, LaStanza stammered, "I knew it!"

"Knew what?"

"Sixth District whores."

He took the rest of the information from Mark. It sounded good.

"Need any help?" Mark asked.

"Naw, we'll handle it."

"Good. I could use a Saturday off."

"Until the phone rings again," he reminded his sergeant.

"I'm gonna fuckin' disconnect it. Call me on the radio if you need me."

Hanging up, LaStanza nodded to his partner. "Eat up. We got a lead."

Jodie's eyes widened. She had a mouthful of chicken salad.

Lizette put her sandwich down and sighed. "I should've known." Moving around the counter, she stepped up to her husband and put her arms around his neck. "I guess I'll just have to amuse myself tonight."

"I'll be back." He grabbed her waist and pulled her to him.

"Yeah," she teased, "sure."

"Aw," Alex complained, "come on, you guys."

LaStanza looked over at his partner.

Jodie's eyes were still wide. She put her sandwich down and said, "We got I.D.'s?"

"Yeah. It was written right on their faces. It said, 'I'm a whore and I stays in the Sixth District.' I knew it."

Three
Baronne Street

Shelby's Fun House occupied the first floor of a two-story stucco building at the corner of Baronne and Clio streets, a block from the Pontchartrain Expressway. LaStanza knew the place. He'd handled a couple fights outside, on the street, back when he was a patrolman.

He parked the Maserati next to the fire hydrant directly in front of Shelby's, climbed out and winked at the very black face of a small boy sitting on the fender of the rusted shell of a 1970 Buick parked right behind the Maserati. The kid was wearing faded shorts and a tee shirt and sat gaping at the Maserati as if it were from outer space.

Jodie climbed out and moved around to the sidewalk. The kid slid off the fender. When LaStanza reached in and pulled out his portable radio, the child ran off yelling, "POLEE! PO-LEE! POLEE!"

The boy disappeared into one of the dilapidated wooden doubles on the downtown side of Shelby's. All of the houses along that section of Baronne matched the same description: shotgun doubles, unpainted for decades with uneven front porches and tiny, unkept front yards. Once, these had been nice homes with their brick chimneys and decorative, gingerbread wood work. But now most were boarded up. The ones still in use were falling apart.

LaStanza took a good look around. Cars were lined wall to wall on the street, most of them abandoned. Some had their hoods up, perpetually waiting for someone to come and work on them.

A couple of middle-aged whores in party dresses were leaning outside the front door of the check-cashing place across Clio Street from Shelby's. They were doing their best to pretend they didn't notice the detectives.

On the uptown side of the intersection, three black males were hanging out next to the mini-market, beneath a large sign that read: FOOD, BEER, LIQUOR. Two of the men, in bebop hats, were sipping bottles of Mad Dog while the third was sucking hard on a cigarette, keeping a watchful eye on LaStanza and especially his partner. A blue-gum-nigger-dog sat beneath the pay phone on the side wall of the mini-market. The phone had no receiver. It never had, even when LaStanza had been a rookie. The dog was also keeping a wary eye on the two white people.

LaStanza took in a deep breath of inner-city air and smiled. He was on familiar turf. He was back in the Sixth Police District, the Bloody Sixth. It was the same old same old.

A large black man with a long, crescent-shaped scar across his chin was sitting behind the register just inside the front door of the Fun House. Well lit from the windows that ran along the Clio side of the place, Shelby's had a long lunch counter on one side and seven tables on the other. The entire rear of the place was wall-to-wall arcade games. The grill behind the counter was manned by a woman, the spitting image of Aunt Jemima. She never looked at the detectives. The two men sitting at the counter looked at them for a second as did the teenagers in the back room.

The man with the scar waited for LaStanza to look back at him before saying, "Homicide. Right?"

"You got it." LaStanza opened his coat to show the badge

clipped to his belt. He put his radio on the counter next to the register.

"Walter Shelby," the man said, extending his right hand.

LaStanza grabbed the hand and returned a strong handshake, responding, "Detective LaStanza. This is my partner, Detective Kintyre."

The man's eyeballs were bright yellow around dark brown irises. Letting go of LaStanza's hand, the man raised his eyebrow and said, "You used to work the Sixth, huh?"

"Yep." LaStanza took out his notebook and pen.

"With that big crazy white boy, huh?"

"Stan Smith," LaStanza said, turning to explain to his partner, but Jodie was already nodding.

"I heard of him," she said.

Shelby pulled out the morning paper and pointed to an article titled: Two Women Are Shot To Death.

"Sounds like the two Pams to me," he said.

"Who?" LaStanza noticed his partner also had her pad out.

"Pam Camp and Pam Dillards. They worked here a couple weeks. They was wearing those clothes. Exactly." Shelby was still pointing to the article. He continued without pause, "Pam Camp. They calls her 'Slow.' She the older one, the one wearing the white tee shirt."

"Number one," LaStanza said aloud. Raising his hand, he asked, "Why's she called 'Slow.'"

"She got what you call a slow brain."

"What is that supposed to mean?" LaStanza had to force himself from smirking.

"She's stupid."

Ask a stupid question. LaStanza asked Shelby to go on.

"Pam Dillards was known as 'Fawn,' 'cause her hair used to be red."

Made sense.

"She the one with the gold star on her front tooth. They didn't show up for work this morning; so I called the Camp family, and her mama say she didn't come home. Mama was

39

all upset. I was sorry about that. She said she's going to the coroner's."

"Can we use your phone?"

"Sure."

LaStanza nodded to his partner. Jodie called the morgue while he secured the girls' addresses.

Shelby gave him the home addresses of both girls, as well as where the girls stayed. He also told them how the girls had left together the previous day at five P.M.

"Which way'd they go?"

"Pair of jacks, man." Shelby shrugged. "They don't got no short, so they walk. Probably down CL-ten." Which meant Clio Street. The street sign read: CL10. Made sense to the boys in the Sixth and especially to everyone in the nearby Melpomene Housing Project.

When Jodie got off the line, she said, "Positive I.D. The family's still there."

"Okay —" LaStanza dug out his car keys — "go get a statement." He held on to the keys a second and added, "Run the names. If they have records, get mug shots and pull the fingerprint cards. And call me on the radio on your way back."

"I'll pick you up back here." She started for the door.

"Call me. I won't be here."

"Huh?"

"I'm gonna canvass Clio."

LaStanza finished interviewing Shelby and then took on Aunt Jemima. She was fairly friendly and, like her boss, knew very little about the two Pams. No enemies. No known associates. No one paying particular interest to the two on the previous evening.

He left his card with each and received another strong handshake from Shelby on his way out.

"Good luck," Shelby told him.

"Thanks for calling."

"Anytime."

He had seen Shelby before, on the street, always in the

40

background, never any trouble. Most of the people in the Sixth were like Shelby. They were no trouble. There were enough of other kinds of trouble to make up for it.

Baronne and Clio were lined with the kind of people who made trouble. One of the whores from the check-cashing place sashayed across Clio, dancing to faint music that echoed from one of the bars down Baronne. She glanced back at LaStanza but not at any traffic. Traffic was supposed to stop if *she* was in the street.

LaStanza spoke to nineteen people along Clio on his way to Euterpe Street. Nobody knew anything. Surprisingly, most of them talked openly to the detective, even a couple mooks sharing a joint on the front stoop of an abandoned house on the river side of St. Charles Avenue. Grinning, they asked if he wanted a "hit."

"I don't smoke," he told them, which produced uproarious laughter. He continued down Clio and turned on Prytania to Terpsichore Street.

A white mook stopped LaStanza at the corner of Terpsichore and Coliseum streets. The man looked like Rip Van Winkle dipped in auto grease and smelled like Advanced Postmortem Decomposition. He asked for a quarter "for a burger." His hand looked like a bleached twig left out in the sun.

LaStanza looked into a pair of vacant eyes and pulled out a buck, folded it lengthwise and handed it to Rip. "You around the square much?"

"What square?"

They were standing across the street from Coliseum Square. LaStanza sighed and walked around the man.

Pausing a few steps later, LaStanza looked over at a small, grassless knoll beneath one of the tired oaks in the square. The body of Lutisha Marie Joseph had been found beneath that tree. That was two springs ago. Lutisha had had the prettiest eyes he'd ever seen on a black girl. That was before the Twenty-two Killer had put a bullet between them. She'd had Egyptian eyes.

The Dillards lived in an apartment on the downtown side of a three-story house at the corner of Euterpe and Coliseum streets. It had long since been carved into apartments. Across from Coliseum Square, the building sported a fresh coat of kelly green paint and yellow trim.

Mr. Dillards answered the door. He was a trim man, just under six feet tall, with dark, angry eyes. He was wearing dress blue pants and nothing else.

Holding up his credentials, LaStanza started to introduce himself.

"I know who you are," Dillards cut him off. The man stood in the doorway with his arms folded.

"I have to tell you something . . ."

Dillards looked toward the square. "Lady named Camp called me already. I know."

He went on without prodding, "I kicked my daughter's ass out two years ago." His eyes expressed no emotion whatsoever, "and I really don't give a damn about her. She was no good."

LaStanza waited until Dillards looked back at him before asking about friends and associates and places the girl frequented.

"I ain't talked to her in two years. I seen her on the street. I seen her out in the square." The man's chin pointed across the street.

"Can I talk to her mama?" LaStanza asked.

"Her mama dead."

LaStanza pulled out a business card and tried to hand it to the man. "In case you hear something."

"Look. My daughter's been gone two years. I don't *wanna* hear nothin'."

LaStanza tucked the card back into his coat pocket and left the man in the doorway. He crossed the street to Coliseum Square and sat on one of the black iron benches beneath an oak that had seen its best days a century ago. Before he could get comfortable, he heard a car door close behind him.

42

Jodie came and sat next to him. He told her about Mr. Dillards and Rip Van Winkle and the mooks willing to share a joint.

"Well, the Camp family won't be much more help," she said. "They're gonna let Jesus solve the case. They don't want any police."

"That's a load off my mind. Christ almighty!" Standing up, he asked, "Where do they live?"

Jodie led the way to the Camps' Melpomene Street house. On the way, she tried to change the subject. "I heard about Stan Smith. If he isn't the craziest cop in the city, everyone thinks he is."

LaStanza didn't want to talk about his old partner.

"I met him once," Jodie went on.

He put his hand up and said, "Only thing he taught me was how to shoot blue-gum-nigger-dogs in the projects."

As soon as the two detectives entered the house, Mama Camp started praising the Lord while the victim's two sisters added Amens. Mr. Camp's whereabouts had been unknown since 1970.

Less obstinate than Mr. Dillards, the Camp family was infinitely more irritating. They listened to LaStanza, all three sitting on their plastic-covered couch, nodding their heads in unison. After each of LaStanza's sentences, they praised the Lord. They even smiled in unison. For all their Christian compassion, they had less insight into the life of their daughter than Mr. Dillards had. LaStanza had Jodie leave one of her cards with Mrs. Camp.

On his way out, he made sure Jodie secured the details of the funeral arrangements. He let his partner thank them and left, quickly.

"Praise the Lord," all three replied.

LaStanza led the way to Camp Street, to the address where Shelby had said the victims had been staying recently. The

House of the Lamb was a three-story, white Victorian house at the corner of Camp and Felicity streets. What once had been a grand home was now divided into twenty "rooms," including three communal bathrooms, one on each floor. The carved wood railing along the front gallery was so filthy, the graffiti was nearly unreadable. Most of the windows had been broken and filled in with cardboard. The front door was missing, but that was okay; each "room" still had a door.

Sister Dawn Abigail, the "house mother," was two hundred and fifty pounds of holy lard with strawlike blond hair and a mole on her right cheek that looked just like the Superdome. She smelled exactly the way she looked.

LaStanza remained in the hall while his tolerant partner interviewed the good sister. He took his own notes:

Fawn and Slow lived, on-and-off, in Room 22, which was upstairs in front. They were both "fallen girls" who sought redemption, although they never asked for it outright. It is suspected that both used illicit drugs and both were lesbians. They sometimes showered together. Slow once "confessed" to Sister Dawn that she was, indeed, a lesbian.

They both had boyfriends. Fawn's is named Leo Morris. He's an old man in his fifties. Slow's boyfriend lives in the House of the Lamb, too. His name is Johnny Loomar. He's almost a midget. Sister Dawn adds that its funny, but he hadn't been seen all day. And that has never happened before.

LaStanza put two stars next to the name of the fifty-year-old boyfriend and one star next to the name Johnny Loomar.

Jodie followed up on the leads quickly and secured whatever information on both boyfriends was available, especially the missing midget. She also asked about any possible pimp, although she was astute enough not to use that word.

"Naw," Sister Dawn said, "they were independents."

When Jodie finished, she turned to her partner.

He had one question: "What religion is this? What's the name of your church?"

"God."

"Church of God?" He jotted the name down.

"No. Just 'God.' There isn't anything else after God."

Cute, he thought to himself, like calling your fuckin' dog . . . "Dog."

"We're from Phoenix," Sister Dawn said, "Arizona." As if that explained it. "I'm from Nogales, originally," she added. "Arizona, not Mexico."

That was another load off his mind.

Room 22 had two windows that looked down on Camp Street. Three of the panes had been replaced with cardboard. There were two soiled double beds, one under each window, and a chifforobe against the wall next to the door. Like the rest of the place, the room had wall-to-wall carpet of an unknown color. Too many stains were mixed in with too much soil for anyone to tell its proper color.

LaStanza searched the two plastic end tables next to the beds, and the chifforobe, combing through the clothes for anything, even searching the light fixtures, but there was nothing.

"No address books, no papers, nothing," Jodie exclaimed. "Prostitutes make phone calls. I've seen it on TV."

"Probably carried everything in their purses."

"Oh, yeah."

"Come on," he told her, "let's see if any of the other fallen know anything about these girls."

It usually took a Mardi Gras parade to bring as many freaks, geeks, transvestites, transsexuals and other creatures of indeterminate sex together in one place. At the House of the Lamb, it was a daily event. In the twenty rooms of the

45

house, LaStanza counted fifty-five occupants. None could be described as a normal Homo sapien.

Jodie had the pleasure of interviewing the most bizarre occupant of the house. In one of the third-floor rooms, she managed to find a creature who resembled a stork, an ear of corn and a skunk rolled into one. And it was an albino to boot.

When LaStanza found them, the creature was explaining about its impending hysterectomy. Jodie was listening patiently until he tapped her on the shoulder and cut in with, "Does it know anything about the girls?"

Jodie shrugged.

"Come on." He led the way out.

Descending the stairs, he told his partner, "Whatever that was, it wasn't a woman."

"I asked her that, and she said she was a woman. She said she'd had a debut."

He looked back at his partner and had to laugh. "A fuckin' drag-queen-debutante?"

God, he was glad to get away from that house.

"Goddam non-denominational, bogus, protestant fuckin' sect," he growled as he fanned his coat in a vain attempt at ridding himself of the smell from the place.

"I'm protestant," Jodie said. "Presbyterian."

"Then the House of the Lamb is all yours from now on," he growled again and started back down Camp Street in the direction of Clio.

Snowood called him on the radio as they arrived on Clio.

"What you working?"

"Batture Case," LaStanza snapped into the radio and then wondered why he was dumb enough to answer.

"You're not missing a leg over there, are you?"

LaStanza handed the radio to his partner, who asked Snowood to repeat himself.

"I got a human leg over here in a dumpster on Dante Street. I think it's a woman's. It's been shaved. And it's got varicose veins."

"What color is it?" Jodie asked.

"Blue now, but it was white."

"Wrong color."

"Okeydokey," Snowood signed off in his best Clint Eastwood voice. "If y'all come across a one-legged fat woman with vericoses, just holler."

"Only in New Orleans," LaStanza said half to himself, half aloud.

They worked their way back up Clio, armed with Camp's mug shot. She had been arrested once, at seventeen, for shoplifting at the Gus Mayer Store on Canal Street, a store that was now closed.

Jodie attracted some serious attention on this walk-through, so he let her do the talking. He was already planning ahead. As soon as they were finished with the Sixth, they would have to recanvass the Lower Coast one more time. Sunday, they would hit the entire Coliseum Square area, hard. Monday evening they would go to the wake of Pam Camp.

Meanwhile, they had a midget to find along the way. But first, they had to walk back to get the Maserati. If it was still there.

Shortly before midnight, LaStanza parked the Maserati back on Milan Street. It had been a futile day. After the initial identifications, they had come up empty: no midget, no leads, nothing but aching feet and the promise of more.

He watched his partner wearily climb out of the car and cross in front of his headlights.

"What time should I pick you up tomorrow?" she asked when she made it to the sidewalk. "Might as well use the city's gas."

"Make it in the afternoon."

She gave him a relieved look and started toward her house.

"You've got a run in your stocking," he told her.

"I'm throwing everything in the garbage."

47

He slipped the Maserati into drive and added, "See ya later, padna."

"Ciao," she managed enough energy to say.

He made it home in less than ten minutes. He found Lizette downstairs, in the library that she'd turned into a study. She was sitting at her new Apple computer, books scattered around her like fallen leaves.

She was wearing one of his dress shirts, a light blue one with a button-down collar. Turning and stretching when he came in, she smiled and said, "Don't I know you?"

Her hair was in a ponytail, her face was free of makeup, and she looked very sexy sitting there with her foot now up on the computer table and her white bikini panties peeking up at him.

"Come here and plant one on me, big boy," she said, reaching her arms out to him.

He crossed the room, dropping his briefcase and radio on the way, and pushed her desk chair back until she was almost prone. Leaning over, he kissed her. Then he kissed her again even longer.

"Did you eat?" she asked when he pulled away.

"No."

He looked over at the books. A drawing of Robespierre was staring back at him. She'd been working on her master's thesis long enough for him to recognize the thin face under the powdered wig.

"How's it coming?" He nodded to the computer.

"I'm on the downhill side." She climbed out of the chair and stretched again. He ran his hand up the rear of her shirt, rubbing his fingers gently across her soft back.

"You feel like getting something to eat?" she asked, reaching over and pushing a couple buttons on the keyboard, which started the computer humming. "I can fix something here." She turned back and put her arms around his neck. "You look beat."

"No, let's go out. It's Saturday night." He was more than

48

beat; but she'd been cooped up, and it would take a while for him to unwind anyway. "Let me take a quick shower first. These clothes are full of Sixth District funk."

A fast shower later, he was dressing when she came upstairs and climbed into a pair of jeans and black Reeboks. He watched her brush a light coat of mocha lipstick over her full lips. He liked to watch her get dressed, watch her in the mirror as she puffed her lips to apply lipstick and then gave herself the once-over before turning to leave.

She drove the burgundy Maserati, and he rested his eyes, letting the breeze from the open sunroof flow over his face. She drove straight to the Camellia Grill and parked in front. He could tell where they were by the turns she made and because it was after midnight. The grill was "it" after midnight. Besides, Lizette loved the place, any time. So he wasn't surprised to see the four large Greek columns and white facade when he opened his eyes.

The Camellia was an old-fashioned grill where everyone had to sit on stools at the counter. There were no tables. A W-shaped counter ran the length of the place with a grill behind and the busiest waiters in the city. All the waiters were black, extremely efficient and very friendly, but none as good as Alfred.

A few years back, a local artist drew a poster for the grill, a pink camellia on a white background. It was sold at the grill for a regular price unsigned. If signed by the artist, it was higher. It was even higher if signed by Alfred the waiter.

"Hello there, Miss Lizette," Alfred said as he flashed a wide smile their way and quickly put napkins and silverware on the counter as they sat.

"And how are you tonight, Mr. Detective?"

"Fine, Alfred, and you."

"I'm *always* fine." The man winked and whipped out his order pad from his back pocket. "The usual?" he asked.

"You know it," Lizette answered.

The "usual" was delivered a few minutes later. Cheeseburgers and fries and chocolate shakes. Taste was what mattered at the grill, not cholesterol or calories. And these were the real thing: grilled burgers with the cheese properly melted and crispy fries and malt shakes foaming over the top of frosted glasses. Alfred whipped out straws, exposed them from their sheaths, and waited for Lizette and Dino to take them.

LaStanza watched his wife beneath the bright lights of the grill. Still fresh-faced with only her light lipstick, sitting on the edge of her stool and swinging her feet while sipping her malt, she looked like a junior high student. For the hundredth time, he felt that rush, that glad he-was-smart-enough-to-marry-this-girl rush.

They rode back home in silence. When they arrived, he armed the alarm and followed her up the long spiral staircase to the master bedroom. Brushing their teeth side by side in the twin sinks in the spacious bathroom adjacent to their bedroom, they remained silent.

Lizette moved to her side of the bed as he disarmed the alarm clock. Facing each other across the wide, king-size brass bed, he watched her eyes as the two of them started to remove their clothes. Her eyes had that mischievous, sexy look as she unbuttoned the blue shirt and pulled it off, freeing her breasts which seemed too large for her petite frame. Her nipples were already erect.

Still standing, she raised her right foot and untied her Reebok, it was tossed across the room along with its sock. The left one soon followed. She wiggled out of her jeans, rocking her hips from side to side, and threw them over the chair next to the blue shirt. Pursing her lips slightly, she pulled her panties down slowly and left them at her feet. Then she reached behind her head, removed the barrette and shook her long hair. Her eyes never left his the entire time. He loved to watch her strip, and she knew it.

He was already naked. They climbed into bed and moved to one another. Lightly brushing her lips, he began to kiss his way down her body, frenching her neck and her right shoulder on his way to her breasts. He kissed each breast and kneaded them gently with the tips of his fingers. He lingered at her navel, kissing her there, cupping her breasts in his hands and squeezing each nipple.

He could feel her breathing heavier as his mouth moved past her stomach to her thighs. Slowly, Lizette spread her legs to allow him between them. He kissed each thigh and moved his tongue along a path up and down the soft inner area of each leg.

He kissed her silky mat of hair and then stuck his tongue inside as she shuddered and began to gyrate her hips in a slow roll. He wanted to continue slowly for as long as he could, but she was hot.

She started to pull on the hair along the back of his head, started to pull him up; but he resisted, and the more he resisted, the more she moaned and pulled. When he started humming the French national anthem, she laughed and yanked him up and guided him inside her.

He held on as long as he could, until he felt her coming in long gasps.

"Come on, babe," she whispered in a voice that sounded hoarse. "Come on."

LaStanza dreamed that night of the river. Of the dark, swirling currents in the big muddy river, of brown water brushing against leveed shores. There were young girls in his dream, brides in Acadian dresses, stooped over the rocks along the base of the levees, washing clothes, beating their clothes on the batture. They were French girls with dark hair and pouty lips, just like Lizette.

Four
Camp Street

Lizette managed to slip out of bed without waking him, which wasn't easy. Dino was such a light sleeper. She wrapped a short, white terry cloth robe around herself, stepped into slippers and eased out of the bedroom.

She brushed her teeth in one of the spare bathrooms, then went down the spiral staircase to the front door. Stepping out on the gallery, she picked up the paper and then looked out at the park. An early-morning mist hovered over the ground. The oaks rose from the fog like huge, gnarled fingers reaching through an endless spiderweb.

She paused momentarily. It seemed so quiet, as if the city had vanished. She had to strain to hear a streetcar rattling up St. Charles Avenue, and then a car's horn echoed from the avenue. The morning air felt cool on her face. Too bad it wouldn't last, she thought. Once the sun burned through the fog, the mist would be transformed into a heavy humidity that could turn starched shirts into sticky globs of cotton and sweat.

She laid the paper out on the kitchen counter, put the radio on low and started breakfast. The kitchen quickly filled with the strong scents of coffee-and-chicory, loss bread, bacon and eggs, sunny-side up.

She cut chilled cantaloupe into little squares and sprinkled powdered sugar on the loss bread when it was ready. For an instant, Lizette remembered her grandmother, her Maw Maw, and how the old woman had taught her to make loss bread. Except, Maw Maw called it by its proper French name, *du pain perdue*.

Lizette was fixing their plates when she saw a wisp of dark hair and a green eye peeking at her from the doorway.

He was grinning like a six-year-old, his hair messed and extra wavy after a good sleep. He had pulled on an LSU tee shirt and gym shorts.

"Ummm," he said, stretching as he crossed the room, "smells great."

He opened his arms to hug her, encircled her, but reached around and started fingering the newspaper. "Murder. Murder. Murder," he said. "They don't even have to change the headlines."

She pressed her nose against the side of his face and bit at his lip. Brushing a finger across the tiny scar on the left side of his neck, where the bullet from the Twenty-two Killer had nicked him, she said, "You want the paper . . . or me?"

"I want breakfast." He draped his arms over her shoulders. "I had you last night."

She poked him in the ribs and turned back to their plates. He kissed her on the back of the neck and wrapped his hands across her breasts.

"Hey," she said, "don't start anything you're not ready to finish."

"After some nourishment." He pulled away and reached for the coffee.

"That's what I get for marrying an old man."

Dino squinted his eyes at her. She'd zinged him again. It was one of the few things she could tease him about, the nearly ten years between their ages.

After half a minute, he said, "Old man, huh? That's not what you were moaning last night."

"I had a charley horse in my leg," she said, passing him his plate. "I didn't have the heart to tell you."

His eyes were so narrow they were almost shut. He leaned over the counter and said, "You're lying."

"Oh, yeah?"

He started rifling through the newspaper. "I can tell when people are lying to me. I'm a trained homicide dick, remember?"

"A *little* homicide dick."

He looked back at her again and tried to look angry, but she could see the corners of his mouth fighting to keep from smiling.

"Liar," he whispered and went back to the paper.

Their breakfast included the Sunday *Picayune*. He read the sports section first and then the metro section. She started with the front page and then moved on to the book page and then the entertainment section. He eventually took the front page after glancing through the comics. He always read SPI-DER-MAN. Neither touched the society sections.

"That's quite a drought they're having up north in the midwest," she said.

"The Yankees are slumping again," he complained.

"Their talking about a salt water intrusion up the river, the water's so low," she said.

"Who ever heard of the Cleveland Indians in first place?"

"The city's had twenty murders in the last fourteen days," she said.

He looked over at her and said, "Seems like more."

He poured himself a fresh cup and asked, "What you got on tap for today?"

"I don't know. After church I'll probably drop by the estate and see what the Louviers are up to." She'd started calling her parents "the Louviers" after the move to St. Charles Avenue. "Might take in a movie with Alex later," she continued. "Then, tonight, I'll be carousing with the boys again . . . Robespierre and St. Just." She looked up at his eyes and asked, "You working late?"

The way he shrugged told her he'd be all day.

He continued staring back at her. He didn't look like a six-year-old anymore. Dino had eyelashes any girl would envy and eyes that looked extra light with the sun streaming into the kitchen, especially against his naturally tanned complexion. He had taut cheeks and a pointed chin, and the way he was looking at her made her want to say, "Hey, let's get the hell out of here. Go back to the Caribbean for another two weeks."

She watched his lips move slowly, "How about a shower?"

Even with his long hours, it was nice being a newlywed.

A black man wearing a soiled pullover shirt and dirty jeans, his face scarred from a recent fight, was sitting on one of the black iron benches of Coliseum Square. He was staring in the general direction of the small playground near the center of the square.

LaStanza moved in front of the man and opened his coat to show his badge.

"Police," he said, sticking the mug shot of Pam Camp in front of the man's eyes. "You ever see this girl?"

The man looked up and said, "Say what?" The man's breath smelled like a Bourbon Street gutter on Sunday morning.

LaStanza moved to the playground area. A maze of untreated logs, held together by large steel bolts, stood in the center of a muddy sand pit. Three little boys and a little girl in a denim dress were playing in the maze. The detective moved over and sat on the end of the maze and watched the kids.

The little girl climbed above him on one of the logs, slid backward and dangled upside down by her legs. Reaching around, she grabbed her heels. She began to swing slightly, turned to LaStanza and said, "You the polee, aren't you?"

"Yep."

"That white lady with you, huh?"

He looked over at Jodie, who was talking to another bench sitter on the Camp Street side of the square.

"She's my partner."

55

"What you want?" the little girl asked as the boys gathered around LaStanza.

He showed the girl the mug shot and let her pass it to her friends.

"You ever see this girl?"

"She name Slow," the little girl said as she swung herself down and landed deftly in the mud. "She a bad girl," she went on. "She uses them drugs and kisses on mens all the time."

"She not nice," a little boy with his two front teeth missing added.

"Why you say that?" LaStanza asked.

"She don't like kids. She always mean."

He let them go on, with a little prodding. Long ago, he'd learned that kids were excellent witnesses. They saw everything. These children had seen Slow pick up men and swap drugs with various people in the park.

But they weren't good with names. They had seen her with several men, but the only name they knew was Slow's boyfriend, Johnny Loomar, the midget.

"She meets white mens, too," the little girl added. "They come by in cars, and she go with them."

Two of the boys, bored with the talk, were already back playing. LaStanza tried a few more questions but came away with only a predictable picture of a dope-fiend whore.

By that time, Jodie was across Camp Street at a small grocery store with a large, hand-painted sign out front that read: CHEAPEREST FOOD. He joined her as she was showing the mug shot, along with a postmortem close-up of Pam Dillards' face. The people collected around Jodie were polite enough to look at the pictures, but none claimed to have ever seen either victim.

"Same thing inside," Jodie said as they turned away and crossed Camp Street back into the square. Jodie was wearing a full black skirt and a white, short-sleeved sweater. The sweater was thick and bulky enough to hide her figure. The skirt was long enough to cover half her calves. He was glad he chose a tan suit that day.

Stepping into the square, LaStanza pulled her aside by the elbow.

"Watch out!"

She barely missed a pile of poo-poo.

"Must be a huge dog." She looked away in disgust.

"Probably human," he told her.

"Yuk!"

A long time ago, someone had planted fine china grass in a square where someone else had planned to build a coliseum modeled after a Parisian dance hall, a coliseum that was never built. Back then, the Victorian and Greek Revival homes along the square were freshly painted and occupied by people who were independently wealthy or who worked as professionals in the new American section of the city, the Faubourg St. Mary. They named the streets after the Greek muses: Calliope, Clio, Erato, Thalia, Melpomene, Terpsichore, Euterpe, Polymnia, and Urania.

By the time Dino LaStanza was a rookie, beating around the streets of the Sixth, the pronunciation of those street names had evolved into their current mook dialect. Clio was now CL-ten. Terpsichore was Tap-si-core; Melpomene . . . Mel-fo-mene; Polymnia . . . Poly-mena; Euterpe . . . U-tap; Thalia . . . Thal-ya. Only Erato and Urania remained the same.

Camp Street had evolved into a skid row, lined with drunks and bums from the central business district to the muddy sand pit of Coliseum Square and beyond. The fine homes were now tenements housing the lower lower class of the city.

LaStanza and his partner were resting next to the large fountain near the uptown end of the square, a fountain that never worked, when Paul Snowood's unmarked Chevy pulled up and parked.

Snowood climbed out and headed straight for them. He was wearing a black, Wyatt Earp coat that almost went to his knees, a black ribbon bow tie with a white shirt, and dress black jeans with a wide belt clasped by a huge Texas longhorn buckle. He wore black cowboy boots, of course.

The son-of-a-bitch had nerve, LaStanza thought, wearing anything that looked remotely like Wyatt Earp. Snowood couldn't shoot worth shit. He carried a Glock 17 automatic with twenty rounds so that he could scare people to death by hitting everything around them . . . except them.

Another man, very familiar to LaStanza, followed Snowood. The broadly grinning black face belonged to a man born in the Sixth District, named for one of the streets, a man who had been LaStanza's partner once, briefly. He was the bravest man LaStanza knew. His name was Felicity Jones, but everyone called him Fel.

"Well," Snowood declared when he arrived, "what in the name of Charles Manson is going on here?"

Jodie stood up and stepped away. LaStanza, still watching Fel Jones, had to ask, "Why are you riding with this pecker-wood?"

Fel continued grinning.

"This here's ma new pardner," Snowood said.

LaStanza's jaw fell open. For the first time in his life, he was certain he'd heard *everything*. It took a second for him to regain control of his lower jaw. Pointing to the black face, he told Jodie, "This man is as *stupid* as the look on his face.

"This fool," he went on, "just transferred out of Intelligence for Homicide."

"You're kidding?" Jodie was incredulous.

"From a do-nothing, glamor-boy job to the pressure cooker," LaStanza added. "Felicity Jones, you must've lost your ever-lovin' mind."

"I got bored," Fel answered, still grinning like a babbling idiot.

LaStanza had never heard of anyone transferring out of the Intelligence Division. People died of old age up there.

"We just thought we'd drop in on the honeymoon patrol for

58

a minute." It was Snowood again. "We just finished with a thirty at Charity."

"The missing leg?" Jodie asked.

"Naw. A douche-bag named Willie Johnson got himself shot to death in a bar on Simon Bolivar. The shit-head was shot three times in three days and decides to die when I got weekend duty."

"Three times?" Jodie said. LaStanza thought he'd taught her better. Now Snowood could take the next ten minutes explaining. And the cowpoke cop did, explaining how ole Willie got shot in the arm Friday but didn't go to the hospital, then got shot in the head Saturday and still didn't go to the hospital, then got popped in the chest Sunday morning and didn't make it to the hospital.

"Shot in the head Saturday?" Jodie had to ask.

"Bullet bounced off."

LaStanza let them talk. He couldn't pull himself away from the jack-o'-lantern grin on the face of Felicity Jones. The man might be brave as hell, could kill an armed robber with a chestful of bullets, but he wasn't . . . bright.

Instead of helping in the canvass of Camp Street, Snowood and Jones tagged along and did their best to distract. LaStanza tried splitting up with his partner, taking Snowood along with him, but that only encouraged Country-Ass to *really* butt in.

"Give me one of them pictures of the dead girl," he said, "so I can scare all the kids."

It was almost dark when LaStanza and Country-Ass joined Jodie and Fel in a decrepit apartment building on Camp, near Race Street. Squeezing into the skinny hallway, LaStanza stopped in the doorway of a room that was actually clean. Jodie was sitting in a folding chair just inside the door while a large black man, who looked like a double of O.J. Simpson, sat on the single bed with his legs crossed and his arms folded across his chest. The man was even wearing a football jersey with his jeans.

They were talking about whores. Not about the two Pams, but whores in general. O.J.'s double was having a good time, talking trash. Jodie looked uncomfortable. But it wasn't the conversation that was making her squirm. It was the leering eyes of the large black man.

Fel Jones was in the hall, leaning against the wall, dozing. Snowood was surprisingly quiet. O.J. II was busy flirting with a pretty white woman, talking about enlarged dicks and wet pussys. LaStanza wasn't sure, but he thought Jodie was breathing a little heavier than usual.

After a couple minutes, he broke in with, "He know anything about the two Pams?"

"No" — Jodie almost jumped — "not really."

"Well, I'm leaving. You wanna come?"

She stood up quickly, almost knocking the folding chair over, and said, "I've got to check upstairs."

O.J. II extended his hand for her to shake. She took it and shook it hurriedly. The man held it a little too long before letting go.

"Come back, anytime," he said, giving her a good look up and down.

LaStanza started down the hall and looked back in time to see Jodie heading toward the back stairs. O.J. II was leaning out his room watching her backside.

"Don't go up there, white girl," O.J. II called out. "Only one couple up there and they jammin' right now."

"They're what?" she turned and asked.

"Jammin'. You know." O.J. II stepped out and began to pump his hips back and forth.

Jodie almost blushed. She had to squeeze by O.J. II on her way out, and her eyes shot a long look at his as she passed.

At least Snowood and his partner hadn't seen that. They were already outside. LaStanza breezed by them. When Jodie looked like she was going to stop and talk, he called back to her, "Come on, white girl, let's get outta here."

Fel Jones took a few steps toward LaStanza and called him back, "Come here. I gotta ask you something important."

He should have known better but went back anyway.

Fel pulled him aside, leaned close and asked, "You hit her a lick, yet?"

LaStanza drove.

"What'd he want?"

"He wanted to know if I fucked you yet."

After a second she said, "So, what'd you tell 'em?"

She was being cute again.

When he was sure that Snowood and company were safely out of the way, he turned around and went back to Euterpe Street, pulling up in front of a wooden, two-story building that hadn't seen a coat of paint since the first world war.

"What is it?" Jodie asked.

"I got a line on Leo Morris," he told her on his way out the door. "He's supposed to stay here."

"Well," Lizette said, "did he know anything?"

Dino had a towel around his waist and another draped over his head. He sat on the bed and began rubbing the towel through his hair. "He's a fifty-five-year-old man who let Fawn spend the night sometimes, take showers, keep some clothes over there."

He reached for the blow dryer and brush.

"Fawn used to let him watch her take a shower. That's all. He knew less about the girls than Snowood."

After drying his hair, he climbed into bed next to her. She was reading a book called *My Friend Robespierre*.

"Any good?"

"So-so."

"So, what'd you do today?"

She told him some more stories about the estate and her mother's newfound society friends and how her father couldn't stand any of them. Dino's eyes were already closed.

61

"Then Alex and I went to see *A Man and a Woman* at the Prytania."

"Did he like it?"

"He sure did." She put her book down and reached over to run her finger over the scar on his neck. Her voice dropped an octave. "Would you drive back to me after a big race, in the middle of the night, over mountain roads, just because I told you I loved you?"

He opened his eyes. "I drive home past four of the loveliest housing projects this side of Paris every night, don't I?"

"Cute, LaStanza. Real cute." She went back to her book.

"Put the book down," he told her, "and roll over here, little girl. I got a little homicide dick for you."

She looked at the clock and shook her head. "Two in the morning and the old man wants a little action?"

He grabbed the book and tossed it across the room.

"Cute, LaStanza," she said as she sank back. "Real cute."

The phone woke LaStanza the following morning. He was in the middle of a dream about the girl in the tight red skirt. He was at her autopsy, watching her intestines squirm around like greasy snakes. He heard her voice whispering again, ". . . old . . . oldie . . ." Then the phone rang.

It was Jodie.

"You awake?"

"Now I am."

"Well, I got the details on Pam Camp's wake."

"Whoa, slow down." He sat up and rubbed his eyes. The clock read eleven-fifteen. Jesus, did he sleep!

Jodie rattled on. Something about how Pam Dillards was already buried, by the city. When she paused to catch her breath, he managed to get a question in.

"Where are you?"

"At the office."

"What are you doing there? We start the evening watch today."

62

"I'm writing the daily from yesterday."

He let out a long sigh. "Well, don't put too much in it. You'll spoil the rank."

"Okay!"

Boy, was she *up*.

"Remember to run the midget on the computer," he told her, "and the address of the House of the Lamb. Let's see how many scumbags live with Sister Dawn. And see if Camp had any criminal associates. And run Shelby's Fun House address, too."

"Right."

He was about to hang up when she raised her voice. "I'll pick you up at four for the wake."

"Right," he said and hung up.

He found Lizette's note in the kitchen.

It read:

Have an early class. Made reservations at the grill for 12:30 A.M.

Catch ya later.

Love, L.

PS: And you only drive past three projects. I checked the map.

The grill for twelve-thirty. No problem, he thought. Unless they found the midget.

The Coliseum Baptist Church was in the thirteen hundred block of Camp Street, across from the poo-poo infested square. LaStanza wore a black suit with a white shirt and gray tie. Jodie wore an equally black suit with a white blouse but no tie. Her blouse was buttoned all the way up, as always. She looked extra blond that evening, but he couldn't tell why.

63

She'd probably done something to her hair, but he couldn't tell what.

No one else wore black, not even the preacher. Most of the mourners wore purple or red or yellow. The victim's mother wore a baby blue, wraparound dress while her daughters were adorned in matching pink jumpsuits. The preacher wore a lavender, three-piece suit with a white tie and a diamond tie tack, the ensemble completed by green, patent leather shoes.

His name was Reverend Stokes, and he ushered the detectives into the back of the church to the glass-enclosed cry room where they put loud babies during the services. It gave them a full view of the wake and kept them separate from the mourners. They were the only white people there.

They had arrived early and were able to watch the crowd enter. The coffin rested at the foot of the altar, on two saw horses covered in blue velvet. LaStanza wasn't surprised to see it was a closed coffin. He was surprised to see the light sculpture on top. It was one of those revolving lights that flashed like a strobe with alternating lenses that shot off different colored lights.

"I wonder where Sister Dawn is?" Jodie asked.

"Can't believe she's missing all this."

The Reverend turned to them and asked, "You think you'll catch who did it?"

"I always catch them," LaStanza answered. His voice was low and smooth without a hint of cockiness.

"Confident, huh?"

"I'm just too stubborn to give up." He turned to the preacher and added, "Ever."

"Good," Reverend Stokes said before leaving.

LaStanza called out to him before he got away, "Did you know the victim?"

"Never seen her or her family before in my life."

The large man headed straight for the pulpit. For the next half hour, the man delivered a sermon that rattled LaStanza's teeth and pricked the hair on back of his neck. With a deep,

64

bellowing voice, the good Reverend belted out scriptures like it was judgment day.

Long ago, LaStanza had become convinced that if God had a voice, He spoke in English with the voice of a black preacher. Reverend Stokes reinforced that conviction.

When the sermon ended, the entire congregation began to file past the coffin, one by one. The light sculpture on top of the coffin bathed each in moving colors as they moved by. The wailing began immediately.

Jodie was startled when the first woman hit the floor. She was a portly woman in her forties, wearing a pink, chiffon dress and a shawl over her head. She rolled in the aisle back to the third pew before a couple people helped her up.

Another fat woman soon followed, hitting the deck and rolling. All in all, five women fell down and took the long roll to the third pew. LaStanza watched the Camp family. They shed a few tears but no hysterics. Probably figured their daughter was in a better world.

The last people in the line were LaStanza and his partner. Most of the congregation hadn't seen them until this point and stared at them as if they were from Mars.

LaStanza made the sign of the cross over the coffin and turned to the Camp family to pay his respects. Mrs. Camp introduced him to some of the mourners. He used the opportunity to question each. He and Jodie talked to anyone who would speak to them.

Most of the people knew nothing of any value. LaStanza worked his way back down the center aisle toward the rear and caught sight of a small figure who'd arrived late. He pretended to not notice until the midget tried to pass.

Turning quickly and bumping against the midget, LaStanza said, "Hey, Johnny, what's happening?"

"Hi," the midget said.

LaStanza grabbed the midget's left hand and twisted it behind the man's back, hard. Johnny's face bulged out in shock, so startled, he could only manage a weak, "Ohhhh!"

LaStanza pushed the left arm up, causing the man to rise up on his toes. Wheeling the midget around, LaStanza walked him out quickly, straight to the unmarked Chevy. Shoving the midget against the hood, he leaned over and snarled, "Don't fuckin' move, Johnny!"

Johnny wasn't really a midget. He was only a few inches shorter than LaStanza. But he was so slight, he looked more like a teenager than a twenty-five-year-old.

LaStanza had the suspect cuffed and frisked before his partner joined him. "Come on," he told Jodie as he opened the back door and shoved Johnny in. Jodie drove while LaStanza sat in the front passenger seat. When the midget started to say something, LaStanza sawed him off with, "Don't say anything, Johnny, until we get where we're going. Understand?"

They brought him in through the police garage and up the rear elevator to the Homicide Office. LaStanza put him in one of the tiny interview rooms, planting him in a hardwood folding chair that had its front legs shaved down a half inch. He left the midget in there for forty-five minutes before going back in, this time with Jodie and a notepad.

"I'm Detective LaStanza," he said, removing the handcuffs, "and this is my partner, Detective Kintyre."

Johnny's chair was alongside the lone table in the room. LaStanza took the other chair. Only the corner of the table separated the men.

"We're homicide detectives; you know what that means?" LaStanza kept his voice smooth and as unthreatening as possible.

Johnny nodded.

"Tell me," LaStanza said.

"Means murder."

"Good. Now I'm gonna read you your rights." LaStanza pulled out a Miranda rights form and read it carefully to the midget. "You understand these rights?"

"Yes, sir."

He had Johnny put his initials next to each sentence of the

rights form and then sign the bottom before leaning back and saying, "I got one question for you, Johnny. Where have you been since Friday?"

The midget blinked twice, looked up at Jodie, who was standing against the door, and then looked back at LaStanza and answered, "You had me."

"What?"

"I been in jail."

LaStanza forced himself not to look at his partner. He leaned forward and asked softly, "Where in jail?"

"Orleans Parish Prison. Can I reach in my pocket?"

LaStanza nodded. The midget withdrew a pink bond sheet and handed it to him, adding, "Police put me in jail last Wednesday. I just got out in time for the wake."

LaStanza picked up the bond sheet and walked out, avoiding his partner's gaze. He went straight for the computer.

Johnny Loomar had been arrested by a Second District patrolman at eleven-thirty P.M., Wednesday, for reckless driving and driving without a valid driver's license and four other previous traffic attachments. He had also been driving a stolen car.

LaStanza printed two copies of the information. On his way back to the interview room, he stopped by the coffeepot and fixed three cups. Stepping back into the room, he put the cups on the table, then sat back in his chair and handed his partner one of the computer printouts.

"Congratulations, Johnny," he said as he passed a cup to the midget. "You've just been cleared of a double murder."

"Good." The midget smiled nervously. "Ca-can I go?"

"Johnny," LaStanza leaned close and said, "tell me everything you know about Slow and Fawn."

Jodie never said a word. She bought the midget a Coke and refilled LaStanza's coffee cup during the interview. When LaStanza was close to finishing, she eased out of the room and waited by her desk.

"Wait a minute and we'll drive you back home," LaStanza

told Johnny when they exited the interview room.

"Can I walk?"

"Sure."

He escorted the midget out of Headquarters. Johnny Loomar was a nervous man. He'd been handled by the police before and handled well. LaStanza had seen it before. Just because a man was nervous as hell didn't make him guilty as hell.

Returning to the Homicide Office, he found Jodie sitting at her desk, her head in her hands.

"I'm sorry," she said. "I just forgot to run him when I ran all that stuff this morning . . ."

LaStanza plopped into his desk chair, kicked his feet up on his desk and covered his eyes with his arms. When she started to apologize again, he told her to stop.

"It's no big deal," he told her.

"Dino, we snatched a man out of a *funeral!*" Her voice rose.

"I know. I'm the one who did it!"

"But it was *my* fault!"

He peeked out at her and grinned. "Did you see his face when we snatched him?"

She didn't see the humor. She crossed her arms and began to stare across the room.

"Lighten up," he told her. "We all make mistakes."

"But at a *funeral?*"

"Hey, the man's a car thief. He should still be in jail instead of out on a quickie bond."

She kicked her own feet up on her desk, carefully tucking a hand beneath her skirt lest he see something he shouldn't. She was so mad at herself she wouldn't even meet his gaze.

He covered his eyes again and said, "Anyway. I've done worse."

She didn't react, so he went on.

"We kicked in a door once," he started and had to fight from laughing aloud, "down in the Ninth Ward. Rampart Street."

Standing up, he kicked his chair out of the way, drew his

68

finger out like a gun and pretended he was rushing in somewhere.

"I stuck my magnum in a lady's face and asked her where her boy was, and she says, 'Don't you know? Y'all got him!'

"Son-of-a-bitch was in *Angola!* Been in jail a *year!* We all looked at each other, and you know what Mark said?"

Jodie's cat eyes were now looking at him.

"He said . . . 'Sorry, lady. We were just making sure.' And then we left. We just *fuckin'* left!"

Jodie's face remained expressionless.

He expected a smile at least. "I don't know," he said, falling back in his chair. "Guess you had to be there."

When she didn't react, he added, "Hell, at least we didn't kick any doors tonight."

Jodie sat up and asked, "You really did that?"

"Sure did."

"You're not just making this shit up?"

"You don't believe me, ask Mark."

She didn't lighten up; she just stared at him real hard and said, "First thing Mark told me when he said I'd be riding with you was that you were the only one with a perfect record up here."

"That don't mean I don't make mistakes. How many times I gotta tell you?" He paused for emphasis. "You're only as good as your last case, partner. And right now I got *two* unsolved on my record."

Standing up, he began to pack his briefcase.

Jodie stood up a minute later and asked, "Who paid for the door?"

"The city. And Mark had to do all the explaining. He was the case officer. I was just his rookie partner."

Five
Lower Garden District

"So, anything new on your girls?" Lieutenant Rob Mason asked. Leaning back in his chair behind his own gray metal desk, Mason's face was partially obscured by a huge cloud of cigarette smoke.

LaStanza shook his head from side to side, then took another sip of the fresh coffee-and-chicory from the FUCK THIS SHIT mug. He was sitting across the desk in one of the three metal folding chairs in his lieutenant's tiny office. Mark and Snowood were in the other chairs. The rookies, Jodie and Fel, were standing in the doorway of an office that was so small, everyone had to take turns breathing, made even more difficult with all the smoke oozing from Mason.

"What about your leg case?" Mason asked Snowood.

Country-Ass spit a wad of brown shit into the Styrofoam cup cradled in his left hand and answered, "You know how many one-legged bitches live in this city?"

With that answer, Snowood guaranteed no one would ask him anything more. He was a master of that art. On this particular day, he was wearing a dusty brown western suit with an olive green shirt that had pearl buttons on it. His boots were genuine Louisiana alligator, not the bogus, Florida pussy-gators, as he so often described them.

Mason turned his lean jaw to Mark and asked about the four suicides, two unclassified deaths, two misdemeanor murders and the three project killings that had made up the work week for their platoon.

LaStanza glanced over at his partner and noticed she was staring at the big board in Mason's office. Jodie was wearing a fitted maroon skirt of the appropriate length for her, below the knee, a white blouse appropriately buttoned up to her throat, and a jacket that matched the skirt. The board she was studying was the unsolved murder board. Cases that had been closed were listed there. The board was large enough to include every homicide detective's name next to the case or cases they had never solved. It was a reminder of past failures. LaStanza was the only dick who'd been in Homicide more than one year whose name had never adorned the big board.

"According to your . . . detailed . . . dailies," Mason was talking to LaStanza again, "I see the families are no help in your case." That was Mason's way of telling Jodie her dailies were too long.

"It's a nobody-gives-a-fuck case," LaStanza said. "Typical Sixth District, dope-fiend whores with no obvious suspects." He let out a long breath and continued, "One family quit on their daughter years ago. The other's waiting for Jesus to solve it."

Mason's chiseled features slowly changed into a semi-grin. "Well," he said, "there goes your perfect record."

LaStanza was surprised to get needled by Mason. He had to smile. It was about time he joined the big boys. Mason, one who never criticized anyone in public, who was known for his gentle prodding in private, reserved his teasing for Mark and the other sergeants, until now.

"Naw, he'll solve it," Snowood injected. "Little bastard never gives up on anything. Besides, he working on his home turf."

"What's your excuse?" Mark said, nodding to the big board that listed Snowood's name twice. Mark's name was up there, too. Even Mason's name was next to a case listed as UNSUB.

71

He'd inherited a bag of bones with a bullet hole through the head a couple years back.

LaStanza turned to Country-Ass and said, "What happened to your fruity ex-partner?"

Snowood spread his arms to the heavens and said, "Keith-the-dick-sucker has been banished to Auto Theft, and now I finally got a partner darker than you."

As usual, no one addressed the rookies until the meeting was over. On his way out, Snowood tapped Jodie on her shoulder and pointed back to LaStanza. "Is he as good a lay as he thinks he is?"

She stumbled to answer.

LaStanza stood up and said, "Don't you know better than to answer him?"

"Come on, now," Mark snapped on his way out. "Cut it out."

Snowood came back with a sentence that froze everyone. He said, "I just don't want us killing this one like we did the last one."

No one moved for a second. LaStanza felt his stomach bottom out. He was the first to move, slowly, to his desk.

"I wish he wouldn't pick on me in front of the lieutenant," Jodie complained to LaStanza a few minutes later after everyone had left and they were alone in the squad room.

He didn't answer. He was thinking about the only other woman who'd ever worked Homicide. Her name was Millie Suzanne. She'd gone on a warrant with LaStanza and Snowood and Mark one evening and hadn't come back. It had been LaStanza's warrant.

"He's so jealous of you," Jodie went on.

LaStanza looked at her and said, "What?"

She repeated her statement.

"Wrong," he told her. "He can be a pain in the ass, all right. Loves to tease people. But he isn't jealous."

Jodie started to make her point, talking about the big board and bringing up the Slasher Case and the Twenty-two Killer. But he wasn't listening. He was thinking about Millie . . . about how she died in his arms. No, she was dead before he got to her. He remembered feeling her warm blood rolling across his hands and into his lap.

He was thankful when he saw his lieutenant coming back into the squad room. Mason walked over and handed him a phone message. It was from someone named Clark with a west bank exchange number.

"Also, I got a call from the lab. Spermatozoa present in moderate numbers on the vaginal swabs from both girls. The other swabs were negative."

LaStanza nodded and looked at the message with the name Clark and the west bank number. He remembered now, the first River Road canvass. It was the pissed-off man with the white hair.

Clark answered after the first ring. Before LaStanza was finished identifying himself, Clark started babbling about the old armory at the end of River Road and Cubans and the Bay of Pigs Invasion.

"Whoa, slow down."

"Okay. Your victims were black, right?"

"Right."

"Could they be Cuban?" Clark asked.

"No, they were Sixth District whores."

"Huh?"

"They were Camp Street whores. Capish?"

"Yeah. But they ended up out here, and those Bay of Pigs guys trained out here . . ."

"Bay of Pigs? Back in the sixties?"

"Yeah." The man was serious. "Some of them trained at the old armory."

"Mr. Clark"—LaStanza tried to be polite—"I don't think the Bay of Pigs people were involved in this."

The man's voice deflated quickly. "Well, if you think so."

"Look, thanks," LaStanza added. "If you come up

73

with anything else, call, okay?"

"Sure. But you better look into those Bay of Pigs fellas. They were bad news."

"Yeah, I remember."

Then the old man hung up.

"Come on," LaStanza told his partner, "let's get outta here before someone links our girls to the Kennedy assassination."

"What?"

The oldest homicide cliche went like this: "You don't solve a case by sitting on your ass."

LaStanza ran the cliche by Jodie on her first day but never repeated it. He knew he didn't have to. It was probably in her little notebook. But he showed her, every chance he got. On that sunny Tuesday afternoon, he took her back to the Sixth for more canvassing. Nothing ever got solved in the Bureau.

They stopped first on Baronne Street, outside a bar with no name on it. They stopped, but the Chevy continued running, clanging and popping as they walked toward the bar.

Better known as the No Door Bar because it had no front door, Freddie's Blue Note was located at the corner of Baronne and Euterpe. LaStanza let his partner walk in first, which succeeded in distracting all the pool players crowded around the two tables in the place.

LaStanza found Freddie, as usual, behind the bar. The old man was bald-headed and his left eye still drooped from where it had been struck by a pool cue wielded by an asshole on angel dust, an asshole who LaStanza and his partner, Stan Smith, had beat the dog shit out of, some years ago.

Freddie recognized LaStanza immediately and gave him the standard line: "I don't know nothin'."

LaStanza thanked the old man and led his partner out to the Chevy that was *still* sputtering. He drove directly to a pay phone on St. Charles Avenue and dialed the No Door Bar.

Freddie answered, "Yeah, man, who is it?"

"It's LaStanza. Can you talk?"

"Yeah. It's about those girls, huh?"

"Yep."

"Word on the street says they was into some bad shit, you know."

"No, tell me."

"Tees and blues and crack and whoring up a storm. Bitches came in here a couple times, but I run 'em out."

"I need to know who they ran with. Where they got their shit," LaStanza said.

"I know. I ain't stupid. I got my ear to the curb on it. You know soon as I know."

"Thanks, Freddie."

"Yeah, call me back in a couple days, all right?"

"Thanks again."

He told Jodie about the conversation on their way to Coliseum Street. She put the information in her notes.

"Put that info from Mason about the sperm in your notes, too."

"Already did."

He should have known. They parked next to the poo-poo square. The Chevy coughed against the curb, like a dying dinosaur.

"I'm not getting in this piece-a-shit again." LaStanza scowled as he got out and kicked the left fender so hard he left a dent in it. The Chevy burped back.

They split up immediately. He sent Jodie up to Prytania Street while he worked his way up Coliseum Street all the way to Urania Street, talking to anyone who'd talk back.

They linked up on Urania in front of a house that had been recently renovated. It was a two-story, wooden house with four square columns out front that supported an upstairs gallery. It was surrounded by a standard-issue, uptown, black wrought iron fence.

Jodie had picked up a couple stragglers, two little black boys.

"Scoot," she was telling them when her partner arrived. The kids both grinned back at her. LaStanza told her to ignore them. "They'll get bored."

"Little mooks keep trying to look up my dress when I walk up the porches."

"Can't be mooks," he corrected her. "Not old enough. Haven't learned to be useless, low-life, scumbag, worthless mother-fuckers. They're still kids."

"Oh," she said, "you didn't explain the subtleties of your Sixth District slang."

"Now you know."

He didn't want to go into the skirt peeking. The kids would have to be on their backs to look up her long skirt.

LaStanza and Jodie started back down Urania toward Coliseum Square, the kids trailing behind, when a voice called out to them. A lady, standing behind the wrought iron fence of the renovated house, waved to them. She was a heavy-set, white woman with wiry, white-blond hair that sported long black roots. She was middle-aged, stood about as tall as the midget Loomar and weighed about twice as much. She had a Chihuahua cradled in the crook of her left arm.

"Yoo-hoo!" the fat lady called out in a sing-song voice. "You there. Come over here." She was wearing a safari suit that was two sizes too small.

LaStanza noticed, as he approached, how much the woman looked like Peter Ustinov in drag, an ugly Peter Ustinov.

"Are you the police?" she asked.

LaStanza nodded, easing behind his partner so that Jodie could handle this important phase of their investigation.

"Didn't I see you over on Terpsickory a little while ago?" she asked Jodie. God, if there was one thing LaStanza loathed, it was the phoney-baloney uptown-white-people's pronunciation of Terpsichore Street as Terpsickory.

Jodie confirmed she had indeed been on Terpsichore earlier.

"Well, what are you two doing?"

Jodie started to explain about the double murder, but the fat woman wouldn't let her.

"Why are you going around and stirring things up?" The sing-song voice rose to a sickening level. "Why are you alarming the entire neighborhood like this?"

Jodie bristled back, "Lady, we're doing our job."

"Didn't that murder happen across the river?"

"Yes." Jodie's teeth were clenched.

"Well, then why are you incensing *our* neighborhood?"

LaStanza put a hand on his partner's arm and stepped up against the fence. Resting an elbow atop the fence, he said, "Lady, you know where you live?"

"What's that supposed to mean?" The woman was getting angrier by the moment.

"Around here, murder's as common as air, lady."

"Now, that's the kind of attitude we've been fighting!" The Peter Ustinov jowls began to reverberate.

"And who's we?" LaStanza was grinning at her just like the kids had grinned at Jodie a minute ago.

"I'll have you know, I'm president of the Lower Garden District Association."

LaStanza pulled out his notepad and put up a hand to stop her, "What's your name, lady?"

"I'm Mrs. Gerrols, president of the Lower Garden District Association . . ."

LaStanza looked over at the street number on her front gate and jotted down her address.

"What are you writing down?" The woman leaned over to look in his notebook.

LaStanza flipped the notebook closed and said, "Where are you from, lady?" He was having a good time.

"I know exactly what you mean by that crack." The woman began shaking a plump finger in his face. "Just because I'm not from New Orleans doesn't mean . . ."

He pulled out a mug shot of Pam Camp and put it in front of the woman's pug nose. "Ever see this whore before?"

Mrs. Gerrols brushed the photo out of the way and shook her finger at him again. This time her dog joined in the jabbering. "We are trying to *lighten* this neighborhood, and you coming around here . . ."

"Lighten?" LaStanza looked at Jodie and said, "Did she say lighten?" He began to laugh out loud.

"Yes," Mrs. Gerrols declared.

"As in lighter-colored people?" Jodie asked.

"Yes, to put it bluntly. We're trying to attract the right kind of people back here, and you're not helping . . ."

Carpetbagger, LaStanza didn't say it, but that was the word. Damn, overweight Yankee, probably got the money to renovate her house from low-interest federal reclamation money. He wanted to stay and *really* make her mad, but he felt hungry and remembered there was a good restaurant a couple streets over.

"Don't you walk away when I'm talking to you!" Mrs. Gerrols called out as he started to leave.

The restaurant had a funny name. Something like the Mad Duck. He kept walking, his partner following, down Urania, back toward the square. The two black kids had run off when the shouting began.

"Come back here!" the fat woman called out behind them. "Come right back here!"

"There's a really good restaurant around here," LaStanza told Jodie.

"What an asshole!" Jodie said.

LaStanza started laughing again. "That was one Republican-looking bitch.

"I think its off Magazine. I only went there once. It used to be a cooking school," he explained. "Stan and I ate there, but he wouldn't go back. He didn't like to eat in nice places."

"An expensive restaurant around here?"

"Not expensive. Just nice. No roaches in your soup."

"Oh."

On Magazine, LaStanza stopped a very fat man who

looked as if he should know where all the eating spots were within a twenty-block radius. The man was wearing a yellow Hawaiian shirt and a pair of shorts the color of an army tent, and just as large.

"It's on St. Mary," the very fat man pointed up the street. "And it's not the Mad Duck; it's the Enraged Chicken."

"I knew it was on a side street," LaStanza told his partner as they walked up to St. Mary Street and took a right. The Enraged Chicken occupied a small brick building sandwiched between a defunct Chinese laundry and a junk shop. The building's facade was painted pink. There used to be a large sign with a duck, no, a chicken on it. Now there was just a small plaque with the restaurant's name.

The menu was modest and inexpensive, but it had a wine list. Jodie ordered roast chicken and mashed potatoes. La-Stanza ordered the same, along with iced tea. Their waitress was Hispanic. She wore a red blouse and a short, black skirt and smiled shyly at them when she took their order.

When the waitress walked off, Jodie put her elbows on the table and cupped her chin in the palms of her hand and said, "I've heard of the Garden District, but what the hell's the *Lower* Garden District?"

LaStanza explained the difference. "It's the low-class garden district. Camp Street, skid row, the St. Thomas Housing Project, the Coliseum, 'poo-poo' Square and now a buncha yuppie whites trying to rewhiten the area."

"God, what an asshole," Jodie repeated.

"Trying to be upper class in a low-class area. Gimme the blacks; give me the *mooks*. At least you can talk to them. They know crime."

The food was very good, especially the iced tea. It wasn't as good as Brulie's tea, but close.

Stepping back out on St. Mary, LaStanza saw something that made him do a double take.

"What is it?" Jodie asked.

He watched the tail end of a new, maroon Thunderbird

disappear down Magazine Street.

"Nothing," he said, "just thought I saw somebody I knew."

They started for the poo-poo square, LaStanza looking back up Magazine in the direction where the T-Bird had gone.

"Who was it?" she asked.

"Guy named Rafferty. Ex-police. He was a friend of my brother's." LaStanza turned back around and continued toward the square.

Jodie was particularly quiet the rest of the way back to the Chevy, so he asked her, "What's up, white girl?"

"Mason told me about your brother."

"Oh." He looked out across the square. It was getting dark now. The drunks and other refuse were collecting big time on the benches of Coliseum Square.

"I went to his grave the other day," LaStanza heard himself say, "and some asshole had used a grease pencil on my brother's tombstone. Right below the inscription 'Killed in the Line of Duty,' someone wrote 'so what.' "

Back at the carcass of the unmarked Chevy, LaStanza lifted his radio and called for a tow truck and a Sixth District unit.

"I'll drive it," Jodie said cheerfully.

"I'm deadlining this bastard," he snapped and then added in a quieter voice, "You can check another unit out of the motor pool tomorrow." But he knew what he was driving from now on. He'd pay for his own gas.

The street lights came on, half of them, anyway. LaStanza leaned against the Chevy's fender and looked around in time to see Mrs. Gerrols approaching.

"Here comes Mrs. Goebbels," he told Jodie as the Chihuahua started yapping and the fat lady started her "Yoo-hoos."

"Officer! See those little Negroes." The woman was pointing to the fountain in the square. "They're not supposed to swim in our fountain."

LaStanza turned in the other direction, refusing to even look at the fountain, but that didn't stop the woman. She wad-

80

dled around in front of him and said, "I want you to get those little Negroes out of our fountain!"

Fuckin' fountain never worked. He wanted to shout it right in her fat face, but instead, he swallowed hard and said, "You know, lady, an hour ago you were funny. Now you're getting to be a pain in the butt."

"Huh? I'll have you know that I represent—"

"All the white people around here. I'm impressed."

Mrs. Gerrols stammered, "I know the new chief of police *personally,* and I want your badge number, young man."

"Lady, I'm gonna ask you one time, polite like. Get outta my face!"

"You heard me! I want your badge number!"

He stepped forward quickly, so close to the woman that she took two steps back.

"The name's LaStanza, lady. I work *Homicide!* I don't give a rat's ass about your freaking fountain. You want a patrolman, call the police!"

"I'm calling your chief."

"Lady, I don't care who you call so long as you take your Lower Garden District White People's Association back to Your-Anus Street and get outta my face. *Now!*"

He wanted to punch her lungs out and drop kick her fuckin' dog all the way to the Superdome, but this wasn't Nazi Germany, even if he was talking to Mrs. Goebbels.

The fat woman wasn't stupid. She could take a hint, especially from a Sicilian with blood in his eye. So she stomped off, huffing under her breath, her nauseating dog yapping back at the detectives.

A couple seconds later, a Sixth District unit pulled up. LaStanza took one look at it and wished with all his might that he had called Mark to come get them.

The car was manned by a sergeant whose uniform shirts had been tailored to show off his muscles. The sleeves had been shortened and narrowed so that his shoulders looked even bigger than they were. His blond hair, touched up with highlighters, was hair-sprayed in place. He wore dark sunglasses, even at night, and smiled at LaStanza and Jodie with teeth that were polished regularly. His name was Stan Smith, Stan-The-Man, legend on the streets of the Sixth, agent provocateur, playboy without portfolio, the ideal policeman, if he didn't say so himself.

Stan paused for dramatic effect before saying, "You called?"

"Drive us to the Bureau," LaStanza said, "and not one fuckin' word!"

He climbed in front, and Jodie went in back. Stan's silence lasted a couple blocks. LaStanza felt lucky at that. Passing up Martin Luther King Boulevard, Stan pointed to an all-night convenience store and said, "Remember that place, Candy-Ass?"

LaStanza refused to answer.

So Stan craned his neck around and told Jodie, "Your padna got in his first fight back there, when he was a rookie. With a big nigger who gleeked him while I was in the store getting a cold drink."

"Gleeked?"

"Yeah, that's when somebody wearing sunglasses puts his chin down and peeks at you over the top of his glasses. Checks you out. Gleeks you." Stan lowered his chin to show her.

"More Sixth District slang," Jodie said.

"Try watching the road," LaStanza told his old partner.

Stan was rolling. "I go buy my cold drink, and the guy behind the counter says, 'Officer, go ahead. You don't have to pay for it.'

" 'Say what?' I tell him.

"He points outside, and says, ' 'Cause your partner's fighting with a big guy out there.'

"Candy-Ass was fighting with a big mulatto-looking nigger. Rolling on the sidewalk. Big nigger had the upper hand but also had hisself a handful of Tasmanian devil. Of course I had to step in and cold cock the big mook, and know what Candy-

Ass says? He says, 'Son-of-a-bitch gleeked me!' I coulda shit."

As usual, Stan left out a couple things from his story, like who threw the first punch, but LaStanza wasn't about to open his mouth. Stan would *never* shut up then.

The rest of the way to the Bureau, Stan told more Candy-Ass stories. As soon as the car stopped in the police garage, LaStanza jumped out. He almost made a clean getaway until he heard the unit's P.A. system crack on and Stan's voice boom, "Don't even tell me you're not fuckin' her!"

Lizette was already asleep when LaStanza got home. He rearmed the alarm, relocked the dead bolt on the cut glass front door and put his briefcase and portable radio in the study. He reached around the wet bar and poured himself a stiff belt of Cutty Sark.

He walked back through the study, across the foyer and through the formal dining room into the kitchen. He grabbed three ice cubes from the refrigerator and put them in the scotch and then took a sip. It was warm and bit at him on the way down.

He looked out the rear french doors of the kitchen, at their well-lit, small backyard, at the Jacuzzi sitting dormant and the magnolia trees and the large leaves of the banana trees dripping down toward the well-groomed grass.

Turning around, he started back through the mansion. Without realizing what he was doing, he was checking out the place, checking out their quiet house. They were safe enough, with their alarm and the dead bolts and barred windows, and with his stainless steel .357 magnum, Smith and Wesson model 66, still riding his hip holster at the small of his back.

He didn't realize it at first, but he felt . . . sad. Not lonely, with his wife upstairs asleep, but sad. It was called the blues. He felt that way every once in a while, especially after the evening watch, when he was still up and the rest of the world was asleep. He never thought much about it because it didn't happen often.

He walked around the house and drank until he finished the scotch. Then he poured himself another. Back in the study, he sat in the big easy chair next to the fireplace and looked up at the mantel where the portrait of Lizette's twin sister used to hang before the Louviers took it with them to the estate. It was Lizette's sister who had brought them together. Lynette Anne Louvier had been twenty years old when she was murdered. He'd been the case officer.

He closed his eyes and thought of another girl. His mind filled with a vision of the electric daughter. He never dreamed of her, but thought of her often. He thought of her dark, Hispanic eyes and the way she smiled at him with her oversized lower lip protruding. He wondered where she was now and what she was doing. But most of all, he wondered if she was all right. It bothered him that she could die and he would never know.

He began to feel the scotch. He could never hold his liquor; that was one reason he didn't drink. That, and the fact his father was already down the road to becoming a drunk.

Lizette woke momentarily when her husband slipped into bed next to her. She rolled over and ran her hand over his chest and sighed. He kissed her cheek, and she snuggled her head in the crook of his shoulder. Her easy breathing soon returned, and she was back asleep.

He closed his eyes and tried to dream himself to sleep. But he never dreamed when he wanted to, and he never dreamed what he wanted to dream. He felt the fuzziness of the scotch working on his brain, but he still could not sleep.

He used to dream of Vietnam, of dismembered yellow bodies and of wounded GIs, mostly black, and of a sweltering sun setting on a river of red-brown water, a river slower and shallower than the Mississippi, but far deadlier. In his dreams, that river ran directly to hell.

He had only been in Vietnam a short while, near the end of the war, back when nobody gave a fuck, not even the South

Vietnamese. Sometimes, in those dreams, he could hear the faint call of cadence that always ended with "I don't want no teenage queen. I just want my M-16."

There was a song they used to sing when they marked time. It went to the tune of the old rock and roll hit "Poison Ivy":

Vi . . . et . . . nam
Vi . . . et . . . nam
Late at night
While you're sleeping
Charlie Cong comes a creeping
A . . . round
Vi . . . et . . . nam

He'd thought he'd been to the infernal regions when he went to southeast Asia, until he returned home and worked the Bloody Sixth District. The dreams of death in the jungle faded quickly, supplanted by dreams of blood on the sidewalk of a city he had thought was the most wonderful place on earth when he was a boy and everything was big and clean and safe.

Now he dreamed of intestines like snakes.

Six
Terpsichore Street

LaStanza had just kicked his feet up on his desk when Mark Land came over and asked, "You guys sign your PANO letter yet?"

"What letter?" Jodie answered. She was sipping coffee at her desk.

"Your PANO 'Get Fucked' letter."

LaStanza began rubbing his temples and decided he might as well get into the conversation.

"What the fuck are you talking about?"

"The sign downstairs. On the naked man."

LaStanza looked cross-eyed at his partner, grabbed his tie and pulled it up like a hanged man, letting his tongue dangle out. Jodie struggled to keep from laughing in their sergeant's face.

Mark went on, "You never saw the sign hanging from the naked man?"

"No." LaStanza regained his composure, adding, "We've been busy trying to solve murders."

Mark continued, "You know that stupid statue downstairs?"

Of course they knew. Everyone knew the large, hammered brass statue of the naked man just inside the entrance to

Headquarters. The statue was holding up a hand as if he was stopping traffic. Although the man was naked, he had no genitalia.

Mark's voice rose. "Well, some smart-ass taped a sign between his legs that said, 'This must be an administrator because he has no balls.' "

"So!" LaStanza said.

"So, the chief saw it and got pissed off, roused Internal Affairs and now we're in the middle of a big fuckin' investigation."

LaStanza pulled his feet from his desk and shrugged. "You're gonna have to handle these little domestic matters yourself, Sarge. You know, we got *work* to do around here."

"That's what the PANO letter's about." Mark was beginning to pronounce each word, one at a time, as if he was talking to his kids. "The chief wants to polygraph people, so PANO's telling him to get fucked, in so many words."

LaStanza put a hand over his eyes and stuck his other hand out. "Just give me the letter and I'll sign it."

Mark growled, "It's in your IN basket. Try lookin' there once in a while."

Sure enough, there was a letter with POLICE ASSOCIATION OF NEW ORLEANS across the top. LaStanza glanced over it. It said something about the Civil Service Commission and due process.

"Jesus," he said as he signed the letter, "it takes administrators to try and punish someone for telling the truth."

Jodie looked up from her form letter and added, "It's like goddam Peyton-fuckin'-Place around here."

LaStanza had to blink. The white girl was coming around, all right.

"Did she say the 'F' word?" Snowood called out from his desk. He was reading the sports section, his boots also up on his desk.

"Sounded like it to me," LaStanza answered.

Jodie's face began to blush . . . slightly.

"When a woman starts using 'fuck' in her language, it's time to call in the poultry!" Snowood added.

Whatever the fuck that meant.

Mark jumped on Country-Ass from his office door, "Don't you have anything better to do?"

"I'm just waitin' for someone to die." Snowood gave his standard reply.

"What about your leg case?"

"My rookie partner's writing up the daily right now for you, *Sarge.*" Snowood liked to drag the word "sarge." "We solved it yesterday."

"Oh, *yeah?*" Mark dragged back.

LaStanza stood up and started packing his briefcase as Snowood began his story: "You see, there's this diabetic old lady who went to the First Presbyterian Medical Center on St. Charles a couple weeks ago and had a leg removed. Seems it was handed over to the Quayle Funeral Home on Oak Street, for disposal. Well, as you can surmise, instead of burying the leg, the funeral home paid this fifteen-year-old black kid to dispose of it. The kid threw it in the dumpster, and presto-magico, we was called."

"You got the kid?"

"Gave us a good statement. Old man Quayle paid ten dollars to the kid, himself."

"You cut a warrant for this Quayle fella?"

"Nope."

Mark had to sit down.

"You see, *Sarge,* ain't no law against it."

Mark started to cite a statute, but Snowood put his hand up. "That law says it's a crime to improperly dispose of bodies and limbs of *dead* people. Says nothin' about diabetic old ladies who are still breathin'."

Mark stood up and bellowed, "I'm getting a *fuckin' migraine!*"

"What are you grinning about?" Jodie asked LaStanza as they left the office.

"The sign on the naked man," he said, but he was thinking about another sign. When he was a rookie, after a series of late-night escapes from the old Parish Prison, some wiseass cop went to the Orleans Parish Sheriff's Office sign shop and had them make up a sign. Then the wiseass put the sign up in place of one of the NO PARKING signs on Girod Street, between the prison and police headquarters. The new sign read:

CAUTION: ESCAPED PRISONER CROSSING

There was a big flap over it, especially when the sheriff discovered his own shop had made the sign. That was how they knew a policeman did it. "It was an N.O.P.D. man," the sign maker said. "A good-looking guy with black curly hair." They never caught the wiseass, although most of the department found out who it was over time. The wiseass was Joseph LaStanza. Dino was never more proud of his big brother.

"By the way," Jodie interrupted his thoughts, "where are we going?"

"Back to the Sixth to canvass."

"Again?"

"Again."

She nodded wearily and then added, "I thought you were going to make a snide remark about that Presbyterian hospital."

"Goddam Protestant sect!"

Smokey Robinson got in three songs before the Maserati pulled up on Terpsichore Street. LaStanza parked against the small neutral ground of the median divider. A host of businesses lined either side of this portion of Terpsichore, just off Coliseum Square. Mixed in between the businesses were the usual, run-down houses.

The first place they checked out was a junk shop with "Algerian Antiques" painted on its glass front door. The place was narrow and dusty, filled with lamp shades and statues of camels and old magazines and the assorted remnants of things thrown out years ago.

The proprietor was standing behind a glass counter. He was an old man in his late sixties. He was wearing a plaid, lumberjack shirt, blue jeans and one of those Arab handkerchiefs on his head with a silk rope around it.

LaStanza's father would call him a "rug head." So the first thing he asked the old man was, "What do you call that thing on your head?"

"It's a keffiyeh," the old man answered, focusing a pair of deep brown eyes on LaStanza. He was a lean man with a rugged face and a full, reddish brown beard generously sprinkled with gray. He looked more European than Arabic.

LaStanza opened his coat to show the badge, put his radio on the glass counter and said, "I'm Detective LaStanza, and my partner's Detective Kintyre."

The old man looked at Jodie and raised his eyebrows. "Not bad. Is she a real girl?"

LaStanza did a double take and then had to laugh. "Far as I can tell."

Jodie moved away and started browsing the store. The old man's gaze followed her. She was wearing a khaki dress with large pockets over her breasts and a matching belt that made the dress snug and showed that she had a figure. The dress had buttons all the way down its front, and when she'd sat in the Maserati, LaStanza noticed, she had left the last button near the bottom of the dress undone.

"What's your name, old man?"

"Marid. And don't call me an old man." The brown eyes were still following Jodie around.

"Last name?"

"You couldn't pronounce it."

"Humor me."

90

"Ahbhu." Then he spelled it out.

"Ever seen these girls around here?" LaStanza pulled out the mug shot and the picture of the other dead Pam and put them on the counter.

Marid finally moved his eyes from Jodie and examined the pictures. "Seen both of them around," he said, "but not lately."

So LaStanza went through the entire routine. When did he see them? Who were they with? And anything else the old man might know or had seen. Marid knew nothing of any value. He was cooperative enough, as he continued eyeballing Jodie.

LaStanza tucked the pictures back into his coat pocket and asked in conclusion, "Where are you from?"

"Uptown."

Everyone's a comedian.

"Before that."

"Algiers. The real one. I used to be a policeman in Algiers. But when the French left Algeria, I did, too. I'm half French."

Jodie eased over and stood next to her partner. The old man flashed his best smile at her and showed off teeth that were still in good shape. If they were his.

Moving around the side of the counter next to LaStanza, Marid started asking Jodie about herself. It was then La-Stanza noticed the man had half of a left foot. He tried not to make it obvious as he examined the half shoe on the foot. The man wore a shoe like Tom Dempsey, the New Orleans Saint who kicked the sixty-three-yard field goal.

LaStanza suddenly remembered something.

"Ever see a punk around here named Cherry?"

Marid looked back at him and nodded. "Place is full of punks."

"Sometimes wears long wigs," LaStanza added, "real long wigs." He looked out at the street. He remembered Cherry used to live somewhere in that block.

"Yeah, you right," Marid said, pointing across Terpsichore. "I think she stays in that green house. Apartment on the left side. Always wears long wigs."

"Thanks." LaStanza nodded to his partner that it was time to leave. "Catch ya later," he told the old man.

"Inshallah!" Marid called out behind them.

"What does that mean?" Jodie asked.

"It means 'if God wills.' "

Jodie smiled at the old man.

Marid winked back at her and added, "Yeah, you right."

Cherry wasn't home, so they knocked on the three other doors of the green house. No one else was home or bothered to answer. So they checked out the massage parlor next door. No one there had ever seen the two Pams or ever heard of Cherry, and they knew nothing about whoring or narcotics or anything. They didn't even know where Coliseum Square was located. One of the masseuses was rubbing lotion on her hands during their conversation. The lotion smelled just like semen.

"Did anything about that Marid fellow strike you as curious?" Jodie asked when they exited the massage parlor.

"Nope."

"Ex-cop. Knows how to use a gun. Algiers? Algeria?" Then she added another homicide cliche LaStanza had taught her, "A good homicide man doesn't believe in coincidences."

LaStanza shook his head. "Unless he can grow a left foot at will, he ain't our boy."

"What?"

"He's only got half a left foot."

"When did you notice that?"

"When you two were making eyes."

Jodie rolled her eyes and added, "Maybe he can wear regular shoes."

LaStanza stopped walking. "Our killer was in his socks."

"Oh, yeah." She turned her cat eyes away from him, really embarrassed at that one. "Can't believe I forgot about the socks."

92

"Nobody's perfect."

"That supposed to comfort me?"

They spent the rest of the afternoon and a good part of the evening along the picturesque streets of the Sixth. They knocked on nearly a hundred doors and entered every bar in the area. They went back to Cherry's three times but still got no answer. Then LaStanza called Freddie right before midnight. Freddie had nothing for them.

"Well, let's go," he finally said. Waiting until she was comfortable in her leather seat, he added, "Pick you up at seven A.M."

"What for?"

"Cherry's got to come home sometime."

At seven-fifteen A.M., the door to the apartment on the left side of the green building opened after LaStanza pounded on it for two minutes. Cherry stood in the doorway blinking her large brown eyes at them. She was wearing navy blue pajamas, her face still smeared with makeup, lipstick smudged across her large lips. She was also wearing a long blond wig. Cherry's skin was so dark, it looked like black satin.

Without a word, Cherry turned around and started back through the apartment. LaStanza followed with Jodie right behind, through a room cluttered with discarded clothes draped over sofa and chairs, a broken coffee table, and enough cardboard boxes to fill a Goodwill store.

LaStanza kept Cherry in sight, through the first room to the bedroom. The bed was covered with more clothes. So was the floor. Cherry turned back to them just outside of the bathroom, opened her pajama top and dropped it on the floor. Two large breasts floated free as she turned toward the bathroom.

"Keep the door open," LaStanza said as he sat on the edge of the bed, keeping his eye on Cherry while she brushed her teeth.

93

Jodie moved around the bed and stood next to the bathroom doorway. She was also wearing navy blue, a smart business suit with a white blouse, buttoned to the neck, and navy blue heels. LaStanza, unfortunately, was wearing a navy blue jacket, but at least he had tan pants.

Headquarters decided to call LaStanza at that moment. He answered, but only after he'd made them call twice. They had a message for him, from a Mr. Clark.

He was acknowledging when he heard Cherry say, "Hey, white girl, looka this."

Before LaStanza could warn his partner, Cherry whipped out a large penis.

"Yuk!" Jodie fell back toward the bed.

Cherry turned her back to them and began to urinate in the commode.

LaStanza tried not to laugh, but it was hard, especially with the sour look on his partner's face.

"It isn't funny," Jodie yelled at him.

"But you're such a white girl." He laughed.

"That's not funny either!"

"I told you she was a punk," he managed to say between laughs.

"So?"

"Don't you know a punk's a fruit?"

"*No!* What's that? *More* Sixth District slang?" Jodie stormed out of the bedroom.

He had thought everyone knew a punk was a fruit. At least, every cop. Oh, well, he thought to himself, she learned something new.

LaStanza watched Cherry climb into a pair of jeans and pull a light sweater over her ample breasts. He had a question for the punk.

"Hey, how do you turn tricks with a dick?"

"All a whore needs is lips, tits and fingertips." It was Cherry's turn to laugh. LaStanza searched her purse before they left.

Back at the Maserati, he told his partner she missed the most important lesson of the day.

"I don't wanna hear it!"

"All a whore needs," LaStanza repeated the saying, "is lips, tits and fingertips."

"I said, I don't wanna hear it!" Jodie was hot.

"What's the matter"—Cherry decided to be cute—"never seen a big black dick before?"

LaStanza reached over, snatched Cherry by the back of the neck and pulled the punk so hard, she almost fell over. "You shut-the-fuck-up until I ask you a question! Capish?"

Cherry tried to nod.

He opened a rear door with Cherry's neck still in hand and shoved the punk inside.

"You could have warned me," Jodie snapped at him.

"It happened too fast," he said as he slammed the rear door and then added, "I'm sorry, Okay?"

"It could have been a gun. And you don't sound sorry."

Sound sorry? He had to force himself to keep from adding, "Gun? It looked like a magnum to me."

"Ouuu weee," Cherry was saying when he climbed in, "where'd you get this car?"

"Drug bust," he said, "and *shut up!*"

Cherry was running her fingertips across the leather backseat. LaStanza popped in a Led Zeppelin tape and turned up the stereo before pulling away. A hard, driving drum started up immediately, followed by screeching guitars until Robert Plant came in with his hollow voice, singing about rain and levees.

He caught Cherry eyeballing him in the rearview mirror. She was making eyes at him.

Before he could snap at her, she asked, over the loud music, "You part black?"

"Shut up!"

"You sure are good-lookin'."

He felt Jodie staring at him for a block before he turned to her with a curt, "What?"

"Don't be such a black boy," Jodie said, turning away to smile in infantile satisfaction at the early-morning traffic.

LaStanza put Cherry in an interview room, put on a fresh pot of coffee and then called Mr. Clark.

"Officer LaStanza," Clark said excitedly, "I'm glad you called. Since one of your victims was named Pam Campo, then maybe she was Cuban after all and—"

"Her name was Pam Camp." LaStanza spelled it out, "C . . . A . . . M . . . P. Period!"

"But the paper said it was Campo."

"Don't believe what you read in the paper. It was Camp, and she *wasn't* Cuban. Understand?"

"I guess so." Clark didn't sound convinced. "I just thought, well, it says Campo in the *Picayune*."

"You want their number?"

"No!" The man hung up.

LaStanza looked at the receiver and yelled, "And Campo's *Italian! You fuckin' idiot!*"

Cherry's real name was Thomas Lee Butler. Arrested for prostitution three times, Butler had also been popped for shoplifting, disturbing the peace, criminal mischief, obscenity, and had one felony arrest for indecent behavior with a juvenile. Butler had also been booked with, of all things, Peeping Tom. LaStanza wasn't about to ask about that one. All in all, Butler had been arrested nine times but never convicted of anything. In fact, according to the police computer, every charge had been dismissed by the crime-fighting D.A. of Orleans Parish.

Armed with a fresh cup of coffee-and-chicory, a cassette recorder and his notepad, LaStanza marched into the interview room with his partner. Cherry had been in the room for an hour.

"We can do this the easy way or the hard way," LaStanza

said as he pulled up a chair on the same side of the table as the punk and sat next to Cherry. "Either way," he added, "you're gonna tell me everything I want to know. Make no doubt about it." He grinned at Cherry and then offered her a cold drink.

Cherry said yes, and Jodie went to get a Coke from the machine in the hall. LaStanza waited for his partner to leave before saying, "Now, we've all had our fun this morning, but now we're gonna work."

It took Cherry three Coca-Colas and two visits to the bathroom before she admitted she knew the Pams, especially Pam Dillards. They used to hang out together before Dillards started hanging out with Pam Camp, who was a "real lesbian," according to the semi-transsexual sitting next to LaStanza.

Two hours after they began, Cherry was flirting with LaStanza again. When she brushed her leg against his, he moved away but didn't snap her head off. They were beyond that. They were friends.

Pam Dillards used to hang out at two bars, George's Love-In at the corner of Euterpe and Prytania and the Fade-Out at Prytania and Melpomene. LaStanza knew the places, especially the Fade-Out. Both were bad . . . very bad. He wouldn't get any information there. Maybe Cherry could. He asked her, and she said she would try; but he'd worked the street long enough to know she was pulling his chain.

They ordered out for pizza and then got down to details. He needed to know who pimped the girls. And more importantly, where they got their shit.

Cherry had anchovies and black olives. Jodie had pepperoni, and LaStanza had Italian sausage. Cherry explained, dripping mozzarella from her lips, that the Pams whored on their own. So he weaseled the names of all the pimps in the area and then the dope dealers, especially the ones dealing tees and blues. Cherry told him about a dealer named Sal Louis who stayed at the House of the Lamb "occasionally" and a fella named Sam who stayed in the Melpomene Housing

Project. Both were "bad dudes." Both sounded small-time to LaStanza.

By the time the evening watch, their watch, was due to arrive, it was time to take Cherry home.

"You don't have to take me home, darling," she told LaStanza as she touched up her makeup. "I got things I can do in this neighborhood." So he escorted her out of Headquarters.

Jodie was at the computer when he returned, running a file on Sal Louis. He was small-time, all right. LaStanza hit the printout button and then asked her to run the streets around Coliseum Square for all prostitution and drug arrests. Then they ran George's Love-In and the Fade-Out. They almost burned out the printer.

"No use running Sam-of-the-Melpomene," he told her. "Must be a fuckin' million Sams."

"Could be worse," she added, still waiting for the printer to stop. "Could be named Tyrone or Leroy."

He was too tired to laugh but patted her shoulder. "Not a bad joke. For a Presbyterian."

"Why don't we call Narcotics?" she asked. "They have to have info on . . ."

LaStanza sat down, put his hands behind his head and told her the story about how he came . . . that close . . . to serving a search warrant on the Narcotics Office because the rotten, no-good, dope-fiend, mother-fuckin' Narcs refused to give him information during the Electric Daughter Case.

"Never mention the Narcotics Division up here," he told her. "Ever! Especially to Mark. He hates them more than David Berkowitz hates pretty girls."

At four o'clock sharp, Paul Snowood and Fel Jones entered, followed by their sergeant. Fel was bragging about this girl he'd met the other night. Something about a fuck-a-thon. Mark was enjoying the story. Snowood was uncharacteristically quiet. Although, he did have a mouth full of Skoal.

Mark finally noticed the material scattered across LaStanza's desk and asked, "Y'all been at it awhile?"

"All day." LaStanza stood up and yawned.

Snowood picked up a Styrofoam cup from the coffee table and dropped a massive wad of brown shit into it. Then he cleaned his teeth with his tongue.

LaStanza started packing up his briefcase and told his sergeant, "I'm going home. I'll be on the radio if something big happens." He grinned at Mark and added, "And it better be fuckin' *big*."

"Capito," Mark said and headed straight for his office.

LaStanza nodded to his partner. "You're going home, too." The relief was evident on Jodie's face.

Snowood stepped up to their desks and tucked another wad of Skoal beneath his lower lip. "You know," he said, "when the bald eagle uses sticks to build its nest, it sometimes uses stickmen."

Whatever the fuck that meant.

Thirteen inches of rain fell between eight and ten o'clock. It was a typical spring downpour. Eyewitness News at ten showed scenes of flooded streets and high water in a city below sea level.

One reporter, in a yellow raincoat, was standing on a sidewalk and pointing to a couple of kids in a pirogue who were paddling along an uptown street.

"That's why we call them banquettes," Lizette said as she rinsed the dishes and passed them to Dino to load into the dishwasher. She was talking about the sidewalks. Since French colonial days, they served as banks for streets that turned into canals when the rains came.

Dino looked out at the rain slamming against the kitchen windows. It felt good being home with a wife whose eyes lit up when he came home and announced he wasn't going back to work, even if someone killed the mayor. Especially if someone killed the mayor.

She was looking out at the rain, too, and said, "Last time it rained like this, we couldn't go out for two days."

Which meant he would have to be bunkered in with her, unmolested, for forty-eight hours. He should be so lucky. He continued watching her as she rinsed the dishes. A strand of her hair had fallen away from one of the barrettes and dangled in her eyes. He liked it when she wore barrettes, pinning up her long hair on the sides, while the rest of it fell lush over her shoulders. She was wearing one of his old Rummel High tee shirts and a pair of baggy shorts. She must have been rooting through one of his old footlockers to have come up with the tee shirt. It was a little too tight for her across the chest, which suited him fine.

"Now, what was it you wanted to ask me?" he reminded her. She'd said she had something to ask him, after they finished supper.

She handed him the last glass, rinsed her hands and grabbed a dishtowel, then said, "In a minute."

He reached over and pushed the strand of hair away from her eyes. Then he leaned over and kissed her, very softly, on the lips.

"Turn on the dishwasher," she told him when he pulled away, "and follow me."

She led the way into the study and pointed to the big easy chair and said, "Sit!" She turned on the stereo and dimmed the lights and then climbed next to him.

The music was low, but he could hear the soft sounds of something classical . . . no . . . someone started singing. It was an opera. It was soothing and sad.

"It's *La Boheme,*" she said, reading his mind again.

It was nice, especially with the rain crashing against the long french doors of the study.

"Giacomo Puccini," she said. "It was composed by an Italian."

No wonder he liked it, he thought to himself.

A few minutes later, he nudged her. "What was it you wanted to talk about?"

"Yeah," she perked up, reached over to the small table next to the chair and handed him a torn ticket stub. "Is this the real thing?" she asked.

He looked closely and recognized it and told her, of course, it was real.

She was leaning up now and eyeballing him. "You were there?"

"Sure. I went with my brother." He handed the stub back to her. She *must* have been rooting to find that thing. "No," he realized, "I didn't go with Joe. He wouldn't take me, so I went on my own."

She read the printing on the stub out loud:

"Admit One. Total $5.00. Good Only Wednesday Evening. September 16, 1964. The Beatles. City Park Stadium. New Orleans, La."

She looked back at him and blinked. "My God. You've got to tell me the whole story." She put the stub back on the table and then settled back with him. "Now, start at the beginning."

He laughed. She elbowed him and said, "From the beginning."

"Well," he put his arm around her and started, "once upon a time, I was a twelve-year-old kid brother." Dino closed his eyes and remembered. "My big brother was an early rock and roller with slicked-back hair and a leather jacket and girlfriends who all looked like movie stars. He was a regular Johnny Angel. Even had Shelley Fabares records to prove it, along with Buddy Holly and Elvis. And when the sixties rolled around, he was the first one to discover the Beatles in the entire city.

"He had all their records. At first I remember I didn't like them. They weren't American. But Joe liked them. He actually said, back in 1963, that they were the greatest. When he

101

found out they were coming to town, he went right out and bought tickets. He bought five tickets. But none of them were for me. He took four dates with him, four girls that looked like teen angels with tight sweaters across their boobs and tight skirts and high heels.

"He told me, since I didn't like the Beatles, then I couldn't go. So me and my friend Gary Early went and got tickets on our own.

"We planned to find Joe and sit behind him and needle him until he lost his temper. But we couldn't find him. The audience was almost all girls, and we couldn't push our way through."

Dino began to laugh. "Gary stopped to look up these girls dresses. They were all dressed up. I guess it was everyone's first concert. I remember there were a couple opening acts. Then the Beatles came out, and the girls started screaming so loud, I didn't think we'd hear anything. Then John Lennon began 'Twist and Shout.' I was hypnotized. I mean it. I couldn't take my eyes off those guys.

"When they started 'Can't Buy Me Love,' a bunch of girls rushed across the field to the bandstand. I remember the cops chasing them. It was so strange, seeing girls screaming like that."

Dino paused a minute and then added, "I remember it was hot and muggy that night. And after, I was a bigger Beatles fan than my brother."

He opened his eyes and looked down at her. Lizette's eyes were closed, but she wasn't sleeping. He saw her smile before she asked, "Looked up the dresses, huh?"

"Gary was an expert."

"Whatever happened to him?"

"He's a lawyer now."

Seven
St. Thomas Project

As Sister Dawn Abigail was telling them how Sal Louis hadn't been around for a couple weeks, a little boy was shot in the St. Thomas Housing Project. LaStanza's radio told the story in sharp, staccato, police language.

A loud beep tone was followed by, "Signal 34S . . . possible 30 . . . 400 block of St. Andrew . . . perpetrator still on scene . . . any Sixth District unit."

Unit 602 responded immediately, followed by a host of others who were cut off by another beep tone from Headquarters. "Perpetrator from St. Andrew fleeing uptown on Annunciation . . . black male . . ." Headquarters began describing the shooter.

LaStanza tapped Jodie on the shoulder, interrupting her conversation with the good sister, who was wearing a Mama Cass muumuu that had once been white but now sported large yellow stains beneath each armpit.

"Let's go," he said, turning around and heading for the door.

The radio exploded with calls from cops in pursuit of the perpetrator, interlaced with calls from Unit 602, which had arrived on the scene and called for an ambulance . . . and a homicide team.

"Where are we going?" Jodie asked as they jumped into the Maserati.

"St. Thomas. 34S . . . probably a 30 by now."

"They need help?"

LaStanza turned down Felicity Street and punched it.

Somehow, a day-shift homicide unit beat them to the scene, quickly calming things down and putting out a detailed description of the culprit.

"Did they ask for help?" Jodie said, hanging on when LaStanza jammed the brakes to keep from running up the rear of a rusty pickup truck.

"Nope," he said, "but we're going anyway."

When they arrived, an ambulance was leaving, in a big hurry.

They had to push their way through the crowd collecting on the north side of the project. LaStanza stopped as soon as he was through. He saw a woman in a bathrobe sitting in the dirt in a courtyard. Her head was bent down, and she was crying, her hand resting in a pool of blood in front of her. Two uniformed men were standing over her. The commander of the homicide day watch, Sergeant Val Buras, was kneeling next to the woman, trying to talk to her.

Three small children behind LaStanza were wailing now, tears streaming down their small, dark faces. LaStanza looked over their heads at another dark face, grimaced in pain. A teenage girl in a Saints tee shirt and blue jeans cried aloud, "I knew they were gonna shoot some little child one day."

Another woman started crying about two other shootings where children were wounded. They were drug shoot-outs, she said.

LaStanza heard the mother begin to talk between heavy sobs. He turned around and stepped closer.

"I was heating his lunch . . . he was playing on his bicycle . . ."

There was a tricycle lying on the other side of one of the patrolmen.

"I called out the window for him . . . he started to come

around to the back door . . . and I heard a shot . . . my baby was on the ground . . . I jumped out the window . . . and Cecil Cornelius was holding my baby, saying he was sorry . . ." Her tears fell in the dirt. "It was Cecil Cornelius. I know him. He killed my baby."

Buras left her alone a minute, got on his radio and gave Headquarters the name of the suspect.

A little boy started pulling on LaStanza's pant leg. The boy had pushed his way past Jodie. LaStanza looked down into a tortured face that looked up at him and asked, "Is Bobo dead?" He was about four years old.

LaStanza knelt down and said, "I don't know."

The little boy buried his face in the crook of LaStanza's neck and started to really cry. LaStanza put his arms around the child and picked him up. The boy's legs wrapped themselves around him.

Buras was standing now and moved over to them. He was a burly man with curly brown hair. He was shaking his head in disgust.

"It only gets worse, don't it?" the sergeant said. Then he said, "What y'all doing here?"

"The Batture," Jodie answered.

"Oh, yeah."

"Is the victim 10-7?" Jodie asked.

Buras nodded and started to move away toward the crime lab technician who had just arrived. "Another hour and a half," he called back to them, "and this woulda been yours."

"Need any help?" Jodie asked.

"Naw," Buras said, "we got it."

LaStanza looked at his partner. She didn't seem to be the least bit upset. Good homicide man, he thought to himself. He turned away because . . . he was upset. He was more than upset. He could feel his hot Sicilian blood rising and knew that he'd better put a quick cap on it. A good homicide man didn't lose his head while others were losing theirs.

Behind him someone shouted, "Come on! *Move!*" It was

Stan Smith, working his way through the crowd, which had grown even larger.

Coming up behind them, Stan reached over for the boy in LaStanza's arms. The little boy blinked his frightened eyes at Stan, then obviously recognized the tall, uniformed sergeant and lunged into Stan's arms.

"Come on, Elroy," Stan said, patting the child's back, "your mama's all worried about you." Stan started back through the crowd, turned around and told LaStanza, "This is one of ma little padnas. So was Bobo." Continuing through the mass of people, he called back, "I'm gonna get that no-good, rotten, dope-head, scumbag *Cornelius! Personally!*"

"Yeah!" someone in the crowd responded.

Another cop started toward them from where Stan was heading. LaStanza saw Jodie look away quickly and move around him. The cop was sporting a flat-top and a pencil-thin moustache, and LaStanza saw a K-9 patch on his shoulder. In the instant before the cop arrived, LaStanza remembered that Jodie used to date a guy in K-9.

"Hey, baby," the cop called out to Jodie, who ignored him. He put out his hand for LaStanza to shake, but didn't look at the detective. The man introduced himself.

LaStanza didn't catch the name and didn't shake the hand. Jodie started walking away, and LaStanza followed.

"Hey," the K-9er called out behind him, "you need my dog to help clear the crowd?"

LaStanza wheeled around and said as he backpedaled, "Take out your dog and I'll shoot him. Then I'll shoot you. Then I'll go tell the grand jury about this stupid K-9 cop I once met!"

The cop's face turned angry before he did an about-face and left.

"Is he gone?" Jodie asked when LaStanza joined her next to the dilapidated, brown-brick project building where Bobo used to live.

"You didn't go out with that asshole, did you?"

106

Jodie pointed to her temple and said, "Tell me I wasn't stupid."

LaStanza remained at the scene. Jodie didn't complain. He watched the day shift process the crime scene and watched the civilians come and go, staring at the pool of blood and Bobo's mother still sitting in the dirt. Some of them were crying. Others just pointed and whispered.

LaStanza caught pieces of conversation from his radio and from Buras and the other homicide men from the day watch. It appeared that the perpetrator was exchanging shots with another man, a running gun battle, probably over drugs, the victim was caught between them. Bobo just celebrated his fifth birthday two days earlier. He was shot once, in the head. He was wearing a Snoopy tee shirt."

Then the reporters arrived, excited men with pencils and notepads, good-looking women with cans of hairspray in their hands, accompanied by television crews that set up quickly as the women with the hairspray primped in mirrors held up by bored assistants.

Everything stopped a moment later when Reverend Stokes showed up in a three-piece, lime green suit and matching patent leather shoes and began singing "Amazing Grace." The man's voice echoed between the tenement houses of the project. LaStanza closed his eyes. He remembered, when he was a boy, the priest at Holy Rosary who would sing "Ave Maria" like God, Himself. A well of emotion rose in LaStanza's chest. He had to force himself to steady his breathing. *A good homicide man keeps his head when everyone else is losing their's.* It was hard, sometimes, when a child was due up next on the autopsy table, and a rich voice boomed, "Amazing Grace, how sweet the sound, that saved a wretch like me . . ."

Then he heard Jodie telling him a homicide team had apprehended Cornelius on Louisiana Avenue and recovered a .32-caliber pistol from the suspect. They were bringing him to the Bureau.

Someone came and took the mother away. Then the cops

started leaving, one by one.

An hour later, LaStanza was still leaning against the three-story, brown-brick building with the green balconies and abundant graffiti. His partner stood next to him. There was still a crowd in the courtyard.

Then the real show began. The new chief of police arrived with his entourage, including his pretty-boy chauffeur, a twenty-year-old kid who received lieutenant's pay to drive the chief around. Everyone knew the kid got his job because he was the nephew of some senator. The entourage also included the fat Chinaman.

Chief Ron Miles wasn't from New Orleans, which was only part of his problem. He was also fat with wispy white hair and a fruity voice. His pug nose and baby-pink complexion gave him the appearance of a hog. To LaStanza, he was a Porky-Pig-looking faggot. Period. No one in the department listened to him and *no one* respected him.

Miles had one friend: the fat Chinaman. Everywhere the chief went, he was accompanied by the fat Chinaman. No one seemed to know much about the guy, except he had lots of po-litical connections.

If the chief and the Chinaman weren't gay, they should have been. They looked the part. Not that being gay, in a city like New Orleans, was much of a problem. *Unless you were chief-of-fuckin'-police!*

The chief decided to hold a press conference at the very spot where the murder occurred. The television crews scrambled to set back up and hurried to catch what was left of the sun. When one of the TV crewmen, backing across the yard for a better shot, stepped in the blood from little Bobo's brain, La-Stanza yelled, "Hey, asshole, watch where you're stepping!"

Everyone turned to him, including the chief.

"Oh, thanks," the TV crewman said, wiping his foot in the clean dirt. Dumb douche-bag thought LaStanza was helping him.

It was definitely time to leave.

Jodie hurried to keep up. "Hey," she called out, "what's wrong with you?"

"I'm pissed!"

"I know that — "She had to run to get in front of him — "but your face . . ."

"Huh?"

"It's all screwed up."

He felt himself breathing heavy now. He stopped and inched up to her and said, "I . . . wanna kill that fuck-head!"

"Which one?" She was trying to be funny.

"Cornelius," he snarled.

"So do I."

"No."

She didn't understand.

"I wanna give back his gun and have him face me, man to man, so I can blow his fuckin' brains all over the project." He grabbed the front of her blouse. "I wanna stick my hands in his brain and squeeze it and then feed it to the blue-gum-nig-ger-dogs."

He let go of her blouse.

"When I say I wanna kill someone, I *really* wanna kill some-one!" He didn't have to tell her he'd done it before. She knew. He never realized just how much he liked it.

Fuck Sister Abigail and her sweaty muumuu! Instead of re-turning to the House of the Lamb, LaStanza headed for the Bureau. He wanted to have a little talk with this Cornelius fella. If it was drugs, maybe it was tees and blues, a drug now out of fashion and not as easy to get as crack. Maybe Corne-lius knew the two Pams. Maybe LaStanza could weasel the name of the other man who was shooting it out with Corne-lius. Maybe *he* knew something about the Batture Case.

Passing Annunciation Square, LaStanza slowed down and looked over at a crowd of St. Thomas Project kids who were lucky enough to be playing in the right park that day.

Then there was another loud beep tone on his radio, followed by: "Signal 64 in progress and a 34S . . . Schwegmann's Supermarket . . . 1325 Annunciation." An armed robbery and a shooting were going down two blocks away.

"JESUS!" he yelled, hitting the accelerator. Jodie grabbed for whatever she could grab and yelled herself, "GODDAM SIXTH DISTRICT!"

Nobody beat the Maserati this time. LaStanza had to hit the brakes hard and cut the wheel sharply to the left to keep from overrunning the entrance to the parking lot on the Melpomene side of the supermarket. The Maserati slid to a stop, blocking the entrance of the lot.

Stepping from the car, he already had his .357 magnum out and cocked and pointed skyward. He called out to Jodie, "Watch the cars"—meaning the parked cars to her right—"might be a getaway waiting!"

He walked forward carefully but purposefully, glancing at the cars parked against the front of the store, looking for any movement. Nearing the door, he saw someone move. There was a large, mountain of a man with a shotgun standing just outside the main front door. It looked just like . . . it was . . . unmistakably . . . Lieutenant Bob Kay of the Training Academy. Kay was barking orders at a light-complected black man with wild eyes and frizzy reddish brown hair puffed out like one of the Three Stooges, like Larry the Stooge. The man was backed up against the brick wall next to the front door. He had his hands in the front pockets of his blue jumpsuit as he batted his eyes like am antelope looking down the snoot of a lion.

LaStanza looked around as he approached the lieutenant from the rear and said, "Hey, Bob. It's Dino. You okay?"

"Yes," Kay answered, "you may approach." The lieutenant was in a lightweight jogging suit, his glasses secured to his head by an elastic band. He was trying to sound calm, but LaStanza noticed a slight shiver in the single-barrel, pump, twelve-gauge police shotgun held like a toothpick in Kay's

110

large hands.

LaStanza eased up to him and thought he'd lost it when Jodie yelled, "FREEZE!" He ducked and turned and saw her pointing her own snub-nosed .357 at the light-complected man.

"Put it away," he snapped at her, "and watch the door. There could be others."

She nodded excitedly and jumped toward the front door. God, she was wired.

LaStanza turned back to Kay, who was saying, "He's got a gun!"

"Looks like you got him covered," LaStanza said calmly.

The lieutenant nodded, the shotgun bouncing up and down like a magic wand.

LaStanza yelled to the man, "Put your hands up!" The man blinked his wide-set eyes at the detective and quickly obliged. "And show me your palms." The man did.

"I'm gonna search him," he told the lieutenant. He waited for the shotgun to rise and point skyward.

"All right," Kay said, his large eyebrows furrowed down, still leering at the man, "go ahead and search the suspect."

Kay wasn't really a man-mountain, he just sounded that way. He was only six feet even but always wore a bullet-proof vest, even off duty, which made him look larger.

"Assume the position," LaStanza told the man. "Come on, you've seen it on TV."

The man obliged, putting his hands against the bricks and spreading his legs, which LaStanza kicked even wider before pulling the back of the man's belt outward so that the suspect was leaning forward, off balance. LaStanza pressed his magnum against the base of the man's skull. Bracing his knee against the back of the man's left leg, LaStanza frisked him, carefully.

LaStanza slipped the magnum back into the holster at the small of his back and pulled out his handcuffs.

"He's clean," he said, slapping a cuff on the man's left wrist

111

and pulling the hand behind the man. "Put your forehead against the wall," he said and then grabbed the right hand, pulled it back and cuffed it.

"Stand up," LaStanza ordered, shoving his prisoner face first against the wall, "and don't fuckin' move."

A Sixth District unit skidded up behind the lieutenant. Two young faces LaStanza had never seen before alighted from the car, revolvers drawn.

"Hey, you!" LaStanza called out to the first patrolman, "read this asshole his rights and put him in the back of your car."

The suspect decided it was time he should start talking, "Yeah, I killed her! *The bitch!*"

"Hey—" LaStanza shoved the man's face against the bricks—"you're not supposed to confess until *after* we read you your rights. Don't you watch TV?"

"She a whore," the man argued back. *"The bitch!* She a *dead* whore now!"

LaStanza noticed blood on the man's fingers and jogging shoes as the patrolman led the suspect away. He waved Jodie over and said, "Stay with the asshole. Don't let *anyone* near him! When the crime lab arrives, have them swab his hands and take his shoes right away. Got it?"

She nodded excitedly.

"And write down whatever he says!"

She nodded harder.

He grabbed the other patrolman and told him to search the area for anyone sitting in a car, like a getaway.

"Then write down the license plates of every car here. Got it?"

"Yes, sir."

"Now—" he turned back to Kay—"cover the door, I'm going in."

"Where's your vest?" Kay asked.

"You sure this was an armed robbery?" he asked back, his eyes scanning the interior of the store through the glass front

112

door. There were plenty of people still inside, most huddled behind counters.

"Don't know," Kay answered. "I was just going in, heard the report of gunfire, retrieved my shotgun from my unit and saw this man running out. He's got blood on him."

"I know. Cover the door." LaStanza took off his jacket so that his badge could be seen and threw it across the hood of the Sixth District unit. Then he pulled his magnum out again and moved forward.

"And don't let anyone leave," he called back to the lieutenant.

"Of course," Kay responded.

LaStanza walked through the automatic doors and moved steadily to the first counter and stopped. A skinny white woman with stringy black hair was crying next to him. He asked her if there were any robbers still in the store. She started crying louder.

While others are losing their heads, he thought to himself. Then he had another thought. "Dino, my boy. You just might have to shoot someone after all."

That thought calmed him even more. He'd already felt a calming as soon as he'd stepped from the Maserati. It was like hitting a plane, a leveling off of adrenaline that made everything . . . smooth and exact and precise. He was in another gear. He wasn't even breathing heavily.

With the magnum cupped in both hands and pointed upward, he moved deliberately and furtively across the front of the store, following the trail of blood that dotted the floor, to one of the side aisles. At the entrance of a wide aisle, he found a bloody footprint from a jogging shoe that turned the corner. He peeked around the corner.

It took a second for the scene to register, especially with the victim's feet sticking in the air out of the frozen-food cooler that ran, waist-high, down the center of the wide aisle. The bloody footprints led to a wide circle of blood next to a mop and bucket on the floor a few feet from the cooler. The body was that of a dark-skinned black woman, her feet sticking straight up, as though she'd been dropped from the ceiling right into the frozen food.

LaStanza uncocked his magnum and moved toward the body. It was hard making out her face for all the blood that had gushed from her wounds, inundating the entire display of Cool Whip where she lay.

He had an even harder time trying to find her carotid artery to check for vital signs. Then he saw why. Besides the hole in back of her head, a bullet had severed the artery. When he touched her neck, what little blood remained in the artery oozed out onto the Cool Whip.

She was wearing a baby blue smock over her dress. The mop gave her away. She was a porterette, probably mopping up some mess when she was shot, at least twice.

He heard whimpering on the other side of the cooler. He wiped his fingers on a clean spot on the smock and reholstered the magnum before calling out, "Hey. It's the police. You can come out now."

A black face peeked up over the cooler and blinked at him. It was another porterette, a very short woman with a flat-top haircut. She started crying louder when she looked at her compatriot, so rudely disposed.

LaStanza inched back away from the body, careful not to step in anything. He stopped when he saw a small, blue steel automatic, also lying in the cooler, atop the only bucket of Cool Whip that hadn't been splattered. It was a typical Saturday night special, looked like a .25-caliber. He also saw a spent casing on the floor next to the blood.

He walked around the cooler and took the crying woman's hand and led her away.

"Is she dead?" the woman wailed.

He nodded. The woman started running in place and wailed even louder. He waited a moment before leading her to the front of the store. On the way, she cried out, "I know who did it! I saw him! It was her husband!"

114

He managed to learn, between more sobs, that the husband had waltzed right in and shot the victim, then shoved her in with the Cool Whip and shot her again and then walked out.

There were seven patrolmen out front now. Kay still had his shotgun at the ready. LaStanza waved them in and told them it wasn't an armed robbery. It was only a misdemeanor murder: a husband/wife killing.

He grabbed a patrolman and sent him to the body, to secure the scene. "Don't let anyone near her. Except Homicide!"

"Yes, sir."

The wailing woman had caught her second breath and wailed even louder. He squeezed her hand but let her continue. She was running in place again.

Then he saw Paul Snowood and Fel Jones walk in and almost started laughing. Fel was wearing, of all things, a golden cowboy suit, hat and all. He looked like Clevon Little from *Blazing Saddles*. All he needed was a fuckin' palomino. From the scowl on Snowood's face, LaStanza could see Country-Ass wasn't amused.

"Nice outfit," he told Fel when they arrived.

"He looks ridiculous!" Snowood said.

"You're just jealous," LaStanza said, "because it looks better on him." Snowood's suit was barely western.

"That's all right," Country-Ass argued back. "He just caught this fuckin' case!"

Snowood had his Glock 17 in hand. It was his famous plastic, Nato gun, twenty shots with big clip. Safest place to be, LaStanza always said, was in front of him.

"Put that away!" It was Kay, who had followed them in. He pointed to the Glock, his large eyebrows protruding angrily over a pair of brown eyes that never seemed to blink.

Snowood obliged, not because Kay was a lieutenant, but because it was Kay of the Training Academy. He'd taught them *all*.

The porterette suddenly regained control of herself and started tugging on LaStanza's white dress shirt, babbling, "I know who did it! Slick's husband did it!"

"Whoa," LaStanza said, "who's Slick?"

"The girl was shot. Georgina. But everybody calls her Slick."

Fel Jones started writing immediately, stepping up and taking over. "And what's your name?"

"Soule Evans." The woman did a double take at the black cowpoke. "You the police?"

"He's the high sheriff," LaStanza assured her. Fel pointed to his star-and-crescent badge, pinned neatly over his left nipple.

"What was the victim's last name?" Fel asked.

LaStanza was about to lead Snowood to the body, when he heard the witness answer, "Snatch." He stopped. Everyone stopped.

Fel looked up from his notes and said, "Say what?"

"Her last name Snatch."

Fel looked over at LaStanza and started giggling.

Slick Snatch! LaStanza never thought he could be floored by a name. He'd thought he'd heard them all. Felicity Jones, who *grew* up in the world of strange names, looked astounded.

Snowood broke the silence with a booming, "Slick Snatch! I don't be-fuckin'-lieve it!"

The suspect was still blabbing when LaStanza joined his partner. Jodie was standing outside the marked unit writing down what the suspect was belting out.

"She a no-good fuckin' bitch! She a *dead* bitch now!"

LaStanza interrupted him. "Your old lady named Slick Snatch?"

"Yeah. She dead, ain't she?"

LaStanza turned away. The suspect continued, "She did me wrong, man. I had to do it!"

It was after dark now, and LaStanza looked over at the line of witnesses that the patrolmen were identifying before releasing.

116

"I took care of business," the suspect continued. Jodie kept on writing.

Snowood joined them. He was looking for the crime lab, which was late.

"I guess we'll call this one the Snatch Case," he quipped, tucking a fresh wad beneath his lip.

LaStanza shook his head. "No way. Cool Whip Murder."

"Yeah," Snowood agreed, "that's got a nice ring to it."

"Cool Whip?" Jodie asked. LaStanza told her to go take a look at the body.

The suspect then asked if LaStanza was married.

"Shut up!" Snowood said.

"I got advice for married men. Watch yourself, 'cause a woman's nothin' but a *whore!*"

"Send it to Dear-fuckin'-Abby! And SHUT THE FUCK UP!" Snowood yelled back. He had no effect on the suspect's soliloquy.

"I work hard all my life and find out my wife's a whore. I heard her on the phone. She was, like, having sexual relations on the phone with some dude. I heard her!"

LaStanza and Snowood started moving away.

The suspect called out, "Hey, how long is this gonna *take?*"

"About six years," Snowood answered.

"Before my trial?"

"No, until all your appeals are gone and we fry you. You owe the state two jolts for this one. You're gonna get the hot squat, my man."

Only, they knew better. Goddam misdemeanor murder. It was second-degree murder at best. Probably end up with a manslaughter conviction. Unless the D.A. fucked it up in court, which happened, too fuckin' often.

The crime lab finally arrived, and Snowood could start processing the evidence from the suspect and the scene. Then, just as everything was calming down, Stan Smith arrived. Bob Kay took that moment to exit Schwegmann's with Jodie.

"Hey," Stan called out to LaStanza, pointing toward Jodie,

"if you're not fuckin' her, can I?"

"She a whore *too!*" the suspect yelled.

Snowood shoved the man back into the seat so hard, he bounced off the other door. It was the crime lab man's turn to start complaining now. He was trying to swab the man's hands for a neutron activation test.

Bob Kay hugged Jodie and then started hugging everyone else. Grabbing LaStanza, he squeezed and, patting him on the back, whispered, "Brother," in LaStanza's ear. There was no use trying to avoid the hug. Bob always hugged his brothers and sisters in blue. When he used to work for LaStanza's father, he used to hug *him,* too, rubbing his ever-present five-o'clock shadow on his commander's face at the end of each shift.

Kay had one more word for LaStanza: "You better wear your vest next time."

"You shop here often?" Dino asked back.

"Yeah."

"Well, stay away from the pink Cool Whip."

Kay almost smiled.

The suspect got to ride to the Bureau in style, in the backseat of the Maserati. Once there, LaStanza questioned the man briefly. Mr. Snatch was a muggle-head, too ignorant to know anything of value about the Batture. He was too busy hating his wife . . . the whore.

Cornelius, who was still at the Bureau, was even worse. He'd been handled too many times to even give any information except his name and address. Cocksucker was on probation for a cocaine conviction and had seven previous drug arrests.

When the Maserati finally made it back to Milan Street, Jodie was too tired to climb out. She'd been sneaking peeks at

LaStanza all evening, and he didn't like the way she was eye-balling him, as if he were going to fritz out and start shooting people. He was going to apologize for grabbing her blouse. But now, with her still eyeballing him in his car, he'd let it lie.

Slowly, she opened the door and climbed out. LaStanza looked toward her house and saw a black cat in the window. He smiled to himself because he thought of another story.

"We used to have a black cat," he told her as she dragged around the front of the car.

"My old man called him 'Nigger.' "

Jodie tried to smile.

"We got him right after the Howard Johnson sniper. By then, my old man was carrying a 30-30 Winchester rifle to work every day. He used to go out on the porch every morning and call the cat, 'Hey, Nigger! Nigger!' "

Jodie stopped to rest against the left front fender.

"One morning the cat was across the street. My old man, Winchester in hand, started calling, 'Hey, Nigger! Nigger!'

"Son-of-a-bitch didn't see the black mailman down the street. The mailman ran up and said, 'Yes, officer. You called me?' "

"Is that true?" Jodie asked.

"Absolutely."

Jodie squinted at him again and said, "What brought that story on?"

"Saw the cat in your window."

"Oh?"

"Didn't know you had a black cat."

"I like cats." She started for the house and added, "I hate dogs." She went through her small front gate and up the steps. Turning back, she called out, "Slick Snatch? Kinda name you'd see in a cheap novel, huh?"

"Naw, it's just the Sixth."

She went in. The girl hated dogs but went out with a K-9er. LaStanza pulled away thinking the whole fuckin' city was crazy.

He raced the Maserati home, blowing up Magazine Street at over a hundred. There was never a cop when you needed one. He popped Led Zeppelin back in and cranked up the stereo. A little song called "Black Dog" screeched.

Lizette was at the computer when he walked in. She turned to him with a smile and said, "So, how was your day?"

Eight
Nuns Street

Sal Louis was dead. It took LaStanza forty-eight hours on the street to discover the man was in Charity Hospital. Forty minutes later, he learned that Sal had expired that very morning of lung cancer.

LaStanza spent the next forty minutes convincing a doctor at the large, public hospital that it was important he view the body of Sal Louis. "You see, doc. There'll be no postmortem. If I don't see it now, it's gone."

Actually, he was angry with himself for being dumb enough to ask, instead of heading straight for the cadaver. He had learned, in the army, that you never ask permission, you just do it.

The young intern agreed but insisted on accompanying LaStanza down to Pathology. They found Sal on the fourth stretcher in the hall outside the lab. Charity was always crowded, even the halls.

LaStanza pulled back the white sheet and looked upon the cancer-ravaged remains of a Rastafarian male. Sal Louis had dreadlocks past his shoulders, old needle marks in both arms, three teeth missing from the front of his mouth and yellowed index fingers on both hands.

"He admitted a three-lid-a-day marijuana habit," the doctor said.

LaStanza added, "He made his living selling it and running dope scams on white boys too stupid to know the difference between pot and ragweed."

He'd also discovered, in his search for Sal, that the man had no car. It would be tough, taking two whores all the way to Algiers without a short. Besides, Sal might have stood six feet tall, but the pothead weighed less than LaStanza, even less than Jodie.

LaStanza measured Sal's feet before leaving. The footprints at the scene were twelve inches long, exactly. Sal's measured eleven and one-sixteenth inches. Not exactly the scientific way to eliminate a suspect, but good enough.

LaStanza was writing a nice, brief daily when Jodie came into the office and told him about their new car.

"It's one of the new Fords," she said, placing her briefcase on her desk.

LaStanza looked up from the gray Smith-Corona and shook his head no.

"It's nice," she went on, "really." She draped her suit jacket over the back of her chair. She was wearing a shoulder holster which required a second look. It was one of the new nylon types with the revolver dangling upside down beneath her left armpit, balanced by two speed loaders under her right arm and a pair of handcuffs in back. She was also wearing a loose-fitting black skirt and her usual white blouse, neatly buttoned to the neck.

Her makeup looked a little heavier than usual, but that was probably the strong, afternoon sunlight streaming in the squad room. Her hair, as usual, looked fresh and fluffed. It probably didn't need much work, he thought to himself, especially with the page boy cut.

He wanted to tell her to lose the shoulder rig but instead told her about Sal Louis. She'd learn about the back pains on her own.

"You should have called me," she insisted when he finished.

"What? And miss that new car?"

She wasn't amused.

LaStanza pulled the daily from the typewriter and spotted Lieutenant Mason coming out of his office. "Good, you're here," Mason said. Trailing smoke like a locomotive, the lieutenant sauntered over and sat on the edge of LaStanza's desk.

"Got a call earlier from a Mrs. Gerrols," Mason said, exhaling a large cloud that floated toward the ceiling.

"Mrs. Goebbels," LaStanza corrected him.

Mason's chiseled face almost smiled. "Claims you told her she was a pain in the butt." Mason paused for emphasis. "Two minutes on the phone with her proved your point."

The lieutenant paused for another deep drag.

LaStanza said, "So?"

"So, I told her there was no departmental regulation in accurately describing people."

"Good," Jodie said.

"So?" LaStanza repeated.

"So, she said she was going to the chief with her complaint. Thought I'd let you know."

LaStanza nodded and reached over to turn up his radio.

Snowood was calling.

"Can y'all mosey over here a minute? I could use a little assistance."

LaStanza asked Jodie to answer. He started packing up.

Mason was still there. His eyes were closed, and he was rubbing his temples. He added an epitaph to his Mrs. Goebbels' story, "Goddam woman started preaching to me about little *NE*groes swimming in some fountain."

Snowood was in a particularly good mood for a man standing in a pile of black mush in the center of a roofless, abandoned warehouse on Nuns Street, a block from the St. Thomas Housing Project. He was wearing a pale green cowboy suit and a cream-colored Stetson. Fel was in a regular suit, only it was red. They looked like Christmas-in-the-projects when they stood together.

LaStanza picked his way between a scattering of two-by-fours and broken glass and the black, oily guck on the floor that was probably some sort of toxic waste. After all, this was Louisiana.

The place smelled like toe cheese from a dead man. Near the center of the wide warehouse, LaStanza couldn't help but notice a naked white woman hanging by her neck from one of the cross rafters.

"Must have used this thing," Fel was saying, pointing to the ladder next to the body.

"Good detecting," Snowood said sarcastically.

LaStanza moved around to get a better look at the dead woman. Her face was covered by her long, dirty blond hair. He counted nine large puncture wounds in her torso, most in the abdomen, one through her left breast. Dark splotches of purpled postmortem lividity ran along her back from her neck to her oversized rear end. A thick, hemp rope was wrapped twice around her neck and three times around the rafter.

"Well," LaStanza said, "what in the name of Alfred Hitchcock is going on around here?"

Snowood didn't answer. He shrugged his shoulders and grinned his dip-stained teeth at his old partner.

"Jesus," Jodie whispered, barely loud enough for LaStanza to hear.

Snowood began whistling his favorite tune as the crime lab technician took photos of the body. He was whistling "Suicide Is Painless" from the original *M*A*S*H* movie.

"Why are you in such a good mood?" LaStanza had to ask.

"Got laid last night. The old lady broke down."

Ask a stupid question.

LaStanza waited for Country-Ass to tell him what help was needed, but it didn't come. So he watched his partner as she followed the technician around, taking private notes. She had a sour look on her face, but she was hanging in there.

"Okay," he finally had to say, "what help you need?"

"Well," Country-Ass added more black shit to the floor by spitting out a long stream of chaw, "a lady name Gerrols called earlier."

"Mason told me."

"She called him, too?"

That kept LaStanza from leaving right away. He stepped over a two-by-four with two rusty nails sticking out and waited.

Country-Ass didn't let him down. "This Mrs. Gerrols—"

"Goebbels."

"Whatever. She said there was this little dago going around her neighborhood pissing people off about some stupid west-bank murder."

LaStanza narrowed his eyes. "Come on, she didn't call me a dago."

"I swear on the memory of Gary Cooper." Snowood teased, but he didn't lie. "Thought you'd like to know."

"You need any help here?"

"Yeah, can y'all canvass?"

"Sure." LaStanza waved to Jodie. "Let's roll."

On their way out, they passed Stan Smith, who was tiptoe-ing in, careful not to ruin his uniform but too curious to stay away.

"Hey, Candy-Ass, where ya going?"

LaStanza kept walking.

"Back to Coliseum Square?" Stan asked.

LaStanza didn't answer.

"You know, some woman's been reporting you as a 107 over there."

LaStanza stopped and turned around.

"She's been calling the district, instead of 911, so we can't trace the calls. Says there's this short, swarthy-looking son-of-a-bitch out in the square starting a revolution. Figured it had to be you."

125

Stan was known to lie, but LaStanza had heard enough.

He stormed from the warehouse but had to stop and drag his feet on the concrete to scrape the black guck off his penny loafers. He was surprised how little got on Jodie's high heels. The girl was learning fast.

Canvass what? That was his next question. There were abandoned warehouses on either side of the one with the body. He checked them anyway, in case there was another body dangling.

Then he went around all three warehouses and jotted down the license plate numbers of all the cars parked in the area. You never knew, the killer's battery may have gone dead. Or a citizen, upon parking his Pontiac, may have seen some lunatic carrying a fat, naked, dead body into the warehouse but figured it was none of his business, until an inquisitive detective knocked on his door. Then the man would say, "Oh, yeah, I saw a guy with a dead white broad . . ."

LaStanza figured he might as well walk up Nuns Street to the St. Thomas and ask the people out on the balconies and stoops if they'd seen anything. The balconies were painted vomit green on this side of the project. Before getting close, he could see the people beginning to melt away.

Jodie seemed spooked when the whistling started. She moved a little closer to him and switched the notepad to her left hand.

"It's just cat calls," he told her. "The polee's here." Whistling was a pretty effective alarm system.

Several defiant-looking men remained on the stoops but pretended they didn't understand English when LaStanza asked his questions. Most of the children peeked at them from around the sides of the buildings. Not only had no one seen anything, no one would even speak to them.

Three days earlier, they had watched Bobo's mama sobbing over the little boy's blood in that same project. Moods in the projects changed like the weather. Most of the time, in New Orleans, it was plain hot.

On their way back to their new tan Ford parked on Nuns Street next to the warehouse, Jodie asked about the body.

"It was moved, wasn't it?"

"Absolutely. Once lividity is set, it doesn't move." There were no purple splotches on the fat broad's legs. But he wasn't thinking about that shit. He was thinking about kicking in a certain Lower Garden District door and ripping a certain telephone off the fuckin' wall.

The gate was locked on the fence at the Goebbels' house. LaStanza rang the bell next to the gate.

He saw her chubby face peek out a side window and then pull back immediately. When she didn't answer his ring again, he jumped the fence, bounced up the stairs and pounded on the carved, wooden front door.

"Tell Headquarters where we are," he told his partner. In case Goebbels got cute with the phone again. He was about to hit the door again when Mrs. Goebbels opened the window next to the door.

He stepped off the porch and leaned against the railing.

"What do you want?" she asked from behind the window screen.

"I wanna talk to your husband."

"He's dead," she shouted back.

"You're not missing a daughter, are you?"

"I have no children."

"Figures."

"What's that supposed to mean?"

"Missing any fat, blond-headed neighbors?"

"No, why?"

"Because we just found the body of a young, fat white woman hanging in a warehouse . . . in this wonderful, brightening neighborhood of yours."

"Dead?" Her voice rose.

"If not, the autopsy'll kill her in the morning."

"That's no way to tell someone." She sounded pissed.

"By the way," he added, "you wouldn't happen to know any-

127

thing about some woman reporting me as a suspicious person to the Sixth District station?"

"I don't know what you're talking about," she answered frostily.

"Fine. If they find out who it is, she's going to jail. If I find out first . . . I'm gonna rip out her larynx."

Aunt Brulie woke LaStanza the next morning, flipping on the overhead light and opening the curtains on the french door of their bedroom balcony.

"Come on, white boy. Get up. You got a phone call."

His eyes had a problem focusing. He felt like he'd just fallen asleep. He reached for Lizette, but she wasn't there.

"What time is it?"

Brulie was already on her way out. "Time to get up. I ain't got all day to pamper you." She continued complaining all the way out the room. "Lazy Italians sleep all the time . . ."

He rolled over and reached for the phone. It was Mason.

"You sleeping?"

"No, waterskiing."

"What time'd you get to bed?"

"I was out late hitting the bars with my partner."

"Oh. Batture Murder, huh?"

You couldn't fake-out Mason.

LaStanza yawned and sat up. "Any particular reason you called?"

"I'm waiting for you to wake up. The chief wants to see you."

"So?"

"He wants to see you and me and your partner—now. Your partner says she can pick you up in a half hour."

"You kiddin'?" Which was a really dumb question which Mason didn't even answer.

"All right," LaStanza started to hang up.

"You in the least bit curious?" Mason asked.

"Nope." LaStanza hung up.

He climbed out of bed just as Brulie came back in.

"What's that smell all over your clothes downstairs?" She was yelling.

"Sixth District funk."

"Say what?" Brulie looked at him for the first time that morning, furrowing the brows of her scrawny black face at him, twisting up her eyes. She gave him a harrumph and walked out again.

He wished she wouldn't smell his clothes. He'd tried to get her to stop washing them, but that was harder than it sounded. He looked at the clock. It was nine in the morning. He'd been asleep three hours. Lizette was already in class.

He took an extra long shower. Somehow, he started thinking about the first day he woke in the mansion. He remembered how he went into the refrigerator while Brulie was fixing lunch and asked, as a joke, where the Grey Poupon was.

Brulie jumped all over him. "Silly-ass boy, we don't use that Poupon shit. We use Zatarain's creole mustard!" Then she threw an oven mitt at him. She never missed with her mitt.

When he came downstairs, Brulie had his coffee ready. It wasn't his typical coffee-and-chicory. Brulie had a steaming cup of cappuccino ready.

He felt like a little toast and made the mistake of reaching for it himself.

"What are you doing?" Brulie was all over him.

He pointed to the toaster.

She snapped the slices of bread from his hands.

"Sit down and drink your dago coffee. I'll get your toast." She popped the bread into the toaster, mumbling to herself, loud enough for him to hear, "Probably electrocute yourself."

"No I won't," he said back.

"Well, it's *my* job." She turned away, adding, "You got murders and shit to solve. I do the work *here!*"

"Yes, ma'am."

The cappuccino was delicious.

129

* * *

Jodie had dressed up in another of her suits, all buttoned up and neat. LaStanza wore jeans and one of the authentic New York Yankees baseball jerseys Lizette had bought him after she discovered he'd been a Yankees fan since Mantle and Maris.

"You going like that?" Jodie asked when he climbed into the tan Ford. He didn't answer. He put on a pair of black, mirrored gangster sunglasses, turned to her, tucked his chin down and gleeked her.

Mason was waiting outside the chief's office, in one of the comfortable chairs in the hallway. He stood up as they approached and nodded for them to follow.

Stepping up to the door, they were all nearly bowled over when Bob Kay burst through and brushed by them like a mad rhino. Kay growled, "The man's a goddam idiot!"

"Hi, Bob," Jodie called out as he stormed off without responding.

LaStanza held the door open for his partner and grinned broadly at her. She looked shook. The chief's secretary waved them in without uttering a word.

Mason tapped LaStanza's shoulder and said, "Lose the glasses."

LaStanza slid the gangster glasses into the jersey.

Superintendent of Police Ron Miles was seated in the large captain's chair behind his large desk. He was wearing a wide-lapeled tan suit with a pink tie. The fat Chinaman was sitting in a chair to the left of the chief. He was also wearing a wide-lapeled tan suit but with a yellow tie.

Miles pointed to the three chairs in front of his desk and waited for them to be seated before clearing his throat and starting with, "We have a problem."

He waited for his words to sink in, as if he were the burning bush. LaStanza fought the urge to put the glasses back on.

Miles continued, "I've just entertained a complaint, a seri-

130

ous complaint, from the president of the—" he looked at the notepad that lay in front of him—"Lower Garden District Association."

LaStanza started shaking his head. He caught the Chinaman smiling, just slightly. He focused on the man's eyes, but they were lifeless eyes without a hint of emotion. The man looked like an overstuffed Buddha doll in a three-piece suit.

"A Mrs. Gerrols." The chief was reading notes again.

"That's Goebbels," LaStanza corrected him.

"Huh?" The chief looked up and then down at his notes. LaStanza spelled the name for him. The chief wrote it down and then looked up at LaStanza with blood in his beady eyes. "As in Joseph Goebbels?" he asked angrily.

"As in 'let's poison the kids so we can be with the Fuhrer in the promised land,' " LaStanza answered.

Miles ripped up his note and snapped at Mason in his high-pitched, fruity voice, "Mrs. Gerrols says that Detective LaStanz threatened to—" he read from his notes again, "to rip out her throat."

Miles turned to LaStanza and asked, "Now, Detective LaStanz, did you tell this lady you were going to rip out her throat?"

"It's LaStanza," Mason said.

"Quit CORRECTING me!" The chief's cheeks quivered when he shouted. "Now, Detective. Did you?"

"No. Unless she confessed to making false complaints to the Sixth District."

"What?"

"I told her that if I caught who was making false complaints to the district, I'd rip out that person's larynx. If she said she was the one, then I did threaten her. Did she confess to you that she was the caller?"

It took Miles a second to realize he was asked a question. He batted his eyes twice and said, "You're not here to question me." He cleared his throat again, leaned over and spit a large glob of snot into his waste basket.

131

LaStanza could hear Jodie gag.

Miles looked back at LaStanza and said, "You're not funny, Detective. I suppose your threatening people is supposed to ensue confidence in the citizens of our fair city?"

Fucker wasn't even from the city. Obviously, because there was nothing fair about New Orleans. LaStanza figured it was futile to respond.

Miles put a real mean look on his face. LaStanza tried his best to keep from yawning.

The chief turned to Mason and said, "Lieutenant, how do you feel about your detectives threatening people?"

"Well, he's shot a couple people, but never ripped out a larynx."

Miles' cheeks began quivering again. He looked back at his notes and fired away with, "And why is this detective alarming the entire Lower Garden District about a murder that happened on the westbank?"

"Because," Mason answered calmly, "that's where the victims were last seen alive."

"Well, I think he's putting too much overtime in on this case, and I intend to talk to the chief of detectives about this."

Mason paused to make sure the man was finished before asking, "Since when do we measure man hours on murder cases?"

"On a case like this one, we do. I know all about that case he's working on. It's a low priority case." Miles went on to elaborate about the rising murder rate.

He didn't say it, but it was clear to LaStanza. Black whores didn't deserve the time of overworked detectives. They weren't nice, upstanding citizens.

Miles finished with, "If I don't see any progress on this case by the weekend, I want it closed."

LaStanza could see the tightening in Mason's jaw as he leaned forward and said, "We close cases in Homicide when I say they're closed."

Miles shot a quick look at the Chinaman and said, "I anticipated that." He picked up a sheet of paper and shoved it across his desk at Mason. "This is an order forbidding any further overtime on this particular case. Period."

Miles sat back as if he'd won something. When he received no response, he added, "And I want Detective LaStanz to apologize to Mrs. Goebbels."

LaStanza shook his head no.

"Is that a refusal?"

"Yes it is."

"That's insubordination."

LaStanza didn't answer. So the chief tried Mason. "That's insubordination."

"If the civil service commission says it is, then it is," Mason said.

Miles tried the Chinaman but got no response there and gave up on it.

Thank God for the civil service commission, LaStanza was thinking when Miles asked him, "And why are you dressed like that?"

"It's my day off, Chief."

Miles started tapping his chubby fingers on his desk and told Mason to stay.

LaStanza led the way out. Jodie followed silently all the way back to the Bureau. LaStanza turned toward the men's room and told her, "I'll be on Camp Street for a minute."

When he got back to his desk, Jodie had already made a sign out of a manila folder. She'd printed CAMP STREET in black Marks-A-Lot. She put tape on all four corners of her new sign, got up and put it over the MEN sign on the men's room door.

"Got a nice ring to it," she told him when she got back.

Mason walked in a minute later, rubbing his temples, trailing smoke like an incinerator. He stopped and sat on the edge of LaStanza's desk.

"So?" LaStanza asked.

"So, our fuckin' chief's turning you in to Internal Affairs.

133

He thinks you're on the take."

"What?" Jodie nearly shouted.

"He heard LaStanza's driving around in a Ferrari."

LaStanza started laughing.

Jodie stammered, "That man's not only stupid. He's *dangerous!*" She slammed her briefcase shut and yelled, "If I see that goddam Goebbels broad again, I'm gonna slap the fuckin' bitch silly!"

LaStanza and Mason exchanged a curious look as Jodie stormed off toward the lady's room.

"How about some coffee?" Mason asked, stepping toward the pot.

LaStanza picked up the FUCK THIS SHIT mug and followed his lieutenant. "I just put in overtime sheets out of habit. Lord knows, I don't need the fuckin' money."

Mason nodded. "Don't worry about it. I'll take care of it."

LaStanza passed the coffeepot and asked, "Think they suck each other's dicks, or what?"

Mason's face soured as he nodded.

"I liked it better when we had an Italian chief."

Mason chuckled. "Especially when it was your father's old partner."

"That fat bastard keeps fuckin' with me, I'll quit and solve it on my own."

"I know."

Lizette was looking forward to a rare night out with Dino when he was on the evening watch. She took her time getting ready, putting on a new, loose-fitting, black cotton blouse with a wide neck and puffy sleeves and a green, full miniskirt that would flow when she walked. She added black pantyhose and spiked heels to the outfit. Dino loved black stockings.

He'd gotten ready early and was waiting downstairs when she descended the spiral staircase. It was like going out on a date, him waiting in the foyer to pick her up. He was smiling at her as she came down, leaning on the stair railing like a short Rhett Butler. He needed a haircut. She liked that. He looked better when his wavy hair was long and out of control.

He was wearing a navy blue, light wool jacket with a European cut, a powder blue shirt with a crimson tie, baggy black pants and black penny loafers. She'd bought his entire outfit. She liked buying his clothes almost as much as buying hers. She was surprised, at first, that he let her. He'd seen the tag on one of the sport coats she bought him once and said, "That's almost a week's pay!"

He must have felt bad, because he quickly added, "It does look good. Just don't tell me the price anymore."

When she reached the bottom of the stairs, he grabbed her around the waist and pulled her to him. He brushed his lips against her very lightly and said, "Let's go."

Lizette looked better than anything on the menu at Commander's Palace Restaurant, which had one of the best menus in a town famous for good dining. Once again she wore barrettes in her hair, pinning it up on the sides, while the rest of her hair fell over her shoulders. She was wearing that dark brown lipstick again, which made her full lips look velvety and sexy as hell.

She might have grown up in a world of garden parties and manicured lawns and cut glass doors, crystal chandeliers and long elegant staircases, fine table settings, works of art and diamond tiaras, but Lizette wore no jewelry, except her wedding ring. She didn't need to. The watch she wore was a Seiko. It was for telling time.

As usual, she ordered for them. He watched her with the waiter, ordering in fluent French. He liked the way she tilted her head when she spoke, the way she rolled her shoulders. He liked the way she moved her hips when she walked or readjusted herself when sitting or standing, the way she'd catch his eye with a flirty glint in her eyes.

Lizette knew instinctively what excited a man, the flash of a thigh when sitting, the roll of her eyes, a feminine sigh, the way she set her lips when listening to him. He liked the way she crossed and uncrossed her legs, sliding them together so that he could hear, faintly, the sexy sound of nylon against nylon.

Dino had known many girls before who turned him on. But these girls had no idea what affected a man, what caused him to feel desire, not just sexual, but the longing to be with her, even at a football game. Lizette was aware of what attracted a man. He'd caught her, again and again, pulling it on him. And he liked it.

"What are you thinking about?" she asked when they were alone again. "Not about the chief and the Chinaman?"

"No, I was wondering what you were like when you were a teenager. You know, like when you made your debut."

"Goes to show how much you know, hot shot. I never debuted. No one in my family ever has."

"I thought all rich, uptown girls made debuts into society."

"Wrong," she said, shaking her head, "debuts are an American invention."

"I've seen plenty French names in the *Picayune*'s debutante section."

"Huguenots," Lizette sneered. "Protestants. Love to see their faces in the paper. Vote Republican every chance they get."

He couldn't hold back from laughing. She stuck her tongue out at him as the bread and wine arrived.

They dined in relative silence, exchanging teasing looks and sexy looks, quietly settling down to a good meal. They had stuffed shrimp, baby veal and some French wine whose name Dino could not pronounce. It was, as usual, excellent.

After, while standing out in the evening air, waiting for the valet to bring their car around, Lizette tucked her arm under his and snuggled against him. The air felt warm and damp, as if another shower was on its way.

Dino looked across the street at Lafayette Cemetery. The place looked extra dark on a night with no moon. He could see, faintly, the outline of crosses looming over the wall surrounding the cemetery. The crosses were set atop the concrete sepulchres and cement tombs of a cemetery built above ground. "The water table's too high," someone figured a long time ago. So the dead were placed in little concrete houses.

"How about some slow dancin'?" Lizette asked.

"Yeah."

They went to a nightclub called Slow Dancin' on St. Charles Avenue, where they danced to Beatles love songs and Streisand and Mathis and Neil Diamond. Lizette had a couple Sazeracs. He had his usual scotch-rocks.

Back at their mansion, Lizette kicked off her heels and led the way to the kitchen, where she opened a new bottle of another French wine, whose name Dino could not pronounce.

He stepped out on the rear deck, fired up the Jacuzzi, and turned the backyard lights on low. He made sure the temperature in the hot tub was on the lukewarm setting before starting to take off his clothes. Lizette joined him with the wine and glasses, which she placed next to the tub before she began to disrobe.

Dino looked around the small yard, at the high, wooden fence along the Garfield Street side of the house. He'd checked it out before. No one could see into the backyard unless they were in the mansion itself. But every time they did this, he looked around again.

He finished first and slipped into the warm, bubbling water, moving around so that he could watch his wife as she removed her bra and then pulled off her pantyhose and then slipped out of her small panties.

Before joining him, she reached over and popped a cassette into the stereo under the canopy. Smokey Robinson's voice eased into "Crusin' " as Dino's naked wife slipped into the Jacuzzi next to him.

He reached around her waist and pulled her on top of him

137

and kissed her. Lizette wrapped her arms around his neck and her legs around his waist. Her tongue rolled over his tongue in a long, wet, french kiss that lasted for most of Smokey's song. Just before she pulled away, he sank back into the water and brought her down with him to the bottom for a moment to get them both completely wet.

"Being With You" was the next song. Dino caught his breath and slid over to the wine, Lizette still straddling him. He deftly poured two glassfuls, passed one to her and then drank the other down.

"Sip it, silly," she whispered. He poured himself another and drank it down, too. It felt cool and tangy and warmed him as soon as it found the scotch in his belly.

"More Love" came on the stereo. Lizette was still nursing her first drink, so he leaned her back and began kissing her nipples one at a time, back and forth, his hands cupped on her rear, pushing her against the stiffness between his legs.

"Ahhh," she sighed in a voice husky with passion. She put her glass down and pushed herself against him and began to ride him slowly, up and down the length of his erect penis, rubbing herself against it until he lifted her slightly to allow himself inside.

Buoyed by the water, heated jets shooting at them, bubbles soaring around them, they continued until he felt he was about to explode. He stopped suddenly and whispered, "Wait! Wait!"

In a couple seconds he had it under control and started the grinding again. Lizette leaned back and put her arms on the side of the tub. Dino stood up, pulling her up to the top of the churning water so that he could see her completely and continued the pile-driving motion against her.

God, she looked gorgeous with her hair wet and her body glistening under the soft light, with her legs open and him inside her, feeling her moving back against him, seeing the glow of pleasure engulf her face. Lizette reached for the pleasure, and it made him feel that much better to see how much it gave her. She bit her lower lip. Her gold-brown eyes opened wide and appeared to soften.

When she came, her voice became shrill, her gyrations rapid and hot. When he exploded, he rode her in and out until he felt his legs slip away. It took another two songs for him to recover.

They remained in the tub for a while, in silence, with their eyes closed, decelerating from the big high.

Lizette was the first to move, climbing out to turn off the Jacuzzi and bending over to pick up the wine and the glasses. He followed her into the kitchen to the towels and grabbed one and began to dry her off. She took the other towel and dried him off. Then she tossed both towels aside and led the way, naked, through the house and up the stairs to their bedroom.

The little exhibitionist, he thought to himself. Just like their honeymoon, when she strolled in the buff across a black pebble beach on Guadeloupe to skinny dip with him in the clear, warm water of the Caribbean.

She pulled back the sheets in the dark and slipped into the bed. He climbed in next to her. She moved her head into the crook of his shoulder. He could feel the naked length of her warm body against him.

Dino closed his eyes and began to daydream himself to sleep. In his mind, he envisioned a sixteen-year-old Lizette in her Catholic school uniform. She was at the Beatles concert in City Park. He was still twelve, sitting in front of her, peeking up her dress.

He dreamed that night, but not of Lizette. He dreamed of the girl in the tight red skirt, slumped over her typewriter. The blood on her blouse was brilliant crimson. He moved her long, sandy hair and saw her blue eyes were open. Her eyes were lifeless. She was dead.

Later, he dreamed of a kitchen filled with smoke, not cooking smoke, but gunsmoke from bullets fired in anger at a killer cornered in the next room with his own gun belching back. Then he saw Millie Suzanne crawling in the kitchen window

139

from the fire escape. He saw her point her stainless steel revolver toward the killer, saw the bullet strike her, saw her head snap to the side and watched her slump, in slow motion, into the room. He reached for her. The blood on his hands was warm and looked dark and muddy, like the waters of an unending river.

When the phone began ringing, he thought he was still dreaming. But it wasn't a dream. It was Mason.

"Take a second and wake up," Mason said.

"What?" Dino felt as if he'd been hit in the head with a hammer.

Mason was patient, adding, "It's important."

Dino sat up and rubbed his eyes with his free hand. He tried to focus on the clock, but his vision was too blurry.

"What time is it?"

"Two A.M."

Dino fell back on his pillow and said, "Okay, what is it?"

"They found another body on the batture," Mason said calmly. "At the same spot. The exact same spot."

Nine
The Batture

She was lying on her back at the base of the levee, parallel to the levee, as if she'd been dropped there. LaStanza knelt next to her and examined the earth surrounding the woman. There was no evidence that she had been dragged nor evidence of a struggle. There was also no mud and no footprints this time.

The drought up north had kept the river low. At this time of year the batture should have been completely swallowed by the river. But this year there was a good fifteen feet of batture left.

"Same spot, isn't it?" Mason said.

LaStanza looked up at his lieutenant and said, "Yeah. Exactly. How'd you know?"

Mason pointed up the levee, to the gaggle of policemen milling about the top of the levee, cracking jokes and leering down at them.

"Patrolman named Kelly told me on the phone an hour ago." Mason was wearing his maroon sport coat, a white shirt without a tie and dress pants. His face looked drawn and tired. It was the first time LaStanza had ever seen his lieutenant unshaven.

He hadn't shaved either. He'd jumped out of bed, thrown

on the same Yankees baseball jersey and jeans that were lying on the chair in the bedroom and pulled on a pair of tennis shoes.

Jodie looked as if she was on a date. She was in another of her suits, buttoned up and crisp. There wasn't even a hint of a bag under her eyes. Her hair even looked freshly blow dried. Standing behind Mason, she was writing feverishly in her notepad. For someone who'd just been assigned her first whodunit, she looked calm.

She must have felt him staring at her because she looked up suddenly and asked, "What'll we call this one? Batture II?"

"Naw, Batture Again," LaStanza answered. He felt a drop of sweat begin to work its way down his back. It was muggy next to the river, and there was no breeze that morning.

"When the technician arrives," he told his partner, "have him bring Kelly down with him."

"10-4," she said. He was sure she also wrote that in her notes next to "Batture Again."

LaStanza turned back to the body. Illuminated by the searchlights from two tugboats anchored a few feet away, the body looked grotesque and fragile at the same time. The woman's right arm appeared to be reaching for the water. Her index finger was extended, like the hand on Michelangelo's fresco from the Sistine Chapel. She was wearing a purple blouse with a matching skirt that had been pulled above her knees. Her pantyhose had been torn apart and dangled, in pieces, below her knees. One of her black high heels had fallen off and was standing upright in the dirt next to her left foot.

She looked about five feet, two inches tall and weighed about a hundred pounds. She had short, light brown hair, with a hint of gray mixed in. From the style of her clothes and the proportions of her body, she looked to be middle-aged. He could not be sure because she had no face. A bloody mass of tissue and bone and maggots occupied the

142

area from her forehead to her chin.

The first layer of her skin was gone, and the dermis had discolored into a gray-brown hue. He found a small amount of epidermis intact on her palms and on the sole of her right foot. She was white. Not flesh-colored or pink; she was chalk white.

LaStanza felt his stomach twisting, not from the stench that floated into his nostrils, not from the sight before his eyes, but from within. The homicide pressure cooker was on, and the heat was rising.

"Ready to take notes?" he asked his partner.

"Shoot away."

He gave her a detailed description of the body. Near the end of his dictation, the crime lab technician arrived. It was Sturtz again. Following behind was the eager face of Patrolman Kelly of the Fourth District, who announced, "I kept everyone on top of the levee this time."

"Good," LaStanza said. "Now, come over here and learn something."

"Yes, sir."

"Don't call me 'sir.' "

"Okay."

Mason announced he was going to search the entire area.

Sturtz pulled his camera out of its bulky case and said, "Haven't we done all this before?"

It was a ritual of death, played over and over again. Photos were followed by measurements, followed by the securing of physical evidence, followed by the inevitable body bag.

LaStanza pulled on a pair of surgical gloves and handled the body himself, turning her over and examining her until he was satisfied he had learned all he could before she was hauled away. He'd found that her skirt, fastened in back, was missing one of its buttons, and the zipper was ripped.

143

He'd found the telltale splotches of postmortem lividity along the length of her back.

Beneath the body he found a pair of red panties, also torn. Unbuttoning her blouse, he noticed she was wearing a matching red bra.

He yanked off the gloves and sat next to the water as the coroner's attendants bagged her and dragged her up the levee. Kelly came and sat next to him. LaStanza leaned back and closed his eyes for a while.

Jodie busied herself, securing a statement from the tug captain who'd found the body. It was the same captain who had found the first victims.

LaStanza overheard the captain's loud voice. "What a coincidence. I was showing my new mate where I found those bodies and son-of-a-gun. There was another one. I couldn't believe it at first."

"How often do you park your boat here?" Jodie asked.

"Couple times a week we moor it here for the night." The man repeated, "What a coincidence."

"It's no coincidence," LaStanza told Kelly, softly enough for only them to hear.

"What?"

He opened his eyes and said, "The killer left it here on purpose. A homicide man doesn't believe in coincidences."

Kelly leaned closer and said, "You think maybe the captain's involved?"

LaStanza shook his head no. "Remember the original footprints leading away from the body? Toward the levee?"

"I mean on this one?"

"It was the same killer," LaStanza stated evenly, without emotion.

"But this looks like—"

"A sex crime," LaStanza finished the statement, adding "It's the same spot. It's the same killer."

Kelly rubbed his chin and said, tentatively, "What if he heard about the bodies dumped on the Lower Coast?"

144

LaStanza shook his head and whispered, "It's too exact. Believe me, it's the same cocksucker."

Jodie finished her statement and stepped up to them. She said, "This scene's so different."

"Only to us," LaStanza quietly argued. "We see two M.O.'s, but who says a dope killer can't be a sex killer?"

Mason had joined them, blowing a cloud of smoke into the morning air. He added his opinion. "Well, we should keep an open mind. But I think Dino's right. Coincidences only happen in old movies."

Then Mason asked Jodie for details for the press release. After getting what he needed, he said, "Okay, we'll say nothing about the panties or 'the exact same spot' stuff."

Kelly politely came up with another what if, about the newspaper. LaStanza cut him off with, "The paper said nothing about the Lower Coast in the article on the first bodies. It just said Algiers."

"Oh."

"Only the killer knew this spot, and the boat captain, and the coroner's office and the police."

"Gee, that's a lot."

LaStanza pointed to the cops atop the levee. "You think they remembered the exact same spot, like you did?"

"As a matter of fact"—Kelly grinned—"only I was sure this was the spot."

"What size shoe you wear?" LaStanza joked. His stomach punched at him, but he ignored it.

"Nine."

"Too small." LaStanza looked at the well-groomed patrolman with the curly blond hair and asked, "You a good shot?"

Kelly patted his revolver. "I shot expert in the Academy."

"Good," LaStanza said, pointing to the levee. "If you see Stritzinger coming over the top, shoot him."

* * *

After the meat wagon had left, along with the curious

cops, Mason led another close search of the batture and the levee. They did not find the missing button or anything else of value. Then Mason headed for the Bureau. "So, what's next?" Kelly asked as LaStanza led the way back over the levee.

"We canvass. Wanna come?"

"Sure!"

They went straight to old man Clark's house and woke him up. Clark answered the door with sleepy eyes. He took a second to say, "Oh, no, you again?"

LaStanza couldn't prevent a mean smirk from crossing his face. "I'll give you two guesses why we're here."

Clark blinked his eyes and then stood erect, pointing to the dead end of River Road. "The Cubans?"

"Nope. Another body on the batture."

"Another one?"

"This one's about five-two, a hundred pounds, middle-aged with short, light brown hair." LaStanza then described her clothing.

"Another Negro?"

"No, a white girl."

"Oh!" Clark sounded concerned now.

"If any of your neighbors turn up missing, call me."

"I got no neighbors. But I'll check anyway."

On their way back to the car, Jodie asked her partner, "You think she's from around here?"

"I'll bet my Maserati she's from the Sixth."

"No, I'd probably lose."

Kelly finally spoke. He asked, "You really got a Maserati?"

They spent the next hour canvassing the Lower Coast.

Mark called on the radio at about five o'clock, just as Kelly was pulling away in his marked unit.

"What's he doing up so early?" Jodie asked.

LaStanza knew it wouldn't be good news. "Go ahead," he answered.

"Can you handle a 29 by 34S for me?"

LaStanza paused a second before answering, "You kiddin'?"

When Mark did not respond, LaStanza said, "We're still working on the Batture. What about the day watch?"

"We are the day watch. We switched this morning."

LaStanza looked at his partner. "Is he fuckin' with me?"

"No, we change today."

LaStanza's mouth remained open.

Mark continued, "I'm enroute to a 30 in the Quarter. Snowood and Jones are already handling a triple 30 in Treme. I'm serious, can you handle it for me?"

LaStanza felt like kicking out the windshield of their new Ford. But what could he say when his sergeant asked, instead of ordered?

He keyed the mike and answered, "10-4, Sarge, I'll handle it. Where is it?"

Mark gave him an address on Kerelec Street in the Faubourg Marigny. LaStanza turned the Ford around and headed back to town. He felt like a ton of bricks had fallen on him. His stomach was imploding.

They found a lone marked unit parked in front of a ratty shotgun house on Kerelec, just off Burgundy Street. The coroner's meat wagon was pulling up behind them.

LaStanza stretched when he got out and walked up the small front porch, past the broken screen door that hung precariously by one hinge, into a living room cluttered with dirty clothes, stained pillows, half-empty bags of potato chips and soft drink cans. Discolored sheets were hung as curtains on the windows of the narrow house.

There was no one in the living room. They were all in the first bedroom. An orange-haired woman in a frilly tee shirt and designer jeans was sitting on the king-sized bed that barely fit in the room. Next to her sat a heavy-set, bearded man with sandy hair. He was wearing a black muscle shirt and identical designer jeans.

He had large tattoos on each arm.

A middle-aged patrolman named Crockett was standing over the two. He was writing in his clipboard. Crockett was an old-timer. He had a potbelly, bloodshot eyes and a drinker's nose. His uniform was in dire need of pressing. He waved LaStanza forward and led him into the kitchen, to the body.

"Looks like the little boy was playing with his daddy's gun," Crockett said, stepping aside.

There was blood on the kitchen counter and brain tissue on the filthy kitchen floor. The body of a small, sandy-haired little boy lay on its side on the floor. Barefoot, wearing a pair of well-worn jeans with holes in each knee, the boy wore no shirt. There was food caked around his small mouth and bruises along his chest and back, some blue, some old and yellow. He was about three years old and very skinny. His large, green eyes were open and glazed in death. The boy had tiny, round lips and a pointy chin. There was a hideous entry wound in the boy's forehead, burnt gunpowder imbedded around the wound. Next to his little right hand was a snub-nosed, Colt .38 revolver with pearl grips.

"I told the boy to quit playing with it." The father had moved up behind them and was leaning against the door frame. "He just got a whipping . . ."

LaStanza pulled Jodie aside and told her to separate the parents and keep them apart. "When the crime lab arrives, have him run a neutron activation test on both."

Jodie was nodding, but her eyes were fixed on the small body. She looked a little green. Bodies of children often had that effect on even the best homicide man. He pretended he didn't notice but kept an eye on her for a couple seconds until she gulped and turned back toward the parents. Her walk was steady enough.

Crockett asked LaStanza if he could leave now.

"Sure."

148

The patrolman pointed to the baseball shirt and said, "Nice outfit. I heard you guys been wearing cowboy outfits lately."

Everyone's a comedian, LaStanza told himself.

Sturtz arrived a minute later and began a careful process of the scene. LaStanza had him run neutron activation swabs over the child's hands as soon as the photos were finished.

When Sturtz started on the parents, the father got huffy. "Don't you need some kind of warrant—"

LaStanza sawed him off with, "This is a crime scene. We'll take whatever evidence we feel like taking."

The father glared at him, so LaStanza came right back with, "You fire any guns lately?"

"No."

"You touch the gun after it went off?"

"No."

"Then, what are you worried about?"

The man was still angry but looked away from LaStanza's stare.

Mason came on the radio a minute later, asking if they needed any help on Kerelec. LaStanza told him no, they had it. He was about to ask Mason to go with Jodie to the autopsy of the Batture Again victim but caught himself. He didn't want her to think she couldn't handle it.

But he pulled her aside and gave her some advice anyway. "Get fingerprints. I don't care what it takes, if they have to cut off her fingers and soak 'em. The lab knows how to peel the skin off to get prints. Get them!"

Jodie nodded and wrote it down.

"And see if they can secure semen. Might be too old a body. And see if the pathologist can give you a date of death."

"I know what to do," she said.

He had to nod. "I know you do."

Damn, he wanted to go to that postmortem, but someone

had to interview the lovely parents of the three-year-old.

He dropped Jodie off at the morgue and drove around the corner to the police garage. He led the parents upstairs to the Homicide Office and put them in separate interview rooms.

He took the mother first and knew, within five minutes, that the father had abused the child from infancy. The mother refused to look him in the eye, and skirted the questions about abuse, but he knew. She only looked into his eyes when she was confirming the boy shot himself. Her eyes looked red, but she didn't cry.

The father had his large arms crossed and said, "It's about time," when LaStanza entered the room. After a careful statement, LaStanza had enough to book the bastard. The man was big and tough-looking but stupid. He was so worried about the abuse and convincing the detective that the boy shot himself, he readily admitted to leaving the gun around, readily admitted to finding the boy playing with it before, to spanking the boy for it and to putting the gun right back in the same place, in the nightstand next to their bed.

When the statement was finished, LaStanza told him to stand up and face the wall.

"What?"

"Stand up and put your hands against the wall."

He was almost twice LaStanza's size, but Dino was ready to kick his fuckin' lungs out if the son-of-a-bitch gave him a hint of shit.

"I'm not gonna tell you to stand up again," he repeated in a voice dripping with anger.

He could see it in the man's eyes. He was a pussy. Big or not, the man was half-a-left-hook and knew it. With his lower lip quivering, the large man stood and started breathing heavily.

"Over there," LaStanza ordered, pointing to the wall.

The man assumed the position. LaStanza frisked him

150

and then slapped on the cuffs.

The man began balling, "My God! My son's dead and you're arresting me?"

LaStanza remembered the bruises and the food caked around the tiny lips and the small hand next to the large pistol. God, he wished the fucker would have resisted!

The man cried all the way down to Central Lockup. He was still whimpering as LaStanza booked him with negligent homicide.

"What's wrong with him?" the jailer asked LaStanza when the cuffs were removed.

"His three-year-old son just died."

"Shit," the jailer said.

"Baby blew his brains out with this douche-bag's gun."

"Asshole!" the jailer snapped, shoving the large man over to the fingerprint table.

The autopsy room reeked of death and chemicals and rotten flesh. The stench assaulted LaStanza's nose as he entered. Goosey Lucy had both bodies, the Batture Again and the little boy, on the tables. He was finishing up with both, simultaneously, dictating into a small tape player.

Jodie began to run down the facts as the morgue assistants tossed the organs back into each body.

The Batture Again victim was beaten to death. "Her face was bashed in. Nasal bones broken, left cheekbone, upper and lower jaw and the hyoid bone." Jodie looked up from her notes and told him, "That's the tiny bone at the base of the tongue between the lower jaw and the larynx."

He knew that, but didn't interrupt.

"She had multiple fractures of her left ribs which lacerated her diaphragm and left lung."

Jesus, she was really beaten!

"Can't tell if she was raped. She's been dead too long for sperm swabs to tell anything, but there was plenty blood

151

around the vagina." Jodie closed her notepad and added, "She also had a hysterectomy scar."

"How long's she been dead?"

"Forty-eight to seventy-two hours."

LaStanza nodded. "What about the boy?"

"Abused and undernourished, no internal injuries. Penetrating wound was very close range."

He didn't respond, so she added, "I also got the toxicology report on the two Pams." She pulled papers from the back of her legal binder. "Dillards had no alcohol but had," she read the rest, "Talwin 0.6 mcg/ml and Dilaudid 1.0 mcg/ml."

She flipped to the next report. "Camp had no alcohol, too, Talwin 0.5 and Dilaudid 0.9. Cytology confirmed spermatozoa present in small number on both vaginal smears but nothing on the other smears."

Tees and blues, he thought to himself. *Cheap drugs may go out of style, but they never go away.*

Aunt Brulie was preparing lunch when LaStanza and his partner walked into the kitchen. Three plates were laid out on the counter. How she knew there'd be three for lunch was beyond him.

"Want a beer?" he asked his partner.

"No, but coffee'd be nice."

He knew better than to try fixing it or even reaching for a cold beer. Brulie did it automatically, pouring the grounds and bottled water into the coffeemaker, popping the cap off an icy Abita beer and passing it to LaStanza.

"You look like hell," Brulie told him.

"I feel like hell."

The first swig felt cold and smooth. The second went down long and easy. He finished the beer in silence, watching Brulie efficiently fix lunch, listening to Jodie raise her cup and take sips and slide her pen across her notepad. Jodie was still writing when Lizette came in behind them.

His wife eased up and kissed the back of his neck before greeting Jodie. She was wearing one of her Ellesse tennis shirts and jeans, her hair in a ponytail. She sat on the stool next to Dino and asked, "Was it bad?"

"Piece of cake," he said and tried to laugh, but managed only a weak croak.

Brulie passed each a large po' boy and iced tea. Lizette dug in, Jodie took a couple careful bites, but Dino ate nothing. There was no use. His stomach was one large knot. He did drink the tea.

"So tell me about it," Lizette said.

He shook his head no. He closed his eyes and began rubbing them.

Jodie briefly described the Batture Again scene, leaving out the maggots. He was thankful for her explaining. Finishing his tea, he poured himself another glass as Jodie told Lizette about the little boy murder.

He watched his wife's eyes grow larger as Jodie related the details.

When his partner finished, she turned to him and said, "On a case like that, when do you know when to wait to consult the D.A. or just make an arrest?"

His voice sounded raspy. "Well, when the kid's got bruises and dried food caked around his little mouth." He took another sip to cool his throat. "When the kid's half-naked in torn jeans and his parents are wearing designer jeans. When the kid's skinny as a rail and the parents are lard asses." His voice rose. "When the baby's fuckin' brains are on the filthy fuckin' kitchen floor and the parents are not catatonic." He looked at his open palms. "When you want to strangle the bastards with your bare hands so much you can taste it." His voice slackened to a whisper. "That's when you know it's time for the cuffs instead of the D.A."

Brulie broke the ensuing silence with, "Ouu wee, that Sicilian shit is some bad."

Jodie took the Ford home. He walked her to the door and told her, "If you get anything on an I.D., call me, no matter what time it is."

"Okay." Then she left. She was beginning to look beat.

He didn't remember falling asleep, didn't remember how he got into bed. But when he woke, it was completely dark. Lizette was next to him, asleep. His throat was on fire, and it must have been the tea that woke him because he had to go to the bathroom like there was no tomorrow.

In the bathroom mirror, he saw a face in need of a shave, in need of a complete overhaul. The small gray hairs that had been sneaking out along his temple were suddenly lined up in a row. He even saw a gray hair in his moustache.

Big fuckin' deal, he told himself. At thirty-two, six gray hairs on his head and one in his moustache were hardly the end of the world. Even the lines on his forehead, where he furrowed his brow at autopsies, weren't worth a second's worry.

He let out a long sigh, splashed on some Mennen pre-electric shave lotion, flipped on his stainless steel Braun electric shaver and smoothed his face in five quick minutes. Then he stepped into the shower and turned up the heat and soaked.

Lizette peeked in later and said, "You okay? I thought something happened to you."

"It did. I'm a new man. I'm clean."

She was wearing one of his pajama tops. Her hair was bunched up on one side where she'd slept on it, and her face was void of makeup. Her eyes looked puffy under the bright lights in the bathroom. When she raised her right hand to rub her eye, he could see the pajama sleeve covered her hand.

"You hungry?" she asked.

"Yeah."

"Meet you downstairs," she said and walked out.

A quick blow dry of his hair and some cologne, a clean tee shirt and pajama bottoms, produced the new-man feeling he sought. He went down to find her finishing loss bread and hot chocolate. The clock read five in the morning.

After eating, they went into the library, where Lizette put on a record and then climbed into the big easy chair next to him.

"Who is that?" he whispered.

"Mozart."

"Ah, I remember him. Woodstock, right?"

She almost smiled at the bad joke.

He settled back, closed his eyes and listened.

Then he felt her sit up. "God," she said, "how could anyone leave a loaded gun around a three-year-old?"

"I wonder," he said, "if he did it on purpose."

"Left the gun out on purpose?"

"No. I meant the little boy."

Ten
Constance Street

LaStanza had an idea. When there was no response to the first newspaper article on the Batture Again Murder, he asked his partner to grab her briefcase.

"Where are we going?"

"You'll see."

When he didn't elaborate on the way, Jodie began to tell him how she'd hit a big zero with missing persons. She also told him that Kelly had called earlier and was conducting an intensive daytime canvass of the Lower Coast while on duty that day.

LaStanza parked the Ford in the fifteen-minute parking zone in front of the *Times-Picayune* Building. He asked the receptionist if he could speak to George Lynn and waited with his partner until a short, balding man in a brown suit came down to get them.

He barely recognized Lynn. Since high school, George had lost so much hair and found so much excess weight, he looked like an exaggeration of the boy who'd sat next to LaStanza in homeroom forty-three at Archbishop Rummel High.

Lynn's face revealed he recognized LaStanza with no problem. He extended a friendly hand. "Son-of-a-gun," the reporter stammered. A familiar, crooked grin crossed the chubby face.

LaStanza introduced his partner, whose dress was the same shade of brown as Lynn's tight-fitting suit. Then he asked for help.

"Anything I can do," Lynn said. "Nice partner," he added as they followed Jodie up the escalator to the second floor.

Once inside the reporter's cluttered office, LaStanza came right to the point. "Can you draw us something like this?" He took out a rough sketch of a woman. He had drawn in the blouse and skirt of the Batture Again victim on the figure with appropriate notations as to color and style of clothing and the physical features of the victim. Over the face, he had drawn a large question mark.

"I'd like it done up right, asking for help in identifying her. This is the woman we found on the batture . . ."

"Sure, we ran something on this case in today's paper," Lynn said.

"Yeah, on the back page. I thought maybe you could put this on the front of the metro section or something like that."

The familiar grin crossed Lynn's face again. "Sure, why not?"

Jodie bumped LaStanza's shoulder gently and pointed to his diagram. "Her skirt and blouse were mauve, not purple, size five. And they were from D.H. Holmes." She ran a hand through her hair and looked up at Lynn. "I think we should be as precise as possible."

"Absolutely," Dino agreed, moving aside to let his partner get a better look at the drawing. After all, he reminded himself, she was the case officer.

"And make a note out here"—Jodie pointed next to the woman's hips on the drawing—"that she had a hysterectomy scar."

Lynn nodded, then grabbed a pen to jot the new information on the sketch. Jodie continued, "And her shoes were Bernardo. That's a brand name. Size six." Lynn added that to the sketch and then sat behind his cluttered desk. Extending a hand, he motioned for them to sit and then said, "I sure got fat, didn't I?"

LaStanza had to smile. He didn't feel like small talk, but he sat down anyway and let Lynn lead them back to the days when they were Raiders together, tearing up the Catholic League.

"We were on the track team," Lynn told Jodie.

That was true. LaStanza had been a runner, the four-forty and the mile. Lynn had been a jumper and, of all things, a pole vaulter.

"I didn't win too many events like Dino here," Lynn added quickly. "Remember those cheerleaders from Donaldsonville? The one with the dark hair and the big boobs that flirted with you?"

LaStanza had no idea what Lynn was talking about.

"Dark hair and big breasts, huh?" Jodie asked.

"Oh, yeah." Obviously Lynn remembered something.

"You should see Dino's wife," Jodie added.

"Really?" Lynn sat up on the edge of his chair.

LaStanza shot his partner an inquisitive look just as Mark interrupted the conversation by calling them on the radio.

"3122 to 3124."

Jodie had the radio and answered, "Go ahead."

"Can you two 10-19?"

"10-4," Jodie answered.

LaStanza stood up and extended his hand to his old teammate. "We have to go." He passed one of his business cards to Lynn and asked for one in return. He thanked Lynn once again and left.

As soon as they were back in the Ford, he called Mark. "What's up, Sarge?"

"We're running papers on the Hanged Lady Case."

"10-4," LaStanza responded and turned to his partner. "Jesus, Country-Ass must have been working."

* * *

Snowood looked like a cast member from *The Treasure of the Sierra Madre*. Leaning back in his chair, dirty boots kicked up on his desk, Country-Ass sported a two-day growth of beard, generously dusted with gray. His tan, Roy Rogers' vest was covered with the funk of the streets, as were his green, double-breasted cowboy shirt and corduroy pants. He looked almost as old as Walter Huston.

Fel didn't look much better. His face, also unshaven, looked weary and beat to the devil. He had thrown his pumpkin-orange suit coat over the back of his chair, along with his pink tie. His equally pink dress shirt was unbuttoned, its sleeves rolled up as he sat typing a warrant at his desk.

"Fuckin' triple murder yesterday and now this fuckin' case . . ." Fel was talking to himself as he typed.

LaStanza picked up Fel's coat sleeve and said, "Where'd you get the suit? Dryades Street?"

Fel didn't look up, but answered, "You just jealous."

"I like your Sheriff Bart outfit better." LaStanza sat on the edge of Snowood's desk and tapped his old partner's boot. "Talk to me, Country-Ass."

Snowood yawned, revealing a mouthful of ka-ka brown saliva. Snapping his mouth shut, he answered, "Once upon a time, an asshole named Tex Watson got released from Angola four days ago. He went straight to Magazine Street and started hitting on this lonely, overweight blond chick who worked in that pet store by Josephine Street."

LaStanza followed him so far.

"The other night, he asked to walk her home, only she didn't make it. They stopped by an abandoned car on Felicity where he killed her. Then he went back and carried her two blocks to a certain warehouse on Nuns Street where he found a rope."

Snowood paused for dramatic effect before continuing. "Then he took her dress to the cleaners. Blood, knife wounds and all. Then he ran his mouth to a couple of his padnas on Magazine."

"Why'd he take the dress to the cleaners?" Jodie asked.

"Who fuckin' knows?" Snowood answered. "Thank God, criminals are stupid."

"Fuckin' dope fiend," Fel added.

Mason came out of his office and crossed the squad room to the new Zenith console television set the Burglary Unit had "liberated" from some burglars. He always watched the twelve o'clock news.

"Hey!" Mark yelled as he stepped into the squad room from his office. "Your killer's name is Tex Watson?" He was carrying a daily in his hand.

"That's right," Snowood said, "only he's from Oklahoma."

"Shit," Mark snorted. "Tex Watson was the name of one of those Manson assholes that massacred Sharon Tate."

"Yeah?" Snowood grinned. "Sorta like naming yerself after Robert Ford, huh?"

Jodie looked at LaStanza, who shrugged and looked at Mark, who interpreted, "That's the guy who shot Jessie James in the back."

"Hey," Mason called out, "pipe down and look at this mook." He was pointing to the TV.

On the tube, there was an unshaven, acne-scarred face the color of pink marble. A pair of vacant, dope-fiend eyes, the color of wet sandpaper, stared into the camera lens as an off-screen voice announced, "This man has been accused of murder and says he is innocent."

The camera moved to the handsome face of an anchorman, who added, "Details after these words."

"MOTHA FUCK!" Snowood bellowed. "That's our killer!"

The squad gathered around the television and waited. After a diarrhea commercial and a word from Jerry Falwell, the anchorman came back on to introduce Alfred "Tex" Watson to the citizens of the Crescent City.

"This man is about to be accused of murder by New Orleans Police and decided to turn himself in on the air," the anchorman said in a voice dripping with concern.

160

The camera panned to the acne face again, who said, "I'm innocent." Watson's eyes shifted around like a kid whose hand was just caught in the cookie jar.

"How do you know about this allegation?" the anchor asked.

"Huh?"

"How do you know the police are looking for you?"

"Oh, I heard it on the street. Some, uh, associates tole me I was gonna be busted for a murder a some broad. In a warehouse. But I, uh, didn't do it."

"What type of business are you in, Mr. Watson?"

"Huh?"

"What do you do for a living?"

"I never sold drugs in my life . . ."

Everyone in the squad room roared and then tried their best to quiet down in order to hear more.

"I, uh," Tex was saying, "yeah, I do drugs, little crack, tees and blues, PCP, you know, and I give it to my friends, make a little money, but I don't *push*."

Felicity Jones was in hysterics. Jodie was trying her best to quiet him.

The anchorman's face filled the screen. "The details of the alleged murder are sketchy at the moment, but we believe this involves a body that was found recently, somewhere in the city."

That got an even bigger laugh. Talk about accuracy!

"Now —" the anchor had one more question — "where were you at the time of this murder?"

"Cleveland."

LaStanza and Jodie left Tex to Snowood and company and headed for the Lower Coast. LaStanza was feeling good for a change, after such a good laugh. They found Kelly at a horse stable in the twelve thousand block of River Road, about a half mile from the murder scene. Kelly was interviewing the

161

large, burly owner of the stable. They were talking about stallions and fillies and all that rot.

Jodie pitched right in and demonstrated, to her partner's surprise, that she knew a great deal about horses. LaStanza stepped away when they started talking about geldings. He waited by the Ford for twenty minutes. When it didn't look like the conversation was near ending, he put a note on Kelly's windshield and left in the Ford. The note read: "I'll be on the batture."

On that particular early summer afternoon, the river was crowded with traffic. A large container ship, riding high in the water, was making its way north while two larger ships, riding low in the water, lumbered south. Behind the container ship, there was a line of barges snaking its way upriver like a long worm.

It was hotter near the water. The air, as usual, was heavy with humidity, and there was no wind. LaStanza stood at the base of the levee and examined the scene before him. It was quiet along the Lower Coast, even during the day. The smell of greenery filled the moist air, along with the smell of mud from the river's edge.

He began to walk around. There was no particular reason for him to be there. But he felt a need to be there, to be where the women had been left to rot next to the brown water. Somewhere, probably across the river, in the concrete mass of a city built on a wide crescent in the river, was a man, his man, his killer.

In movies and novels, the cop sometimes tried to think like the killer, to get into the killer's mind and find a clue. But in real life, LaStanza knew that getting into the mind of a man who would do such a thing could not be done. A good homicide man went with the facts. Speculation was for amateurs.

He would find the killer, but not through the concentration of a good idea, not by the spark of a light bulb illuminating in his mind. He would find the killer through the victims. That was the only way.

He looked back at the river and said aloud, "I'm gonna get you, mother-fucker. Period."

LaStanza grabbed the morning paper, stopped by Cafe Du-Monde for a thermos of café au lait and beat everyone, including Mason, to the office the next morning. He poured a steamy cupful in the FUCK THIS SHIT mug, kicked up his feet and opened the paper.

It was on the front page. The drawing was at least five inches tall. Above it was written, "Who Is She?" The newspaper artist did a great job on the sketch. She looked like a real woman, instead of the scarecrow that LaStanza had drawn. In the center of her blank face was a large question mark.

"Who Was This Woman?" was the title of the accompanying article. LaStanza stared reading: "She was middle-aged. Found on the Algiers river batture last Wednesday morning, her identity still unknown, she lies unclaimed in the Orleans Parish Morgue . . ."

The article went on to describe the clothing and the fact that the victim was beaten to death. Then it asked anyone with information to call N.O.P.D. Homicide.

LaStanza reached for the phone and called the *Picayune*. Lynn wasn't in, so he left a message of thanks with the senior editor. As soon as he hung up, the phone rang. It was Fat Frank Hammond from the crime lab.

"That father's neutron activation test came back negative," Frank said.

"Uh?" It took a half second to realize what Frank meant. "Okay," LaStanza acknowledged.

"The little boy's came back positive."

"Fine. Thanks."

"I just thought you were in a hurry for it."

"Yeah, I was. Thanks a lot."

Well, there would be no rebooking of the asshole father with murder. LaStanza and the state would have to be satisfied with negligent homicide. It was not satisfying at all.

The phone rang again, and LaStanza took their first lead on the Batture Again victim. A lady who worked in a bakery called to report her friend who hadn't shown up for work for three days. After a couple minutes, the lady asked, "Did she have a bridge. In her mouth?"

"No."

"Oh, well. Then it wasn't my friend."

LaStanza thanked her anyway and prepared himself for a long day of answering the phone. Mason came in after LaStanza eliminated two more leads. Mason was wearing his navy blue blazer that morning and sported a fresh, Marine Corps haircut. He was happy to lend a hand. Not two minutes later, LaStanza hit pay dirt.

"I think it's my tenant," said the voice of an elderly woman. "She's been missing for three days, and when she left, she was wearing a mauve outfit." The voice began to quiver as the woman added, "Her name's Margaret Leake, with an "e" on the end. She wore Bernardo shoes just like that. And she had a hysterectomy four years ago."

"And what is your name and address, ma'am?"

"I'm Mary Roberts."

LaStanza jotted quickly, adding the woman's address and phone number next to her name in his notes. Then he told her they'd be right over.

"I've got a good lead," he told Mason. "Landlady on Constance Street." Nodding, he added, "Sixth District again."

"Good—" Mason let out a long drag of smoke—"I'll keep logging calls until you get a positive."

Jodie came bouncing into the squad room with a paper tucked under her arm. She was wearing a full pink skirt and a light, pale yellow sweater. She stopped as soon as she saw him packing up his briefcase.

"Let's take the Maserati," he said. "I wanna piss off the chief."

"Where are we going?" She was always asking that.

"To talk to your victim's landlady."

Her wide-spaced eyes shot open.

Margaret Leake had lived ten years in an apartment on the uptown side of a one-story, wooden double in the fourteen hundred block of Constance Street between Euterpe and Terpsichore. Her landlady occupied the other side of the narrow shotgun house with the small front porch, gingerbread overhang and tiny front yard. The place looked very much like the double where Jodie lived.

Mary Roberts had once been a handsome woman. Her eyes were still clear and blue, even though her face had wrinkled like a raisin and her hair had turned cotton-candy white. She was eighty-seven, born and raised in New Orleans, attended Sacred Heart Academy before going to Sophie Newcomb College where she met her husband. He was an engineering student at Tulane at the time. They married and lived fifty-five years of a childless but happy marriage until he died of lung cancer eleven years earlier. Mary Roberts told LaStanza and his partner her life's story in the first few minutes of their conversation.

Mrs. Roberts wore an old-fashioned, seersucker dress with a high collar and long sleeves, even though it was close to a hundred degrees outside. She wore black oxford shoes, a pearl necklace and matching earrings, a silver and gold wedding set on a finger that was speckled with age and stockings rolled up just below her knee, which was visible when she sat on the high-back sofa in her neat home. She served them hot tea and pralines. LaStanza passed on the pralines but nursed a cup of tea through the interview.

When Jodie showed photos of the victim's clothing, the landlady nodded her head and let out a small sigh. "Yes. I believe that was Margaret's." She turned to LaStanza and asked, "Would you like to see her apartment now?"

"Tell us a little about her."

"Margaret was from Tennessee. Had a son there who died four years ago in a car wreck. That was the only family she had."

"What about her son's father?" Jodie asked solemnly.

"He died in the Korean War."

The landlady waited a moment before continuing, "She was forty-nine but didn't look a day over thirty-five. Such a petite girl." The old woman almost lost it for a moment but went right on. "She was a barmaid, by profession, but not a wild girl at all. She worked up and down Magazine Street but was on unemployment for the last year. Monday night, she went out in that outfit." The woman nodded to the photos lying on her coffee table. "She walked up to Magazine Street. She didn't have a car. She was going drinking. She did that sometimes and sometimes didn't come home for a day or even two if she found a man. But she never brought anyone here."

When the woman stopped, Jodie asked about boyfriends and enemies and locations where Margaret had worked and anything else she could think of. There were no steady boyfriends. Then the landlady led them next door.

"Don't touch anything," LaStanza said politely after Mrs. Roberts unlocked the door. He led the way into an apartment that was even cleaner than the old woman's place. After slipping on surgical gloves, the detectives spent the next hour searching the apartment. LaStanza found a photograph of Margaret Leake atop her bedroom dresser. It was an old-fashioned black-and-white picture of a young woman in her twenties, sitting with a boy of about ten with a cowlick at the back of his head. They were both smiling at the camera lens. The date on back of the picture read 1962.

LaStanza called Mason on his radio and told his lieutenant it was looking good. Then he asked Mason to run Margaret on the police computer and then call Baton Rouge to get a driver's license photo of her, if she had a D.L. Then he called the crime lab over to dust for prints and to secure Margaret's hairbrushes and comb, containing samples of her hair which could be compared to that of the victim.

After two hours, the crime lab technician was unable to locate, much less lift, a fingerprint. "The place is too clean. Even the telephone receiver is clean. All the dishes are clean. The ash trays are spick-and-span."

LaStanza had been standing near the front window of the apartment, peering out of the venetian blinds at the passersby on Constance Street.

"Come here," he told the technician. Pointing to the venetian blinds, he said, "Dust the blinds."

"You kiddin'?"

"No. Dust them right here." LaStanza pointed to the blinds at eye-level.

The technician found four neat, clean prints on the blinds right where LaStanza had pointed. Shaking his head, the man lifted the prints carefully.

"How'd you know?"

"I'm a detective," LaStanza answered and winked. He had seen his mother separate their venetian blinds a thousand times to peek out their front window. He'd just used his ballpoint pen to do the same thing.

"I'll check them out with the victim's prints ASAP," the technician said on his way out. LaStanza joined his partner in searching the rest of the place. He went through the kitchen, but left the clothes to Jodie. An hour later he was sitting in the living room when Mrs. Roberts came in with more tea. Jodie soon joined them.

LaStanza could have really used a strong coffee-and-chicory but didn't mention it. He listened to his partner and the old woman exchange stories. The conversation started with the tea and then moved to where the old woman shopped for her groceries to shopping for clothes on Canal Street. By the time the phone rang a half hour later, they were talking about, of all things, Tulane Stadium and the Superdome.

LaStanza answered the phone. It was Fat Frank from the crime lab. "Bingo," Frank said. "You got your victim. It's a positive I.D. on your prints."

"Thanks, Frank."

"Anytime, my man. It's what I live for." Frank hung up laughing.

LaStanza hung up, removed his surgical gloves and nodded to Jodie.

"The lab?" she asked.

"Yep."

The old woman looked into his eyes and nodded herself. She finished her tea and stood up.

"Would you be so kind as to tell me who I should contact about the body."

"It's at the coroner's office," Jodie said.

LaStanza took out a business card and jotted the number for the old woman on the back. He handed it to her.

Mrs. Roberts looked at him with eyes that were now red. "I'll take care of the burial," she said.

"Are you sure?" Jodie asked.

"Yes." The old woman continued looking into LaStanza's eyes. "No need to worry about me. My husband left me . . . comfortable." Her eyes began to mist as she stepped forward and put her forehead against his shoulder. "I just don't know where I'll find another good tenant like Margaret."

Mrs. Roberts began to cry softly. He didn't move for a moment, then raised his hands and placed them on her back. He closed his eyes and waited for the woman to finish.

Margaret Leake's trail was easy to follow. On the last night of her life, she walked up Constance to Euterpe, where she turned right and walked up one block to Magazine. The first bar she visited was a half block from Euterpe on the river side of Magazine Street.

Two witnesses, both who knew Margaret slightly, said she was alone. She had two drinks before she took off her shoes, placed them on the jukebox and began dancing alone to a

168

couple slow songs. Apparently she did this often.

Margaret caught two more bars before Jackson Avenue. She used to work at both. The owner of the first remembered she was there but didn't remember much else, except she was alone. The bartender at the second one said she stayed for two drinks and danced alone again to a slow song before leaving.

The owner of a bar on Jackson Avenue didn't know Margaret by name but had seen her in there often enough to know her routine. "She looked depressed," he said. She left alone.

The trail turned cold after she turned up Prytania Street. The only bar they could place her in there was a dive that was usually frequented by sailors from the nearby Scandinavian Seamen's Home. The owner of Thor's Bar remembered she came in, sat at the bar, had one bourbon and then left alone. "She looked down in the mouth," he said.

"Which way did she go when she left?" Jodie asked.

The man pointed downtown. LaStanza grabbed Jodie's arm when they got outside and pointed down Prytania. "Those are all black bars," he told her. "Let's go back to the other bars. I got an idea."

They retraced their steps all the way back to the first bar and learned that Margaret Leake's usual routine was to drink and dance and get picked up, mostly by strangers. She shied away from regulars. And yes, as LaStanza thought, she liked black men, especially. Whenever a black would stray into the bar, she would immediately hit on him. On more than one occasion, she left with a black man.

It was near midnight when they finished. LaStanza started up the Maserati and told his partner he'd pick her up early the next morning.

"How early?"

"Seven. We're gonna call on Cherry again, if you're up to it."

"Of course I am," Jodie answered indignantly.

He popped in a Johnny Mathis tape and cruised back to Headquarters. When Jodie climbed out, she looked back and said, "Led Zeppelin and Johnny Mathis? You are strange."

"Tomorrow's program includes Pink Floyd and *La Bohème*. That's an opera."

"You're very strange."

He drove home thinking about the black bars on Prytania they were gonna have to hit next.

Lizette was at the computer. Hair in a ponytail, she was wearing jeans and a baby blue crocodile shirt and no shoes. She had a pencil behind her left ear and six books laid out on the wide desk next to her.

He lifted her ponytail and kissed her nape. She made a yummy sound and quickly followed it with, "I'll be finished in a minute." She completed a sentence on the screen and looked up at him. "Did you eat?"

He shook his head no.

"Good. Aunt Brulie left supper for both of us."

"Good." He put his briefcase and radio aside and headed for the kitchen.

Brulie had fixed two large plates of red beans and rice and breaded pork chops. She'd put a large note on the refrigerator which read, "Put them in the microwave. One at a time. Heat it for four minutes. Don't overheat. Fresh iced tea in the pitcher." He smiled and took settings out and placed them on the counter.

Lizette came in just as he was pouring the tea. She threw her arms around his shoulders and french kissed him softly. He kissed her back and ran his fingers across her large breasts.

"I'm hungry," she said, pulling away to sit across from him. She picked up her fork and said, "So, how are your batture girls coming along?"

"We identified the third victim."

"Oh, tell me about it."

Lizette was a good listener. She always was. He told her everything they'd discovered about Margaret Leake, and

170

when he finished, she said, "Sad, isn't it?"

"I think she picked up the wrong guy. Now all we gotta do is find out who."

"Then, you're close?"

"Maybe. Those bars on Prytania aren't too friendly."

"Oh."

After supper, they went up and took a long shower together. When she asked him to lather her back, he took his time, moving his hands around front as often as he could. Lizette started laughing after a while and said, "You wanna wash me or screw me?"

"I love it when you talk dirty."

She splashed him and pushed him aside to rinse off. When they got out of the shower their fingers were wrinkled. He dried her off, and she returned the favor. He pulled on a tee shirt and pajama pants. She climbed into a pair of white bikini panties and a hot-pink, satin pajama top.

He had wanted to go to bed early that night but wound up downstairs on the sofa with Lizette, watching a late movie on HBO. She fell asleep halfway through *Evil Under the Sun,* but he stayed awake to watch Peter Ustinov's Hercule Poirot solve the murder.

It must be nice, he thought as he carried Lizette up to bed, *having a limited number of suspects sequestered on an island with you like Poirot.* It was also nice having a script.

He dreamed that night of the batture, of muddy water and swirling currents of blood. The French-Acadian girls were back. They were beating their wash on the rocks at the base of the levee. They didn't seem to be bothered with the blood.

One of the girls stood up and began removing her dress. The others, at first shocked, soon joined in. Dark-haired girls with svelte, young bodies bathed in the river that was now bright and turquoise blue like the Caribbean. He could see the girls clearly in the clean water. They were beautiful.

Eleven
Melpomene Street

They didn't get to Cherry's until after ten the next morning. LaStanza had trouble getting up, and Jodie wanted to wait until Margaret Leake's driver's license photo arrived from Baton Rouge. Actually, Margaret had a state I.D. card, which looked just like a driver's license, except she couldn't drive with it. State I.D. cards were used for cashing checks.

Cherry answered the door without her wig. When she saw who it was, she wrinkled her nose, sighed and then let them in. "I was just going out," she said, putting an impatient hand on her hip. She was wearing a red halter top that barely contained her large breasts and an extra-tight pair of acid-washed jeans and the kind of shoes LaStanza's mother called pumps.

"Yeah? Where ya going?" LaStanza asked as he examined a statue of Napoleon sitting atop the lone end table in Cherry's front room. It was a statue of Napoleon crossing the Alps. Lizette had a copy of the painting hanging in their study. Cherry's statue was made of some sort of heavy plastic. Instead of a broken cannon beneath the horse, there was a gigantic penis.

"I was going to eat."

"Then, come on," he said, turning back to the door. "Lunch is on me."

He took them to Delmonico's Restaurant on St. Charles. It was a very nice place. He asked for a table in a corner and watched Cherry's reactions to the waiters pampering them with warm bread and fresh rolls, melted butter and fine wine.

Jodie looked perplexed. Sitting quietly across from LaStanza in her prim, executive, two-piece cream-colored suit, she buttered her bread and sipped her wine but left the conversation to him.

Cherry downed four rolls in quick succession. Licking her long fingertips after the fourth, she grinned at LaStanza and then started in on her third glass of wine.

He grinned back and pulled out Margaret's photo. "Ever see this woman around?"

Cherry gave the photo a bored look. "Nope," she said and passed it right back. He was about to take it, when she pulled it back and took a longer look at it. Then she nodded.

"Yeah. She a barmaid on Magazine. I seen her around."

"Tell me about her."

A waiter arrived with Cherry's baked chicken and Jodie's broiled trout. His fried shrimp came last. He picked at it while Cherry dug into her half chicken and told him what she knew of Margaret Leake. It wasn't much.

LaStanza was more interested in what she didn't know of the woman. Margaret, as he figured, was exactly what she appeared to be, a lonely woman who ran on the wild side occasionally. Margaret didn't run with whores or dope fiends, and Cherry knew of no connection between the dead barmaid and the two Pams.

"Did you ever see her with a black man?"

"No," Cherry answered and then added smugly, "not like I seen your friend with black boys."

"What friend?"

"The president of the Garden District."

"Mrs. Goebbels? I mean Gerrols?" He had a mouthful of shrimp and had trouble chewing and talking at the same time.

"Whatever her name is. That fat white broad with the dyed

173

blond hair and the little rat dog. Lives on Urania Street by Coliseum."

"Don't tell me." LaStanza managed to swallow the shrimp.

"She likes young bucks. Lets them in her back door. Little boy who lives on the other side of my house, he's fifteen. Him and his sixteen-year-old cousin go there to do odd jobs. They do jobs on her. She takes them both at the same time." Cherry turned to Jodie and added in a lower voice, "You know, one in the mouth and the other doggie style. Then she kicks them out."

"How much she pay them?" LaStanza asked.

"Ten apiece. She cheap."

"Yeah." He had to laugh.

"But I hear she sucks a mean dick."

Jodie was trying her best to give no reaction, but he could see her squirming.

After the meal, as they were climbing back into the Maserati, LaStanza reached over and pulled off one of Cherry's pumps. He looked inside and saw that it was a size seven. He took a closer look at her foot and handed the shoe back. She had smaller feet than he had, and he wore a man's size eight. His feet were exactly nine and a half inches long. He'd measured. That made Cherry's feet more than a few inches too short for the Batture.

He looked up and saw Jodie giving him the eye. "You look like you've got a foot fetish," she said.

He tossed the pump to Cherry and answered his partner, "Hell, I even went back and checked out ole Shelby."

Jodie was shaking her head.

"What was that all about?" Cherry asked as they drove off.

"It's for my diary."

"I sure like you, white boy." Cherry added, pulling open her blouse to let her breasts out.

LaStanza grimaced. "Put those fuckin' things away. I just ate!"

Cherry cackled. LaStanza interrupted her revelry by asking about the two bars where Cherry had said Pam Dillards used to hang out. "What about George's Love-In and the Fade-Out? Did you come up with anything there?"

"I went there, but nobody knew nothing."

Jodie waited until they dropped Cherry off before stammering, "That no-good Goebbels bitch!"

"I don't know," he said. His opinion of Mrs. Goebbels was changing. Somehow, her getting banged by the young bucks made her almost human.

"Bitch raises hell about *Nee*groes in the fountain and then sucks and fucks two at a time." Jodie was getting pissed.

Goebbels was certainly a two-faced cunt, LaStanza agreed, but her having sex, no matter how disgusting the picture seemed, made her almost pathetic. He turned up Pink Floyd and told himself he must be getting soft. Goebbels, all fat and naked with two black dicks in her, made a helluva sickening vision.

"I wonder if she swallows it?" he added, which made Jodie retch. He started laughing, so she slugged him in the shoulder. Pink Floyd followed immediately with a little ditty called, "Careful With That Ax, Eugene."

LaStanza went through his usual routine with Freddie up at the Blue Note. He showed the old man the photo of Margaret Leake and then called back. Margaret had never been in the Blue Note. Freddie had no useful information on the two Pams either, except he was getting word on the street about a bad dude named Sam. Freddie said he'd been checking on this Sam, but was beginning to think the name was an alias.

"I got both ears to the ground on this one," Freddie assured him.

"Thanks again," LaStanza told him.

"No problem."

It was time for a break. Later that night, they would canvass the bars on Prytania Street.

At ten o'clock, LaStanza picked up his partner and headed for Prytania. Four hours later, hours spent meandering in and out of seven predominately black bars on Prytania from Josephine to Erato, LaStanza and Jodie strolled into George's Love-In Bar. Occupying the first floor of a wooden building painted bright blue at the corner of Prytania and Euterpe, George's was the only local bar that featured dancers. It was always crowded.

A long bar ran along the right wall of the place with tables along the left wall. The dance floor was in a rear corner. Behind, there was a lighted stage with mirrors along two walls. A white girl was dancing when they entered. She looked about seven months pregnant. She had long hair and wore a black cape over her black Danskin as she gyrated to Prince's "Little Red Corvette." When she turned to face the mirrors, she would flop out a tit and rub the nipple.

LaStanza leaned against the bar and watched his partner in action. Jodie had changed clothes after their delightful lunch with Cherry. She was now wearing a light-weight, fitted sweater dress with buttons that ran down the entire front. Much to his surprise, she had left several of the buttons undone to actually show she had a cleavage and to show a surprising amount of leg.

There was a remarkable difference in the men talking to Jodie than the earlier attempts they had made in canvassing. Everyone talked to her, and many of them actually looked at the picture of Margaret Leake and the pictures of the two Pams, when they weren't staring at Jodie's chest.

When the pregnant broad finished dancing, she was replaced by an overweight black girl in a purple Danskin. At least she could dance, even with her large breasts hanging out. LaStanza watched the pregnant girl head straight for the bar

176

and down a stiff belt of bourbon.

Jesus, he thought, *the poor fetus.*

Under the sporadic lights, Jodie's billowy blond hair stood out. She looked damned good, and he kept a close eye on her as she bent over the tables and asked her questions.

The black girl finished her dance and was replaced by a tall, thin, big-breasted white girl with long brown hair. The crowd cheered as the girl opened her wraparound skirt to show off her red panties. There was something wrong with her, La-Stanza thought. Her shoulders were too large, her breasts too firm, and her Adam's apple was the size of a golf ball. She did have nice legs, but she had a skinny, male ass. She was also a bad dancer, which didn't seem to matter to the crowd.

He caught sight of the black dancer making her way through the crowd toward him. Her boobs were still hanging out when she leaned over to him and said, "You wanna tip me for my dancing?"

"No."

"I saw you watchin' me. You got a tip for me?" She pressed closer.

"Put your tits back in," he told her. He wanted to give her a real tip, to tell her to get fuckin' lost, but decided that giving her a five would be better.

"You ain't Vice," she said, tucking the five into her crotch.

"No. I'm the real police. Homicide." He handed her his card and asked her to step outside with him.

"Why not?" she responded.

He signaled for Jodie to follow. Outside, under the street light, the whore looked much worse. She took a look at the pictures of all three victims but said she'd never seen any of them. He thanked her anyway and led his partner down the street to the worst bar in the Sixth District.

He had already warned Jodie about the Fade-Out, which rested on the uptown corner of Prytania and Melpomene. He had to watch himself in this place. LaStanza and his old partner, Stan Smith, were well known in the Fade-Out.

He went in first and remained just in the doorway. When he didn't recognize any overtly hostile faces, he eased to the side and slipped on a pair of gangster sunglasses. He took them off a second later. He couldn't see a damn thing. He turned around and waved his partner in.

Jodie waltzed in like she belonged, and he liked that. She caught every eye and went right to work with her pictures. He stayed in the background, still wondering how those guys in the movies wore dark sunglasses in bars at night.

LaStanza watched one large black guy hover over Jodie. The man began rubbing his crotch as soon as she turned away; but that was all he did, so LaStanza let out a small sigh of relief. All he needed was to get into more shit at the Fade-Out.

There were no dancers in this bar, but there were two pool tables. Jodie broke up each game when she approached. A couple of the men asked her to join in as they ogled her. She declined and passed out her card before leaving them gaping.

Outside the bar, the usual amount of street people were hanging out. Jodie approached some. LaStanza stayed out of the way. A second later he caught sight of a girl leaning against the street sign on the corner. The girl was staring at him, real hard.

She had long brown hair that looked reddish under the amber light. Her hair looked natural. It wasn't a wig. She was black, but her skin was as light as LaStanza's. She had a high forehead and classic, sensual Negro lips and light eyes. She was wearing a hot dress, a fire red, strapless minidress that was way too short. It was also snug fitting, revealing a well-shaped body. She looked about twenty, give or take a few years. LaStanza always had trouble aging whores.

After a minute, she shot him a haughty look, turned and walked across Prytania. His eyes followed as she continued down toward Thalia Street.

"You ready to go?" Jodie asked.

"Yeah," he answered, glancing at his partner. When he

178

looked back down the street, the whore was gone.

He had parked the Maserati on St. Charles, so they turned up Melpomene after leaving the Fade-Out. They walked along a block of half-empty parking lots and ragged-out cars on a street named for the Greek muse of tragedy. The lots serviced the businesses on St. Charles. After midnight, they were a gathering place for winos, dope dealers and other creatures of the night. There was no one out on the street, except a woman in a white dress walking about twenty yards in front of the detectives.

A few steps later, a burly-looking man stepped out from behind a parked car and moved up behind the woman. A second later, the man leaned over and said something to her. LaStanza couldn't make out what it was, but it couldn't have been anything nice because the woman turned quickly and slapped the piss out of the man.

LaStanza was already moving forward. The man was retreating almost as quickly, as the woman continued pummeling him and shouting in Spanish. Two slaps later the man crashed into LaStanza, who shoved the big bastard against the fence of a parking lot on their left and then started pushing the angry Hispanic woman away. Jodie took control of the shouting woman, pulling her out toward the street.

LaStanza wheeled as the man came off the fence. He pointed a threatening finger at the man and shouted, "POLICE! Don't move, asshole!"

"Good. Then, bust that bitch. She hit me."

"Shut the fuck up! And stay up against that fence!"

The man's eyes began to bulge as he took a step forward. He was bigger than LaStanza and much more solid. His fists were already clenched.

LaStanza raised a defiant fist and said, coldly, "You don't want any part of me, pal."

"You gonna stop me, little man?"

LaStanza's eyes answered for him. He braced himself and waited. When the man hesitated, he knew he'd won. He

179

waited another three seconds before saying, "Just back up against the fence."

The man didn't move. Unclenching his fists, he crossed his arms and started nodding his head, like he was cool now, man.

LaStanza took a step back to keep a cushion between him and the man. He glanced at his partner. Jodie had the woman calmed now. Turning back to the man, LaStanza caught sight of the girl in the fire red dress. She was walking along Prytania. She was eyeballing him again.

The man started to move. LaStanza wheeled like a tornado and screamed, "One more step and I'll kick your fuckin' ass!"

The man clenched his fists again.

"Come on," LaStanza challenged.

When the man didn't, LaStanza added, "I oughta let that woman finish you off, you fuck!"

LaStanza was mad now. And he was ready. Obviously, the man wasn't and stepped back against the fence.

"Now," LaStanza was still yelling, "ask her if she wants to press charges!"

"She doesn't," his partner answered.

"Then, run her up the street!"

He was still leering at the man against the fence and said, "You, put your hands against the fence!"

The man shook his head no.

LaStanza kicked the man in the chest. It was a straight kick, a karate kick as taught by Bob Kay. It sent the big man tumbling against the fence.

LaStanza told his partner to take out her gun. "If he moves, blow his fuckin' brains out."

He stepped up to the man, grabbed his shoulder and wheeled him around to face the fence. The man automatically put his hands against the fence. LaStanza kicked his feet out and frisked him.

He came up with a pack of pills, a half lid of marijuana and the man's driver's license. Stepping back, he called the Bureau on the radio and ran the man on the computer.

"I just got out of Parish Prison," the man said before the results came back. "I been out two days."

He hadn't lied. He'd served a month in the Orleans Parish Prison for aggravated assault. There were no outstanding warrants.

LaStanza dumped the pills and pot into a nearby drain and then gave the man his license and told him to get lost. Without another word, the man turned and walked off toward Prytania.

The whore with the fire red dress was nowhere to be seen.

"You sure know how to use your temper," Jodie told him as they started back up Melpomene.

"Temper? What temper?"

After climbing into the Maserati, they took another drive down Prytania. He was looking for Fire Red, but stopped when they were flagged down by a skinny black man outside the Fade-Out.

The man stepped around to Jodie's side of the car and asked to see those pictures again. Jodie dug them out and handed them to him. LaStanza watched the man carefully, but the guy was more interested in Jodie's chest and legs than anything else.

When seated, Jodie's dress opened almost all the way to her panties. The guy was probably getting quite a view. After a minute, LaStanza started to race the engine. The man handed the pictures back and thanked Jodie.

He popped *La Boheme* in the tape player and headed straight for Milan Street.

"Well," Jodie said a minute later, "I guess Felicity was right. He told me to show a little cleavage and leg. They'll talk to cleavage and leg before they'll talk to a cop."

So that's where the white girl had gotten the bright idea. Part of LaStanza didn't blame her for using every tool she had available. Another part told him a good homicide man didn't need a cleavage to solve murders.

He could see her looking at him for a reaction, so he pointed to her legs and said, "Unbutton one more button and they'll start confessing to crimes that never occurred."

"Yeah, I am sure."

"You'd be surprised what the flash of a little panty will do to a man." When she didn't react, he added, "Well, you asked my opinion."

She looked away quickly and closed her dress. "What makes you think I'm wearing panties?" She was being cute again.

"That dress is awfully tight. You can see the panty lines along your rear end."

"You can?" She started to roll over to look but stopped herself. "Even through pantyhose?"

He had to laugh. "There isn't anything you can't see through pantyhose. Didn't your K-9er ever look up your dress; tell you these things?"

"I don't wanna talk about him!" That frosted her.

"You want advice on flashing, ask my wife. Lizette's an expert."

"What's that supposed to mean?" Jodie's voice was icy.

Oh, shit, he thought. He was misreading her again. So he explained his remark.

"You've seen the way she dresses. Believe me, when she climbs out of a car in a miniskirt, bends over and flashes, it's no accident."

"Oh? Does that bother you?"

"Why should it? I'm the one she flashes."

"But what if a spectator sees?"

"Let 'em eat their hearts out. I carry a .357 magnum, don't I?"

That seemed to defrost her a little.

Surprisingly, even to him, it didn't bother him when Lizette dressed sexy or flashed a hint of panty when they were out in public. It should, he thought, only secretly, deep down, it excited him.

182

"Look, you did a good job tonight," he told his partner. "Everybody talked to you. Even if we didn't come up with anything, at least they talked to you."

Jodie was looking at her watch.."How about we take tomorrow off," she said, "after all, it's Saturday."

"Why not?"

"Good."

"Refresh the gray cells," he added a Hercule Poirot line.

"What?" She hadn't seen the movie, obviously.

"Never mind."

As soon as he pulled up on Milan, she jumped out and waved. "See you Monday."

"*Ciao.*"

He watched her ·go in before leaving, then turned up the volume and gunned the Maserati. He started thinking about the girl in the fire red dress again. He wondered about that haughty look. Then he wondered just how much Jodie knew she was showing with her buttons undone.

Then he thought about Lizette strolling naked across a beach in front of those black boys who had stood stunned, their eyes glued to her breasts and between her legs. Lizette had been in no hurry with her towel to cover up. She'd made sure the boys got a good look.

"I always wanted to do something like that," she'd admitted later.

That night they'd had the best sex of their honeymoon up in the wicker bed of their weather-beaten, airy French hotel room on the beautiful isle of Guadaloupe.

Still later, she'd whispered another fantasy in his ear, a fantasy about suntan oil.

Lizette was asleep when he got home. It was so dark in their bedroom, he couldn't even see her. He slipped into bed and managed to find her face in the darkness and kissed her cheek. Then he rolled over and closed his eyes. Stretching, he realized how tired he was. He ran the image of Lizette on the beach through his mind again, in slow motion. The sun reflected off her body as she moved. She smiled at him and winked as dark eyes glared at her.

He dreamed, and in his dream, a young boy, about eight years old, was standing out on Garfield Street, looking up at Lizette's balcony. It was at night, and there was a light in her window. Then the french doors opened and Lizette came out on the balcony. She was naked. She stood on the balcony and brushed her long hair, her figure bathed in the bright light from her room.

He could see her through the little boy's eyes. In fact, they were Dino's eyes. He was eight years old, and she was the first naked woman he had ever seen. She was gorgeous. His eyes examined her breasts, the rosy area around each nipple, the full swell of her bosom when her arms moved as she brushed her hair. Then his gaze moved between her legs, to the soft, black pubic hair and the hint of pink within.

Dino's hands were on Lizette. He could feel her. When she sighed, he woke up. His hand was in her panties, rubbing her ass. She sighed again and rolled to face him and kissed him. He pulled her panties down and moved over her and kissed her flat belly and then down to her silky pubic hair. He opened her legs and kissed between them, slipping his tongue inside her. She curled her back and began to breath heavily. He reached under her pajama top to her breasts and kneaded them, running his finger over her erect nipples.

"Oh," she cried as she began to gyrate her hips with the movements of his tongue. He licked her again and started working his way up her body to her nipples and then to her open mouth.

She reached down and guided his erection into her, and after the initial flash of pleasure of the insertion, they both moved in rhythm. It was a hot one that rose to a crescendo of pleasure quickly before Lizette climaxed in short, quick spurts, crying in ecstasy and struggling to catch her breath.

He came immediately in long bucking jerks that left them both exhausted.

"Jesus," Lizette gasped.

"Yeah, wow," he said.

She ran her fingers over his back and added, "Hey, you'd better get up before my husband comes home."

Twelve
Conery Street

At noon, he woke to an empty bed. The bright sun of a hot summer day filled the room. Lizette had pulled open the heavy curtains on the french doors before leaving. He sat up, stretched and then climbed out of bed. After brushing his teeth, he climbed into a pair of gym shorts and went downstairs.

On his way to the kitchen, he picked up the newspaper from its usual place on the dining room table. Lizette had tacked a note to the paper which said she was going shopping.

Yawning, he walked into the kitchen to find Jodie sitting at the counter, sipping coffee. He stopped and blinked, but it was his partner all right.

"Good morning," she said, turning around to face him. She was wearing a plaid, button shirt and jeans.

"Uh," he said, "did I miss something?"

She smiled broadly and said, "Your hair's a mess."

He heard the doorbell ring and turned around. Stepping back through the dining room, he heard Lizette letting someone in. When he saw it was Carolyn Snowood, he figured it was time to beat feet.

He went back through the kitchen and asked Jodie to tell his wife he was upstairs.

"I like those shorts," Jodie teased.

He went up the back stairs to the bedroom. Lizette peeked in a minute later to explain.

"We'll be shopping," she said. "We'll probably be late." She was also wearing a button shirt and jeans.

He reached over, unbuttoned the center button on her shirt and said, "I'll tell your husband when I see him."

She pursed her lips and blew him a kiss goodbye.

He locked the door and took a shower before going back down to the paper.

Three bored hours later, he parked his Maserati on Camp Street and strolled across Coliseum Square. He'd brought popcorn for the pigeons. Sitting on one of the wrought iron benches, he fed the birds and talked to anyone who would talk to him.

An hour later, he spotted a man heading straight for him. The man didn't look like a drunk. He walked too straight. Wearing a dark blue jumpsuit, the man sported a full beard as dark as his face and bright brown eyes.

The man asked if he could sit next to LaStanza.

"Sure."

"You the police workin' on the murder of that girl named Pam, ain't ya?"

"Yes, I am."

The man extended a hand calloused from overwork. LaStanza shook the hand as the man said, "I'm Jose Brown. I'm a janitor for Mister Joseph who owns six buildings along in here."

LaStanza knew Joseph. He'd met the landlord once when he was a patrolman. Joseph's buildings were a cut above the regular tenements in the area.

"Well," Brown continued, "a couple days ago a white man in a Mercedes flagged me down and asked about that Pam girl, the one called Fawn. I told him I ain't seen her around. I wrote down his license number." Brown handed LaStanza a slip of paper with a Louisiana license plate number on it.

"Thought you might like to know about it," Brown added.

LaStanza thanked him and then asked if there was anything else the man knew about the Pams that might help. Brown shook his head no. Then LaStanza pulled out the photo of Margaret Leake. Brown took his time looking at the picture but swore he never saw her before. "Officer, if I knew any more about any of this, I'd tell you."

"What did this Mercedes man look like?"

"Blond hair and blue eyes. Clean shaven. Looked like a lawyer."

"What did he say, exactly?"

"I don't remember the exact words, but he was looking for Pam."

"You know what for?"

"Pussy."

"He say that?"

"He didn't have to."

LaStanza thanked the man again and then asked Brown what size shoe he wore.

"Nine and a half."

Too small.

The Mercedes was registered to a Dr. D. K. Duke on Conery Street, a half block off St. Charles Avenue, two blocks from Commander's Palace. It was a Garden District address, still in the Sixth District. The Bloody Sixth not only had four housing projects, it also had the Garden District. In New Orleans, it didn't matter what neighborhood you lived in; it was which house you lived in.

Nestled between an estate that faced the avenue and a mansion twice the size of LaStanza's Exposition Boulevard address, Dr. Duke's mini-plantation home sported seven white columns and a gazebo in the side yard and its own cut glass front door.

The doctor answered the door himself. He was about six feet tall, medium build with blond hair styled in a wave across his forehead. He was wearing a white sport coat, gray pants and a blue dress shirt that matched the color of his eyes. He also wore brown sandals.

LaStanza introduced himself, showing his credentials, and asked to speak to the doctor alone. The doctor's face lost the smug, comfortable look it'd had when he'd answered the door. He led LaStanza into a study and closed the door.

LaStanza had Fawn's pre-autopsy picture out and showed it to Dr. Duke.

"Ever see her before?"

The doctor gulped and nodded slowly.

"This girl was murdered. I want you to tell me everything you know about her. It's important."

The doctor sat down and began to shake his head. When he started speaking, his voice was faint. LaStanza asked him to speak up. The doctor shook his head harder and pointed up. "My wife's upstairs."

LaStanza took a step closer and waited.

"I'm a podiatrist." Duke passed a business card to LaStanza, who noted the doctor's office was on Prytania near Napoleon Avenue.

"I met Fawn while cruisin' around Coliseum Square about a year ago. She works—" he caught himself and said, "worked the square. I called her over and she propositioned me. She was wearing a yellow dress that day. We went off and I dropped her back."

The doctor's voice, still faint, was rattling nervously. "I paid her forty bucks each time. I never took her anywhere. We did it in my car. I never screwed her either. It was always fellatio.

"Last time I saw her was in February, right before Mardi

189

Gras." Duke gulped again and stopped talking.

"Okay," LaStanza said and then rattled off a series of questions. Who did Fawn hang out with? Did he ever see her with anyone? Did she ever tell him she had a pimp? Did she ever tell him anything? Were drugs ever involved in their relationship? How many times did he meet Fawn?

Duke answered every question "no," except the last one. He guessed he'd seen Fawn maybe twenty times.

"Do you 'see' any other girls?"

The doctor blinked once, slowly, and said, "I have a girl over in the Ninth Ward."

"What's her name and where does she stay?"

The doctor's shoulders sank. He only knew the girl by her street name of Stilt. She was about six feet tall, about twenty years old. She was a very dark-skinned black. He always found her hanging out in the park near St. Roch Cemetery.

LaStanza finally sat and wrote out some notes. The doctor offered him a drink which he turned down. Pulling out pictures of Pam Camp and Margaret Leake, LaStanza asked if Duke had ever seen them. The answer was no.

"What size shoe do you wear?"

"Huh. Um, size ten."

Still too small, LaStanza thought as he stood up and asked one final question.

"Know anyone else who was a client of Fawn?"

"No, sir."

LaStanza nodded and passed a business card to Duke. "What does the D. K. stand for?"

"David Keith."

Another fuckin' Keith. LaStanza forced back a smile as he turned to leave.

"Um, Detective. Is there any way to keep my name out of this?"

"I'm not a reporter, doc. If you're not involved in murder,

I don't care what you do, and I'll do you a favor."

"What?"

"Your story checks out, I won't even write a daily on it. It'll be between us."

"Oh, thank you. Thank you." Duke extended a nervous hand to shake. LaStanza remained polite and shook it.

"You think of anything else," he told the doctor, "call me."

"Oh, I will. And I appreciate the favor."

LaStanza smiled and said, "One day I might call in the chip, doc. Remember."

Duke's face looked puzzled.

LaStanza loved pulling his Sicilian out every so often. At the front door, when Duke put a friendly hand on his back and tried lightening up the atmosphere by saying that it sure was a strange world, LaStanza nodded and fought the urge to tell Duke that maybe he should switch to sheep.

On his way home, LaStanza put "A Hard Day's Night" in the tape player and made a mental note that he had to spend more time around Camp Street, much more time.

It was dark when LaStanza opened his own cut glass front door and walked into his house. There were shopping bags on the dining room table and more on the kitchen counter. Moving around the counter he could hear the Jacuzzi running. Peering out the french doors he saw Jodie climbing into the tub. She was in her bra and panties.

She didn't hear him come out, so he moved closer and said, "Hey, partner. What's up?"

Jodie sank quickly into the churning water.

"Jesus, what are you doing here?" she snapped, sinking all the way to her chin.

"I live here. Where's my wife?"

"She went upstairs for towels."

He looked back toward the kitchen and nodded. Then he

kicked off his penny loafers.

"What are you doing?" Jodie asked anxiously.

"Getting in." He started removing his socks.

"Oh, no you're not!"

When he began to unbuckle his belt, she put her hands in front of her eyes and turned away, which made him laugh. He left his belt buckled but rolled up his jeans, sat on the edge of the Jacuzzi and stuck his feet into the water.

Lizette came out of the kitchen with a bottle of wine and two glasses. She patted him on the head on her way into the tub. "Hey, babe," she said, "want some wine?" She was also in her bra and panties.

He shook his head no. Jodie, as far away from her partner as she could get, peeked out between her fingers and then pulled her hands away.

"That was cute, LaStanza!"

He leaned over and kissed his wife on the mouth and then settled back down.

"So, you girls had fun today?"

Lizette answered, "We sure spent enough to have fun for ten. What'd you do today?"

"Had a nice talk with a doctor who used to get regular blow jobs from Pam Dillards. He was a real charmer."

"You serious?" Jodie asked.

"Yeah, on his lunch break he cruises Coliseum Square in his Mercedes for blow jobs. He did confirm that Fawn was an independent." Narrowing his eyes, he added, "Come on, padna. Stand up and let's see what you look like in wet panties."

Lizette reached over and pulled his toe but didn't say anything.

"Go get me one of the towels in the kitchen," Jodie told him.

"Oh, I don't think so. I'm just getting comfortable."

Jodie turned to Lizette, who put her hands up and said,

192

"Don't look at me. A good police wife doesn't get between partners."

He threw back his head and really laughed at that one, especially with the strange look Jodie gave his wife. Then, after catching his breath, he stood up and went into the kitchen for the towels.

He put them on one of the chairs next to the tub, grabbed his shoes and socks and turned back to the kitchen.

"Be a darling and go get us some Chinese for supper," Lizette called out behind him.

"Why not?"

He grabbed the Chinese menu from the cabinet and went out to the Jacuzzi.

"What do y'all want?"

"Surprise us."

It took almost twenty minutes to get through on the phone to their favorite Szechuan place up on Carrollton Avenue. After ordering, he went back outside. The girls were both sitting up now and laughing hysterically. He turned right around to go back in. Lizette managed to catch her breath long enough to ask for another bottle of wine.

He brought it to them and turned down the heat on the Jacuzzi before going back in. Glancing back, he saw Jodie sticking her tongue out at him.

Forty-five minutes later he was back with their dinner in neat, little white cartons. The girls were still at it, laughing uncontrollably. They were out of the tub now, sitting on the edge, soaking their feet. Their hair was now wet.

He opened the door and said, "Supper's on."

They both stood up and came into the kitchen. Lizette moved up against him and planted a long, wet kiss on his mouth and then handed him her bra. Putting a hand on his shoulder she pulled off her panties and then draped them over her head before grabbing a towel and heading for the counter.

193

Jodie moved up against him, put her hands on her hips and said, "Turn you on or what?"

Lizette started laughing so hard behind him, he thought she'd fall out of the chair.

He raised an eyebrow at his partner and then gave her a good looking over. The bright kitchen light hid little of the wet body standing in front of him. Jodie had larger breasts than he imagined and big, round nipples that were pointing at him like loaded popguns, right through her bra. Her small, white bikini panties were extra sheer when wet and were pasted against her, revealing hair a few shades darker than the hair on her head.

Looking his partner back in the eye, he shrugged. But he was thinking, *Oh, Shit!*

Jodie took another half step forward and raised a finger in front of his face. "Eat your heart out, mister." Then she grabbed a towel, wrapped it around herself and went into the small bathroom just off the kitchen.

"Bring me another towel for my hair," Lizette called out to her.

Jodie came out a moment later with a towel around her, which barely covered the essential parts of the woman. She also had a towel wrapped around her head. Sitting next to Lizette, Jodie passed her another towel.

LaStanza found himself sitting across the counter, passing the white cartons to a pair of those evil genies from the *Arabian Nights*, the ones who enjoyed playing tricks on mortals.

LaStanza's mind was racing. He'd been to Vietnam, been inside every major housing project in the city on search warrants in the middle of harrowing, fear-filled nights. He'd been in shootouts, been shot, even shot a couple people. But he figured he'd never been in real trouble before that evening. You see, he was thinking of the old police saying that a hard-on had no conscience. He had absolutely no idea what would happen next, much less what he would do if the towels started opening.

"Arc light," someone should have shouted. The B-52s were overhead, and they were open for business. Turning slowly, he reached for the coffeepot and extra scoops of coffee-and-chicory.

He had an uncomfortable meal. He wished Lizette would close her towel and that he would stop looking. Most of all, he wished there was an easy way to sit on a bar stool with an armor-piercing erection. No sense in trying to get his mind to tell the hard-on to go away. It didn't work like that.

Thankfully, the girls barely noticed he was even in the room. They downed their food and the strong coffee and talked about everything from art to literature, from food to wine and back again.

They never spoke to him, until the meal was finished and the coffee was beginning to have an effect on them. Jodie was the first to feel it and began to make sure her towel was closed tightly. Lizette followed suit thirteen minutes later. He was counting.

"I'm going to watch TV," he said as soon as he finished.

Lizette stretched, which opened her towel to show off her full pair and nipples that stared back at him. "I need more coffee," she said, reaching for the pot. She caught him looking and stuck her tongue out at him. He smiled because he would settle up with her later.

Jodie stood up, put her back to him and rewrapped the towel around herself. Then, as he was leaving, she called out to him, pointed her finger again and said, "Not a word to anyone about seeing me in my panties."

He let out a long sigh and answered, "Hey, I never squealed on a partner in my life."

Early Monday morning, LaStanza walked into his

195

kitchen to find, of all people, Stan Smith standing behind the counter. Lizette was pouring coffee into a mug for his old partner.

"Hey, Candy-Ass," Stan teased, "I was just trying to get your wife to take off her blouse, but she won't."

Lizette was trying her best not to laugh in Stan's face. She stepped over to LaStanza, put her arms around his neck and kissed him good morning.

"She can keep her bra on, long as it's one of them French ones where I can see her nipples through it."

Ignoring the big man in the uniform never worked, but LaStanza tried anyway. He reached over and poured himself a cup.

"I'm leaving," Lizette said as she picked up her books and turned away. She was wearing a white blouse and a tan, full miniskirt, her hair fluffed out and flowing. LaStanza envied her classmates. He knew, for a fact, she was wearing a low-cut, sheer bra and matching panties. He turned to his ex-partner and grinned.

Stan was watching Lizette leave and added, "Bet you didn't know I been meeting your wife like this for months."

LaStanza shook his head and thought, *Here we go again.*

"She keeps shooting me out of the saddle, but I'm not giving up," Stan continued without missing a beat. "Yep, ever since I saved her life, she lets me drop by."

"Saved her life?" Son-of-a-bitch was talking about the Twenty-two Killer again. "You guarded her porch while I shot the bastard."

Stan's jaw dropped open in mock disbelief, which was followed by a quick retort. "So, sue me."

LaStanza figured he might as well ask, "All right, what do you want?"

Stan held up the front page of the *Picayune*'s metro section and pointed to a large story. "You made the paper again, big shot."

Next to the story, there was a picture of the House of the Lamb and Sister Dawn Abigail sitting on its front steps. In her muumuu, she looked like a tent with a head sticking out the top. The title of the article read: "Friend Of Dead Women Missing."

LaStanza began reading, "An acquaintance of two murdered women has been reported missing over the weekend. Thomas Lee Butler, an occasional resident of the House of the Lamb, disappeared over the weekend. Butler, also known as Cherry, is a transsexual . . ."

The article went on to elaborate how Sister Dawn had spoken to Cherry, who was making inquiries about the double murder. Then the article mentioned the police.

"According to persons interviewed by New Orleans Police Detectives Dino LaStanza and Jodie Kintyre, the two officers have established contacts throughout the lower Sixth Police District, a high crime area that the women were known to frequent.

"The investigation has taken the detectives through the run-down community of housing projects, corner bars and flophouses. The detectives have been seen mingling with homosexuals, prostitutes, pimps, transsexuals and transvestites in an attempt to seek clues in the murders."

God, LaStanza's mother was gonna love that. His aunts and cousins were probably already on the phone with her.

The article went on to retell the story of how the bodies were found. He read it carefully, and as he figured, the Batture Again case was not mentioned. Margaret Leake might as well have been found in Gretna. That suited him fine.

Sister Dawn described the two Pams as nice girls. "They did some hooking on the side," the lady from Arizona explained, "but by no means were they wicked."

Cherry was last seen leaving the House of the Lamb on Saturday. Sister Dawn discovered, Sunday morning, that

Cherry had "vanished" from her apartment on Melpomene Street.

Well, LaStanza knew what he'd be doing that day, as soon as he got rid of Stan, which was never easy. He called Jodie as Stan started up another of his stories of gore and glamor in the Sixth District. Jodie was still home, so LaStanza gave her the information on Dr. Duke's girl named Stilt and asked her to follow it up right away. Then he told her to read the front page of the metro section to see what he'd be up to.

"Meet you later at the Bureau," he told her.

Stan finished his story and poured himself another cup. "Come on"—the tall sergeant grinned—"tell all about them transvestites you been mingling with."

To hell with questioning Sister Dawn, LaStanza told himself. He went straight to Melpomene and parked in front of the Algerian Antiques Shop. Old Marid was wearing his keffiyeh, a khaki work shirt and jeans. Grinning at LaStanza, he held out a friendly hand to shake.

"You here about that article in the paper, huh?"

"That's right."

Marid began to chuckle, pulling on his red beard. "Well, it ain't no mystery. I saw Cherry leave Sunday afternoon, about four o'clock. She climbed into a yellow cab with a host of suitcases. She was all dressed up."

LaStanza leaned on the counter and began to rub his chin. "You didn't happen to notice the cab's number."

"Sure did." Marid handed him a note with the taxi's number on it. "The driver was white, about forty-five, and bald. They turned on Coliseum and headed uptown." Marid was proud of himself and had every right to be.

"You're still a cop," LaStanza told him as he shook the man's hand again.

"Yeah, you right. Want some coffee?" the French-Algerian offered. "It's Moroccan."

"I'll take a rain check," LaStanza said on his way out.

"Hey," Marid called out to him, "you need any help?"

"No."

"Okay. But I'd sure love to kick ass with you sometime."

"All right."

"*Inshallah!*" Marid added.

"Same to you."

Across the street, LaStanza found Cherry's landlady in one of the front apartments. He showed her his badge and then the article. The woman, at first cold, changed when she read the report in the paper.

"Damn," she said, shaking her large Afro. "Cherry never told me nothing."

"Can I look in her place?"

"I don't have a key. She put new locks on. If you break in, you gonna have to pay."

He rubbed his chin again and then had another idea. "You know anything about her family?" he asked the landlady.

"Her mama lives in Mississippi. I think I got her number." The woman went in to get it. LaStanza stepped around to Cherry's window and peeked in. The place looked as messy as usual.

"Here," the landlady said, handing him a note with Mrs. Butler's phone number, which began with a Mississippi area code.

"If I need to break in," he told her, "I'll let you know first." He walked back across Melpomene to the Maserati and headed for the Yellow Cab Company.

The cabbie had taken Cherry to Union Passenger Terminal to catch a train. She'd been alone. "Not a bad-looking girl," the cabbie remembered.

"She's not a girl."

"What?!"

"She's got a nine-inch dick as thick as my wrist."

"SHIT!"

A couple calls from the Bureau located the missing transsexual. LaStanza first spoke to Cherry's sister at the Butler home in Hot Coffee, Mississippi. "It's between McComb and Jackson," the sister explained. Then she told LaStanza how her mama was in the hospital and that Cherry was with her.

Cherry's mother was dying of emphysema. Cherry answered the phone in the semi private room. She was more than surprised.

"Well, hello, white boy. What it is?"

He told her about the article, and Cherry laughed so hard he could hardly get a word in. He finally managed to tell her he was sorry about her mother and promised to mail her a copy of the article.

Cherry thanked him, still laughing.

Stilt was just as easy to find, Jodie explained when she arrived. At six feet tall, the twenty-year-old girl stood out easily in the small park across the street from St. Roch Cemetery. A native New Orleanian with a sixth grade education, Stilt readily admitted knowing Dr. Duke and anything else, which didn't amount to much.

"She's never heard of Coliseum Square," Jodie explained as she kicked her feet up on her desk. She didn't have to worry about anyone peeking. She was wearing pants that day. "She didn't recognize either Pam or Margaret Leake. Hell, she doesn't even know where Camp Street is."

"Did you get her shoe size?" LaStanza asked as an afterthought.

200

"Sure did. Size eight, which makes her feet about nine and a half inches long."

He nodded and then told her about Cherry and Hot Coffee, Mississippi.

"Such distractions," Jodie complained when it was time to put Cherry and Stilt out of their minds.

"Gotta cover every base," he told her.

"Well," she replied, "I picked up Margaret Leake's toxicology report on my way back."

"That was fast," he said.

"I sweet-talked Dr. Lucy."

She passed the report to him. It revealed Margaret was legally intoxicated at the time of her death. It also revealed no illicit narcotics.

"We figured that," LaStanza said as he passed the report back.

He looked out the dirty windows of their office and added, "You didn't say you'd go out with Lucy, did you?"

"No, why?"

"Because I heard he'll make you soak in a tub full of ice first."

"Cute, LaStanza, real cute."

Thirteen
Euterpe Street

Another week of hanging around the Sixth produced one good result. People talked to LaStanza. Not just some people, but almost everyone. Sitting in the Maserati with the windows down, with Motown rocking on the tape player, LaStanza easily collected kids, like a pied piper. And when the kids accepted you, the teenagers weren't far behind. Before long, LaStanza was leaning against his fender and having nice chats with passersby.

"You the man, ain't ya?" he would be asked. "You the one workin' on the murder of them girls, huh?" Which was followed by, "Man, you sure don't give up, do ya?"

"Never," he would answer. "I always get my man."

That usually produced a laugh, but a friendly one.

Two days into the second week of soaking in the warm sunshine of summer in a terminally urban environment, LaStanza found a witness, or rather, she found him.

Jodie had court that morning, so he was alone, sitting on the left front fender of his Biturbo 425I, the heels of his penny loafers resting on the bumper. A thin white girl with long stringy hair came out of a laundromat three doors down from George's Love-In. She carried a full laundry basket under one arm and pushed a baby carriage with her other hand. Smiling at LaStanza as she passed, she said, "I guess it's about time we talked."

"Yeah?"

"Yeah, I saw Slow on the night she died. Sooner or later I knew you'd find me."

LaStanza recognized her right away. She was one of those faceless witnesses with valuable information who waited until the police came and asked them, personally. He climbed off the Maserati and stretched. Reaching over for the basket, he said, "Let me help you."

"Okay."

She smiled shyly at him and passed the basket. He could see that her teeth were bad. He gave her a good look-over while trying not to appear he was doing so. She was more than thin. She was emaciated. Her bones protruded from her pale skin at hideous angles. Her small eyes, khaki colored, were clear but bulged from their sockets. She had the figure of an adolescent basketball player. She appeared to be in her late twenties.

Her child looked healthy enough. He was a plump boy, about a year old, with dark brown eyes and kinky hair. His mulatto skin was darker than LaStanza's.

"His name is Martin," she said.

"How old is he?"

"Thirteen months."

"My name's LaStanza."

"I'm Abby Marshall," she said, turning the corner of Euterpe as he followed. "I was a friend of Slow. I knew you'd come to talk to me sooner or later."

She lived in a two-room efficiency above George's Love-In, on the Euterpe side of the building. LaStanza passed the basket back to her and carried the baby buggy up the two and a half flights.

"Thanks. It usually takes a couple trips," she said when they arrived.

Her living room held a well-worn sofa and a broken recliner covered with a soiled sheet. There was also a small end table next to the recliner which supported a black-and-white television set. The windows, which looked down on Euterpe, had no curtains.

The second room was a combination bedroom and kitchen with a tiny stove, an even smaller refrigerator, a single bed and two particle-board chests of drawers. At least there was a bathroom, too, on the other side of the kitchen area.

Abby Marshall sat in the recliner, pulled out a bottle and fed her child as she rocked and told LaStanza the story in one long monologue. He listened and jotted some sparse notes, but did not interrupt her until she finished.

"I'm from Los Angeles. I moved here two years ago with my old man. He's from Bogalusa. We used to live there, but a black guy with a white chick don't go over well in Bogalusa."

No kidding, LaStanza thought, Bogalusa had more Klan assholes than Pulaski, Tennessee.

"We moved here and, well, to make a long story short, we busted up." She shrugged and looked down at her child and then kissed the baby. "But my baby sure is a darling."

Looking back at the detective, she added, "So, I'm on the check now."

Welfare, LaStanza jotted down.

"I don't go out much, except downstairs on the weekend sometimes. On the Friday night that Slow and Fawn disappeared, I met Slow downstairs. She was wearing a white tee shirt and her new black boots.

"Fawn was wearing a red jersey, blue jeans and her new black boots, the same kind. I remember because that's what the paper said she was wearing when you found her.

"We had a drink, and Fawn said she was gonna shoot up. She went outside a little while and came back in all excited.

"The band was playing, and Fawn said something in Slow's ear; but Slow didn't look scared. Fawn was scared. When the band stopped, this dude came in and told Fawn she had to go with him. He grabbed her arm and she stood up.

"That's when Slow got up and said if Fawn was going, she

204

was going, too, and they left."

Abby paused a moment as she readjusted her baby. "I followed them out in time to see them get in an Oldsmobile Ninety-eight. It was brown with a tan top, and it had a Louisiana plate; but I didn't get the number.

"That's the last time I saw them."

"What time was it?"

"A little after midnight. I was worried but not that worried. You see plenty shit like that around here. Then the barmaid downstairs told me what happened and showed me the newspaper. Then I got scared. I ain't been back in George's since."

Abby lifted her child, who was now asleep, and placed his little head against her shoulder as she continued to rock. The baby burped right away but didn't wake up.

"Do you know the man with the Oldsmobile?"

"No. I've seen him around, but I don't know his name."

"Have you seen him since?"

"No, thank God."

"Can you identify him if you see him again."

"Sure."

"Describe him."

"He was a mulatto, but definite black features, high forehead, kinda bald in front, and tall, about six-four, and muscular. He had a moustache and a goatee, and I think he had a gold tooth in front."

"What's the barmaid's name, the one who told you about the murders?"

"Judy. She's black and short. Got both front teeth missing."

Abby seemed to relax. "Well, at least one good thing came of this. When I told my mother, she wired me enough money to get us to Los Angeles. It should be down at the Western Union office today. When Martin wakes up, we'll walk over."

She was talking about a couple miles. No way, LaStanza was already planning.

"I'll pack tonight," she said, "and we'll be off with Greyhound in the morning."

"How would you like to fly," he asked, "first class?"

"You joking?"

"I never joke about murder." Then he put his proposition to her. Then he helped her pack.

LaStanza drove his witness and her baby to the Western Union office on Carondelet Street before bringing them to the Bureau, where he called a pizza delivery place and ordered enough for them, his partner and his sergeant.

It was a bribe for Mark, who loved pizza and was the best composite man in the Bureau. While waiting for the pizza, Mark took Abby into his office with the composite kit and constructed the face of the man who had taken the Pams out of George's.

LaStanza tried to amuse little Martin. The baby wasn't crying, but looked terrified until Jodie scooped him away. That left LaStanza free to call Delta Airlines and charge two first-class tickets on one of his credit cards. Having all that money sure was convenient, he thought as he hung up.

By the time the pizzas arrived, Mark and Abby had finished the composite. "It looks like him," the girl from California declared as she munched on a piece of sausage and pepperoni pizza.

LaStanza logged in the numbers from the composite sheets in his notes and then helped himself to some pizza before Mark scoffed it all down.

"Can he have some?" LaStanza asked, pointing to Martin, who looked like he wanted some. The question brought howls from Jodie and Mark. Abby seemed to think all of them were funny. Martin soon gave up on the pizza and began playing with Jodie's handcuffs.

After lunch, LaStanza drove the entourage to the Quarter to the police artist whose art gallery was on St. Peter Street, a half block from Jackson Square.

Johnny Dee called himself the starving artist. He looked the part. Always in jeans and an old shirt, his face was perpetually in need of a shave. But he was an excellent artist. Once, when LaStanza was a rookie dick, Dee had drawn a face from a witness that looked so much like the perpetrator that they received five calls the day the face hit the paper. Four of the calls came up with the killer's name. The killer had turned himself into Central Lockup that very evening, figuring it was no use.

Using the composite as an outline, Dee composed a likeness of the man that had Abby shaking her head. He embellished the drawing with Abby's help until she declared, "That's him, without a doubt. Looks like he sat for a portrait."

Back at the Bureau, Jodie took Abby back up to the Homicide Office to look through the volumes of mug books of black males, in case the man had been arrested recently. LaStanza took Dee's drawing to the crime lab for a quick set of eight-by-tens and a "shit load" of four-by-fives.

Abby was still at the mug books, ably assisted by Martin, who was examining the faces almost as intently as his mother, when LaStanza walked back into the Bureau.

"Probably looking for his old man," Mark whispered to LaStanza, who ignored the remark.

"I was just kiddin'," Mark added as LaStanza walked over to his desk to call the *Picayune*. He punched the number and got Lynn on the phone. He'd been trying to thank his old classmate for over a week.

"Hey, we helped each other," Lynn declared. "We got a good follow-up and scooped the TV stations."

"Well, I got a couple more things for you. We got a drawing of the killer's face now. Maybe you could run it."

"We damn well can!"

"Good, I'll drop it by with a little write-up."

"Good, put my name on the envelope if I'm not here. Okay?"

"Fine," LaStanza agreed and then told him the other thing. He told him about Cherry and a sleepy village called Hot Coffee, Mississippi. Lynn enjoyed the story, adding that the reporter who wrote the Cherry article wasn't known for following anything up.

"Good," Lynn went on, "I'll get to rub it in."

After, LaStanza called Lizette to ask if she wanted to join the entourage for dinner.

Aunt Brulie answered the way she usually answered the phone. "Yeah, what is it?"

"Hello, Brulie, is Lizette there?"

"No, who's this?"

She was playing with him again, so he played along, "It's that little guy with the moustache, streak of Sicilian a mile long . . ."

"Oh, yeah. What you want? I'm busy."

He asked for his wife again.

"She gone. Left you a note. Want me to read it?"

Oh, she was asking for it. But he wanted to know what the note said, so he remained polite. "Please," he said.

Brulie dropped the receiver, which clanged across the kitchen counter. She came back a few seconds later and started reading, "Darlin', I have to drop by the estate this evening. I'll probably be late. Call me when you get home. Love, Liz."

Brulie cleared her throat and said, "She always call you Darlin'?"

"Sometimes" — he couldn't resist — "she calls me God. Oh, *God!*"

Brulie hung up.

So he took his partner, Abby and Martin to dinner at a northern Italian restaurant in Metairie on the way to New Orleans International Airport. The place was a little on the fancy side, and they weren't dressed up enough, especially Abby in her jeans; but LaStanza started rattling off Italian phrases and slipped the maitre d' a twenty, and a spot was found for them in a corner.

"Wow," Abby said when the vino arrived, "this is so nice. I always thought New Orleans was a cheap town. Not the people"—she was quick to sound apologetic—"but I thought the city was broke."

"It is," LaStanza assured her. "But we don't pay for this."

"We don't?"

"Naw, I got a gun and she's got a gun." He pointed to Jodie, who didn't react. She seemed to be far away. So he left her there.

Abby answered with, "I don't know what to believe with you."

They had an enormous meal and followed it with spumoni and cannoli. LaStanza passed on the ice cream but had two cups of cappuccino.

They made it to the airport with time enough to spare. He made sure he had Abby's mother's address and phone number and elicited a genuine promise from Abby to keep in touch, close touch.

They had a quiet moment, just before loading began.

"You think you'll get him?" Abby asked.

He nodded his head and said, without reservation, "I always get them."

Jodie was still a pickle puss, so he left her alone on the way home. Pulling off the expressway on Carrollton, she finally broke the silence.

"That was nice, um, putting her on the plane and all. But . . ." She let out a sigh and said, "Would you quit paying for everything. I mean for me."

"Sure." He hadn't thought.

"I'd like to pay once in a while, or at least pay for myself."

"Fine. Really." He meant it.

"Good. Tomorrow, lunch is on me."

"Good."

He decelerated in order not to ram a public service bus and put a tape on.

A few minutes later the scowl was back on his partner's face.

He turned down the music and asked what it was.

"What the hell kinda music is that?"

Iron Butterfly was in the middle of the drum solo from "In-A-Gadda-Da-Vida." He wasn't surprised she didn't recognize it.

"It's rock and roll," he said, turning it down even lower, "the kinda music that makes kids run out and have premarital sex."

"Jesus, it sounds like something a maniac would put on while he's torturing someone to death." She sounded just like his father, who used to throw a tantrum the second Dino put on "In-A-Gadda-Da-Vida."

"Put on something quiet!" His father would bellow.

"Okay, Pop. I'll put on something smooth." Then he'd put on Cream.

LaStanza finally had something to work with. He had a face. He took copies to the *Picayune* and to each TV station in town. He made up wanted posters and sent them to each police district. Then he took the posters to the Sixth District with a staple gun and posted one on every telephone pole within a five-block radius of Coliseum Square.

He carried the face with him everywhere, even out to dinner with his wife, to ask the waiters at the Camellia Grill if they'd ever seen the face before.

He studied the face carefully. He memorized it, seared it into his mind. If the cocksucker came within six blocks of LaStanza, he would recognize him. Only the man didn't come within six blocks, not during the day, not at night. And no one, absolutely no one, recognized the face.

The barmaid, Judy, at George's Love-In had never seen the face before. Hell, Judy wasn't sure she'd even seen the two Pams before. Freddie didn't recognize the face, neither did Shelby, nor Marid the French-Algerian, nor anyone in the Camp family, nor anyone at the House of the Lamb nor any of the people milling around Coliseum Square day after day.

LaStanza's concentration was interrupted near the end of

210

the week when he had to attend the retrial of an armed robber he had caught while a patrolman in the Sixth. It was the third trial for the asshole. Each time they convicted him, some court found a technicality to overturn the conviction. At least no judge had let the douche-bag out of jail on some sort of bullshit bond.

Dressed in the same three-piece blue suit he had worn in his first two trials, the "underwear robber" sat defiantly in Section "H" of Criminal District Court, an extra-hard look on his face. Three years in Angola State Penitentiary did that to some, turned pantywaists into tough guys. Get tough or get gang banged.

When LaStanza took the stand, the robber glared at him with a look he must have practiced in one of the stainless steel mirrors in the pen. LaStanza ignored the hard stare. He faced the jury and told his story:

LaStanza was alone that night, sitting in his marked unit, parked along Dryades Street, when he saw the underwear robber walk out of a convenience store across the street. He couldn't help noticing a silly-ass white boy with a pair of drawers over his head.

Peeking out of one of the leg openings of the Jockey shorts, the robber had strolled into the store, pulled out a Saturday night special and demanded money, netting thirty-one dollars and three Snickers bars.

LaStanza watched the idiot exit the store and stroll off down the street. He never lost sight of the dumb shit as he made a quick U-turn through the neutral ground on Dryades and crept up behind as the man pulled the drawers off his head and tucked them into his pocket.

Easing the unit closer, LaStanza turned on the public address system and said, "All right, put your hands against the wall."

The fool started looking up at the sky.

"Hey, this isn't God. There's a police car behind you, stupid."

The white boy wheeled and stopped and stood staring with his mouth open.

"Now," LaStanza said, "put your hands up against the wall before I blow your fuckin' brains all over the sidewalk."

The man professed his innocence as LaStanza frisked him, coming up with the gun, the money, the three Snickers bars and the Jockeys.

"Shut up," LaStanza moaned. "I don't even wanna talk to you. You're going to jail."

Shoving the dipshit into the back of his unit, LaStanza heard Headquarters put out a beep tone and the armed robbery call. LaStanza grabbed his mike and announced he had the culprit.

At Central Lockup, the underwear robber asked to talk to the cop who'd caught him. So LaStanza Mirandized him and took his confession. The man said he held up the convenience store because he was out of money. He also liked Snickers.

Now it was the defense lawyer's turn to cross examine LaStanza. He tried to rattle the dick. When the detective would not rattle, the lawyer decided the jury had heard enough and got LaStanza off the stand as quickly as possible.

On his way out, LaStanza winked at the robber, who jumped up and shouted, "I should have shot your ass!" Realizing he had the rapt attention of the jury, the underwear robber quickly added, "If I was the one who did it."

Half the jury laughed aloud. The assistant D.A. buried her face in her hands to keep from laughing aloud. The exasperated defense lawyer fell back in his chair. Even the judge could be heard snickering.

The underwear robber was convicted a third time. The judge decided that the original fifty-seven-year sentence wasn't good enough and sent the man back to Angola for ninety-nine years, without benefit of parole, probation or suspension of sentence.

Well, LaStanza thought as he left the courtroom, *chalk up one for the good guys.*

"Well," Lizette said, late one night in the darkness of their bedroom, "I thought it would be downhill after you came up with the face."

He turned over and put his arm around her. He had thought she was sleeping. "Tell you the truth," he answered, "so did I."

She rolled her leg over his and put her head on his chest. Her steady breathing almost put him to sleep, until she said something that woke him up right away.

She said, "Are you happy?"

"What?"

"I don't mean with me," she said. "I know we're happy together. I mean, sometimes, when you're all wound up, like tonight, are you happy? Know what I mean?"

"Uh huh." He hadn't noticed he was particularly wound that night.

"I just wonder about all the autopsies and deaths. It's got to get to you. Like that little boy." She paused a second before adding, "At night, when you sleep, sometimes you toss and turn so much you almost knock me out of bed."

"I do?"

"And sometimes, you shake. Really bad."

He had no idea.

She began to rub his stomach. "Does it still knot up?"

"Not as much." He was having a hard time about the shaking and tossing. He stared at the ceiling, although it was so dark he could see nothing but blackness.

A minute later he heard himself ask, "Are you happy?"

"Can't you tell?"

"I mean," he cleared his throat and added, "is marriage what you thought it would be?"

"It's exactly what I thought it would be."

He could feel her yawn before she added, "It's just a little hectic now with my school and teaching and your job."

"When you get your M.A., it should get better, huh?"

"Nope. Not until I get the Ph.D."

He adjusted his leg a little and said, "Maybe we should just run away."

"We could, you know."

He nodded and said, "As soon as I catch my killer."

She began to giggle. "Signore LaStanza. Sometimes, you are so romantic."

He rubbed his hand across her back. A minute later, he asked another question.

"Is there anything that would make you happier?"

"Yes." She lifted her chin and said, "A baby."

It took a while, but he managed to catch his breath.

"I don't mean now," she added, laying her face back on his chest. "I want a few years alone with you."

That, he could manage.

Lizette became quiet and fell right to sleep. He would have fallen asleep as quickly if he wasn't thinking about a baby.

She wasn't saying, "Oldie . . . oldie." She was saying, "Hold me. Hold me."

He knew it was a dream because the girl in the tight red skirt was dead when he found her. Slumped over her type-writer, her white blouse was streaked with blood. When he brushed her long, sandy hair from her face, he found a pair of dull eyes, milky with the unmistakable look of death. Care-fully, he replaced her hair, covering the lifeless eyes. Then he turned off her typewriter.

Dreams that ran in sequence gave no indication that time had passed. His next vision was of the electric daughter. She was standing in an open-air cabana bar at the edge of a lush, tropical jungle. On the other side of the bar was a beach and a sea the color of the lapis lazuli from the death mask of King Tut.

It was very late at night. They were the only two in the place, except for a faceless band and an equally faceless bartender. She turned to him and smiled. She was still seventeen. Her dark, Hispanic face never looked more lovely. Her eyes were still chocolate brown, her lower lip still a little larger than her upper lip.

She was wearing a strapless, black evening gown, and her lips were the color of hot lava. She held out her hand, and he took it, pulling her to him to dance when the music started.

He thought it was raining, but it wasn't raining. It was the song. They were dancing to "Riders on the Storm," dancing a slow, sensuous dance that went on and on. After the song ended, they continued dancing. She was pressed against him. It was as if they were in a trance.

Then she moved. In slow motion, she leaned her head back. He opened his eyes. Her head tilted toward him. She closed her eyes and parted her lips. And then she kissed him.

When the bartender began to applaud, Dino looked back at the man and saw it was his brother. Joe gave him a smart-assed smile and said, "That's it?"

There was a girl standing next to Joe. It was the girl in the tight red skirt. Her white blouse was pristine, without a hint of blood. She had her arm up on Joe's shoulder. Her long hair was flowing in the breeze that rolled in from the sea. Pursing her lips, she kissed his brother on the cheek, leaving a dark red mark.

Fourteen
South Broad

An obese woman came storming down Prytania Street, running everyone off the sidewalk. LaStanza and Jodie, standing outside the Fade-Out, hurriedly moved aside as the woman pushed her way through the midnight crowd collected outside the bar. Yelling in an unknown tongue, the woman appeared as mad as a hippopotamus with a bee up its ass.

The woman was of indeterminate race. Well over three hundred pounds, she was also very ugly. There was nothing about her that wasn't ugly. She had a flat, bulldog face and slanted eyes. Because she was so fat, her thighs rubbed together in a loud rasp that sounded like a mouse getting squashed. The cellulite in her arms prevented them from falling to her sides like a normal human. Rolling through the crowd like a runaway taxi with its doors open, her arms brushed everyone aside. The woman had black straw hair that stuck straight out as if her finger were in a light socket. She also had a wart on her nose the size of Rhode Island.

"Mrs. Goebbels in ten years," Jodie said after the woman blew by and the people began moving from the street back on the sidewalk.

LaStanza was watching someone else. In the same fire red dress, she was leaning against the front of a defunct furniture store on Melpomene street, a half block from the Fade-Out Bar. Her long hair, pinned on one side with a barrette and curled into ringlets, gave her a sultry look. And she was staring right at him.

LaStanza touched his partner's arm and then started for the girl. Fire Red didn't move. She ran her tongue over her large lips and waited until he arrived.

Before he could say anything, she said, "I know who you are."

"Yeah?"

"You're LaStanza. You're the one looking for Sam."

He nodded slowly and said, "We gotta talk."

"Yeah? Why?" Her voice was high-pitched and nasally and sounded as if she'd been on the street long enough to know the score.

"Because you want to talk to me."

"Oh, yeah?" Her voice rose. "What makes you think that?"

"Because you mentioned Sam."

Her large eyes, so brown they looked black, darted away from him. She took in a deep breath and said, "We can't talk here."

"I got my short around the corner," he said.

"I got work to do tonight, my man." She looked back at him and narrowed her eyes. "Know what I mean?"

"How much you make a night?"

"I'm not gonna tell you that."

"State secret?"

"Huh?"

"Lady, I don't give a rat's ass about selling pussy."

"I make five hundred a night," she said.

Sure. She was pulling his string, but at least she was still talking. LaStanza passed his keys to his partner and asked her to get the Maserati.

"I'm not going anywhere with you," Fire Red declared.

"Oh, yes, you are." He nodded for Jodie to get the car.

"Man, you really wanna mess me up, huh, leavin' with you two?"

"Not if I throw you in the backseat. Like we snatched you." He grabbed her wrist and pulled her to the edge of the sidewalk. She didn't resist.

The Maserati was there in a flash. LaStanza shoved the girl into the backseat and climbed in with her.

"Take us to the Camellia Grill," he told Jodie, who quickly punched the accelerator and pulled away from the gaping faces and the ogling eyes of the street people.

"So," he said, leaning back in the deep seat, "what's your name?"

She looked at him with fish eyes, the kind of eyes that said he wasn't registering. He reached over and grabbed her purse and began to look through it. She didn't react. He found a lid of marijuana along with nine vials of pills of assorted colors and size, a pack of Kleenex, three tampons, cigarettes, a lighter, an address book in some sort of code, a pocketbook with twenty-two dollars and change and a heap of photos. None of the photos looked like the killer's drawing or the two Pams. He also found makeup, lipstick and a nickel-plated .25 automatic. It was a cheap one, a Raven Arms MP25 with plastic grips. He unloaded the gun before returning it to the purse. He put the cartridges in his coat pocket.

He found her driver's license. Her name was Violet Clay, and she was all of twenty years old.

"You're gonna have to slap me around," she said, "so they see marks on my face."

"First things first. What do they call you?"

"Bunny." She leaned back and ran her hand over her knees. She gave him that sultry look again. She was a pro

218

all right, he told himself. He'd have to be sharp with this one.

Jodie cleared her throat and said, "You sure you don't wanna go to the office?"

"The grill," he said. "I'm hungry. It's your treat anyway."

Jodie flashed him a little smile in the rearview mirror. In her white dress shirt and jeans, Jodie looked very casual that night. He had worn jeans also, with a blue dress shirt and a gray jacket, his magnum on his hip.

Bunny was eyeballing him, real hard. So he reciprocated, and they spent most of the ride uptown staring each other down. It wasn't one of those blinking contests. It was a search of the eyes. LaStanza automatically kicked into Sicilian and let his eyes stare back, revealing absolutely no emotion.

Alfred, Lizette's favorite waiter, served the group but shied away from his usual chatter. Alfred could tell business from pleasure.

"Okay," LaStanza finally said, as he pulled out a four-by-five photo of the drawing of the killer's face, "this is Sam, right?" He didn't have to worry about being overheard. The only other people were across the cafe.

Bunny took the photo and studied it. "Of course it is," she said, handing it back.

"So, tell me about him."

Under the bright lights, her eyes had a purplish tint to the black irises. They were the darkest brown he'd ever seen. She had them opened wide now as she spoke, "I gotta do this my way. And don't tell me how you can protect me and all that shit."

Alfred deposited three Cokes before withdrawing quickly.

Bunny continued, "His name is Sam Brooks. He used to stay on Saratoga, by the Melpomene Project. And he's bad. Real bad." She let out a sigh and added, "He's a mulatta." She said it with contempt, as if she wasn't one.

219

"His daddy was white and his mama was black as hell. I know what you thinking, but I ain't white. Both my parents were black. I'm just light-skinned."

She put her elbow up on the counter next to LaStanza's and asked, "What's your excuse?"

"I'm Sicilian. We're all dark."

Bunny fought back a smile.

The sandwiches were ready. Alfred served them without comment, until LaStanza started up a conversation with him. The waiter asked politely about Miss Lizette before withdrawing.

Bunny dug into her club sandwich. After a couple bites, she looked like she was ready to talk again. She was prevented when a group of college kids stormed into the grill and spilled onto the stools on both sides of LaStanza and company. One of the students gave Jodie a good looking over but lacked the courage to strike up a conversation with her.

She looked like she wouldn't have minded, LaStanza thought, but the boy hesitated and wasn't old enough to know that if you hesitate too many times, you never catch the brass ring.

Jodie paid. LaStanza drove while Bunny took the front passenger seat, her skirt crawling way up her legs as she leaned against the door to watch LaStanza. Jodie climbed in back and said nothing. She took notes.

"Where does Sam live now?" LaStanza asked once they were on their way.

"I don't know."

"Can you find out?"

"Maybe."

"What kinda short does he drive?"

"Oldsmobile. Big one."

"What color?"

"Brown."

220

"How tall is he?"

"Big. Real big."

Abby Marshall had said he was six-four.

He asked about the two Pams. She said she never heard of them. So he asked Jodie to show her the pictures.

"Nope. No, yeah. I seen them. On Prytania. They whores."

When she passed the pictures back and glanced at LaStanza, he saw something in her eyes before she looked away. He saw fear. He made a mental note about hitting her again with the two Pams.

Jodie showed Bunny the picture of the Batture Again victim, and Bunny shrugged. "Never seen her before, ever."

Then Jodie hit her with a good question. "Why are you doing this?"

"Doin' what?"

"Talking to us."

He could see Bunny looking hard at him now. She answered, " 'Cause I hate that bastard."

She clammed up after that and asked them to drop her off at Lee Circle. She refused to tell them where she lived, refused to be dropped off anywhere near Prytania Street.

"Drop me off at Lee Circle. I'll walk."

She hadn't noticed he was taking a different route back to the Sixth until she noticed him turn off Tulane at South Broad and drive around to the police garage. She had one thing to say when they pulled in: "Uh, oh."

The Homicide Office was empty. LaStanza put a chair next to his desk and sat Bunny in it. Jodie sat at her desk and prepared for more notes.

LaStanza kicked his feet up on his desk, put his hands behind his head and asked, "Why?"

"Why, what?"

"Why do you hate Sam Brooks?"

She looked away at first and avoided answering the ques-

221

tion directly, but her story was anything but boring. She used to live with Sam on Saratoga Street, until he beat her once too often. He was her pimp and supplier of tees and blues and crack cocaine. Sometimes, when he got mad, she wouldn't sleep until he left the apartment.

In short, punchy statements that would have sounded sad if there were any sadness to her high-pitched voice, she told them about her life with Sam. But tough years on the street rid voices of any sentiment.

LaStanza asked her about the two Pams again. He also asked her about the Batture Again victim, but Bunny continued to say she knew nothing about the murders. She did not look him in the eye when she answered, but that could have been because of her nervousness. The Bureau seemed to make her nervous as hell. LaStanza liked that. At least the street hadn't hardened her into concrete yet.

He didn't push her. He just accepted her story and told her he'd take her home. She was so relieved she stood up first and actually smiled.

On the way down, in the elevator, Jodie asked, "You enjoy living like this?"

"When you're young, baby, have fun because you'll get old before you know it."

"You have any kids?" Jodie asked.

"No way." Bunny wasn't angry at the questions, but she answered Jodie as if the policewoman were a two-year-old.

Pulling up at Lee Circle, LaStanza had one more question. "You still live on Erato Street?"

Her eyes immediately said yes, but she said, "No." Then she gave up and said, "How'd you know?"

"Your driver's license."

"Oh."

"You want us to drop you there?"

"No. Here's fine." And with that Bunny climbed out. Leaning back in a second, she said, "You sure you won't hit

222

me? Slap me around a little?"

"No," he said as he reached into his coat pocket and handed her the bullets from her .25, "but I'll be seeing you around."

Bunny took the bullets and flashed a hard glint at him and walked away.

He waited for Jodie to climb in front. He followed Bunny's figure as the whore walked away. When Jodie got in, he said, "Thank God criminals aren't smart."

"Yeah," she agreed, looking at the whore.

"Not her. I mean Brooks. Mess over enough people, it catches up with you."

Sam Brooks was also known as Billy Brooks. According to the police computer, he stood 6'4" exactly, weighed 195 pounds, had black hair and brown eyes, with tattoos of "Sam" on his left arm and "Brooks" on his right arm.

"In case he forgets his name," LaStanza pointed out to his partner.

Brooks was arrested for receiving stolen things on three occasions. He was also arrested for simple burglary, theft, possession of cocaine and various traffic charges. His only conviction involved a juvenile arrest for simple burglary. He never served time.

There was one feature of Brooks' record that was out of the ordinary. He was always arrested alone. He had no running padnas. Brooks was a loner. He was a sneak thief, scumbag-burglar-dope-fiend, who just may have moved on to killing women.

"No known criminal associates," LaStanza told Jodie. "He's either antisocial or just smells that way."

LaStanza ordered twenty mug shots from R&I. He asked Jodie to pick them up while he ran Brooks' driver's license record. He discovered that Brooks' driver's license and late-model Oldsmobile were registered on Saratoga Street.

He started up a list of checks to be made to locate the man's new address: post office for a forwarding address, the power company for any electricity in Brooks' name, the gas company for the same, the telephone company, too, welfare records, unemployment records and finally, any record of parking tickets for the Oldsmobile. Then he wrote the word "Bunny" at the end.

He ran the name Violet Clay on the computer and was surprised to find that she had no criminal record whatsoever, not even a juvenile record.

As soon as Jodie returned with the mug shots, LaStanza looked into a face that matched the drawing of their murderer, exactly. Abby was right. It looked as if he had posed for the police drawing.

He asked Jodie to make a photo lineup with six other mugs of similar-looking black males with goatees from the extra photos at the rear of the mug books.

He got on the phone and called L.A.P.D. Homicide.

"I need you to run a lineup for us," he told the detective who answered. "We got a witness in Westwood by the name of Abby Marshall . . ."

As the California dick took down the information, LaStanza stared into the face of Sam Brooks. Brooks didn't look so tough. In fact, his face looked expressionless. That was probably the exact same expression he'd had on his face when he'd pulled the trigger on the two Pams. The Fuck!

"We'll Fed Ex a memo along with the lineup," LaStanza added, concluding his call to Los Angeles.

"We'll get right on it."

"Thanks."

Then he called Abby Marshall at her mother's number.

"So what does it mean?" Lizette asked, passing the

224

candied yams. Dino didn't seem happy at all. He seemed distracted.

"If Marshall I.D.'s him, then we got a suspect." He took a bite of breaded veal and added, "The trick will be in getting Bunny to tell us what she knows."

"She's holding back?"

"She lived with him and she's scared. There's got to be more." He looked at her and shrugged.

Lizette saw no sense of accomplishment in her husband and no relaxation either. He was too focused. He'd barely spoken since coming home, unless she prodded him. His mind seemed far away, probably on the batture again.

She knew he'd solve it. If there was one thing she was sure of about her husband, it was his persistence. He'd never give up until he solved it. Now he would never give up until he caught the man. This was always the hardest part for her. Just like the Twenty-two Killer and the Electric Daughter Case, Dino was on another plane; he was in another gear, a calm, steady gear with no hitch. His father described it as the leopard. It was a cold Sicilian trait. It was the mark of the hunter.

After the meal, after they'd put up the dishes and relaxed on the sofa in front of the big screen television in the living room, watching Bogie in "The Big Sleep" on the video player, she asked another question.

"Is Sam Brooks dangerous?"

He thought about it for a few seconds before answering. "I don't think so. He's a sneak thief who likes to pick on women. He's a bully, and bullies are cowards. We'll see what he's like up against the police. People like him are usually easy to take down."

"You're not just telling me this, are you?"

He looked into her eyes for the first time that evening, really looked into her eyes. Without blinking, he said straight out, "I'm not just telling you this. I showed you his rap sheet, didn't I? I think he's a pussy. Really. I bet Jodie could take him down by herself."

"The Big Sleep" was one of his favorite movies, but he didn't seem to pay much attention to it. He watched it, but he was far, far away. Maybe he'd seen it too many times. Or maybe, he was too focused on the batture. Maybe that was best. A sharp and focused Detective LaStanza was what she wanted, after all.

There was a sealed envelope on LaStanza's desk the following morning. It was from the chief of police. He ripped it open and read the formal memorandum within:

> To: Detective D. LaStanza, Homicide
> FROM: Superintendent Ron Miles, Administration
> RE: Superintendent's Hearing
> You are hereby notified to report to the Office of the Superintendent, 715 South Broad Street, New Orleans, Louisiana, on the following date for a Superintendent's Hearing.

He looked at the date. It was today. He had to report at ten o'clock. The chief had signed the memo. LaStanza looked hard but couldn't find the Chinaman's signature.

Apparently Mason had received a copy of the same memo. He came out of his office, trailing smoke, and said he was going along. Jodie wanted to come.

"You better wait here," Mason told her. "We can't afford having everyone fired in one day."

At ten, the lieutenant led the way up with a relaxed LaStanza in tow. The chief's secretary was her usual icy self, waving them in without a word. The chief was sitting behind his desk, as usual, and just as usual, the fat Chinaman

226

was planted at his side, a perpetual Buddha smile on his pasty face. Miles was wearing a yellow suit with a brown tie. His pink, Porky Pig face looked extra bloated that morning.

"You are not to speak," Miles told LaStanza before the detective could even sit. "You are not to say one word. I have something to read to you, and after, you will leave without comment."

LaStanza winked at him.

"Sit," the chief ordered, pointing to the two chairs in front of his desk.

"If this is a Superintendent's Hearing," Mason said before sitting, "I protest that someone outside the department is in attendance."

"I'm the superintendent!" Miles boomed. "I can have Genghis Khan here if I want to! I looked it up!"

LaStanza thought that was funny. Genghis Khan, ha! Mason apparently saw no humor in it and sat angrily to LaStanza's right.

Miles cleared his throat and pointed to a sheet of paper in front of him. "This is a formal letter addressed to Detective LaStanza. I will read it aloud."

He looked at the sheet and began to read; "As a result of an investigation by the Internal Affairs Division, Detective LaStanza has been exonerated of improprieties involving his privately owned automobile."

Big fuckin' investigation, LaStanza thought.

"In investigating Detective LaStanza's past, it was determined that his penchant for violence is unacceptable."

This was getting interesting.

"Detective LaStanza has been directly involved in five shooting incidents in which seven people have succumbed to gunshot wounds."

Seven? LaStanza started to mentally list them, but didn't have to. The chief listed them for him, aloud.

227

"On Mardi Gras Day . . ."

That was the cop killer LaStanza gunned down as a rookie.

"On Mazant Street . . ."

LaStanza never fired a shot. His partner killed the man.

"On Dryades Street . . ."

Again, he never fired a shot. Hell, he and Felicity Jones barely escaped from being shot by the other police at the scene.

"In Audubon Park . . ."

Guilty. He shot the Twenty-two Killer. No doubt about that one.

"On Iberville Street . . ."

Miles was talking about the Hotel Nenos now. Millie died there, along with her killer. Again, LaStanza never fired a shot.

"Detective LaStanza's penchant for violence . . ."

The man was repeating himself.

". . . makes him an unstable member of the department. He is now officially notified that if he becomes involved in any further act of extreme violence, be it justified or not, he will be immediately transferred from his present duties and assigned to the records section."

Miles looked up at LaStanza and added, "Since this will not be a demotion in rank or pay, it is not under the jurisdiction of, nor can it be reviewed by, the Civil Service Commission."

LaStanza opened his mouth to answer and was cut off by the chief. "This isn't Tombstone or Deadwood!"

You could have fooled Paul Snowood with that one. He even called LaStanza "Wyatt" on occasion.

"That is all," Miles concluded, shoving the letter across the desk toward LaStanza.

"You keep it," LaStanza said as he stood up.

"One more word and you're suspended!"

Mason was so angry, he mumbled profanities all the way back to the Bureau. LaStanza felt for the man. He wasn't in the least bit upset. He tried telling Mason on the stairs, but the lieutenant was huffing so loud, he probably didn't hear.

Mason went straight into his office and slammed the door shut. Jodie was bouncing in her chair, so LaStanza told her while pouring himself a fresh cup of coffee.

She couldn't believe it.

"It's true, all right. I shoot one more person and I'm a gelding, off to the record room. Hell, if you shoot someone, I'm a gelding." He had to laugh.

"Jesus," she stammered. "That man's crazy. How can you work? What's he trying to do, make you hesitate? Get you killed?"

"Don't worry about me hesitating," he said, sitting in his chair. "Fuck that Porky-Pig-looking faggot. I may shoot someone on purpose, just out of spite."

"Can he do that, just transfer you?"

"I really don't care. He tries and I'll make Lizette the happiest woman in New Orleans. I'll fuckin' quit."

Fifteen
Erato Street

The sun rose at exactly 5:47 A.M. Six minutes later, La-Stanza donned his dark, gangster sunglasses and readjusted himself in the driver's seat of the Maserati. Jodie, who was wearing shorts for the first time since teaming up with La-Stanza, put on her sunglasses, too. Even though the fourteen hundred block of Erato Street was narrow, with tall houses on both sides of the street that kept it in semi-shadow, it provided no relief from the bright heat of an early summer morning in the subtropics.

There were no front yards in the fourteen hundred block. The houses were sandwiched together on skinny lots that left no side yards either. Most of the homes were beat up and in dire need of paint. Most were single-family dwellings with small front porches and gingerbread overhangs. Once they had housed the upper middle class of a city just sprawling out from the French Quarter and Central Business District. Now they housed low lifes.

Jodie yawned and stretched, catching LaStanza's eye with her movement. She was wearing a short-sleeve, khaki shirt with her white shorts. She looked like an uptown shopper, especially in her white Ellesse tennis shoes. As usual, she looked crisp and unaffected by any lack of sleep. LaStanza was wearing jeans and a red LaCoste shirt. His magnum was in an ankle holster.

At one minute after six, Violet Clay, known to her friends and neighbors as Bunny, rounded the corner of Erato from Coliseum Street. She was wearing a baby blue sundress and black spiked heels. After taking three steps, she spotted the Maserati and stopped. LaStanza leaned out his window, tucked his chin down and gleeked her. Bunny mouthed the word "Shit" and put an aggravated hand on her hip and waited.

LaStanza started up the car and eased over to her. Smiling, he asked, "How about some breakfast?"

Before she got in, he made her hand over the .25, which he unloaded and tossed back into her purse. Bunny didn't speak until they were settled at an outside table at the Cafe DuMonde.

"Beignets?" he asked.

Bunny nodded. Jodie also nodded and yawned again. LaStanza ordered three café au laits and two orders of beignets and watched the young oriental waiter walk away. The clock at St. Louis Cathedral chimed out the half hour. Pigeons rose in a swarm from Jackson Square to circle the lower Pontalba Building. Behind the cafe, a boat's whistle moaned as it made its way along the river.

"So," Bunny finally said, "what you want this time?"

"Thought we could have a nice coffee together, that's all."

"Bullshit."

The waiter dropped off their orders, picked up the five LaStanza had placed on the table and walked away.

Bunny went right to work on her beignets. Jodie took a casual bite of one of the hot, solid donuts with powdered sugar sprinkled over it. LaStanza poured two teaspoons of sugar into his steamy coffee and stirred.

"When was the last time you saw Sam Brooks?" he asked casually.

Bunny closed her eyes in defiance as she took another bite

231

of beignet. She chewed it a couple times and then said, " 'Bout a week ago. He was passing in his short. He didn't see me."

"Was he with anyone?"

"He works alone."

"What makes you think he was working?"

"He always works. Like you."

Turning to Jodie, Bunny asked, "You two ever get it on together?"

Jodie was caught with a beignet in her mouth. She glared at Bunny, a small cloud of powdered sugar rising around her nose, which caused her to sneeze, which sent more sugar billowing. LaStanza thought she was gonna punch the whore. He'd never seen such a look in his partner's eyes before. But Jodie did nothing except snarl at Bunny and furrow her eyebrows all the way to the top of her nose.

Bunny turned to LaStanza with an inquiring look. He wasn't even about to answer. He knew what she was doing. She was avoiding the subject.

"You ever have a black woman?" she asked him, her eyes large and innocent-looking.

He took another sip of coffee.

"You don't know what it's like until you get some black pussy."

The waiter was approaching with LaStanza's change, but must have heard Bunny's remark because he pirouetted and walked off quickly.

"Come on," Bunny goaded LaStanza, "you wanna talk to me, don't you?"

"Brooks," he said, "talk to me about him."

"I told you all I know."

LaStanza put his cup down and looked out across Decatur Street to Jackson Square at a tall woman artist who was setting up shop along the wrought iron fence of the square.

"Bullshit," he said. "You hear the same thing about Italian men. Being good lovers. Believe me. It ain't so." He looked at Bunny again and added, "And you ain't begun to tell me all you know about the wonderful Mr. Brooks."

Bunny picked up another donut and started in on it.

LaStanza noticed that his partner never took another bite.

After they dropped Bunny off on Erato, Jodie finally spoke. She was fit to be tied.

"You know, I've been a cop for five years. I've had lots of partners, but you're the only one I ever had where every single person, police and civilian, wants to know if we're fuckin'!"

"Well, don't look at me." He was tired of hearing it, too. "You wanna work with Snowood? Nobody'd ask you about him because nobody'd fuck him!"

"Hell no!"

It took a while, but he was sure a hint of a smile came to her lips, just a hint.

Abby Marshall identified Sam Brooks as the man who left George's Love-In with the two Pams. LaStanza immediately cut a search warrant for Brooks' Oldsmobile.

"Now," he told his partner, "we gotta find where he lives."

They spent the rest of the day in the Sixth District, talking to Freddie and then Shelby, the occupants of the House of the Lamb and finally, Marid the French-Algerian.

Freddie had seen Brooks around, so had Shelby, but neither knew anything about the man. No one at the House of the Lamb recognized Brooks' face from the mug shot. One of the transsexuals wanted to see it again, making a yummy sound, but LaStanza left the creature drooling on the front porch of the mission. Marid had never seen Brooks before, but asked to keep one of the mugs, just in case.

"We can't pass them out," LaStanza told him.

Jodie gave one to the smiling French-Algerian, along with her card. "Call me," she said, "anytime." She wasn't flirting with the old man, exactly, but her statement had the same effect. Marid's dark face turned a shade darker with excitement as he tried his best to get them to stay for lunch, coffee, anything he could think of. Jodie left him longing.

At dawn, on the following morning, they snatched Bunny from the corner of St. Charles and Melpomene. Like a bad cliche, she was leaning against a light post. This time he took her purse away and cuffed her before shoving her into the backseat of the Ford. She was in a blue, body-snug jumpsuit, so he didn't bother frisking her.

"Hey," she complained, "you're hurting me."

"Good."

"What's the matter with you?" she asked as they sped off.

He turned around and said, with a cold smile, "Fun time's over, young lady. Sam Brooks murdered those girls. I know it and you know it. And we're gonna have a nice long talk about it."

Cutting her off as she was about to answer, he growled, "I don't care if it takes a fuckin' year; you're gonna tell me. Period!"

They put her in an interview room with the cuffs still on and let her cool it for an hour. LaStanza made coffee. Jodie started up a daily.

When Snowood came in a half hour later, both looked up at him in surprise.

"What the fuck are you doing here?" LaStanza had to ask.

"I'm in my wife's shit house again," Snowood said as he reached for some coffee.

"What'd you do this time?"

"Who has to do anything? She's a woman, ain't she?"

Jodie closed her eyes and pretended to take a nap.

Snowood pulled a chair up next to LaStanza's desk and continued his soliloquy, "She told me I'd have to kiss her ass hard enough to leave a bruise to get outta the shit house this time."

"Look," LaStanza cut in, "we got an important interview. We were gonna bring her out here, but if you're gonna whine."

"I'll be quiet," Snowood promised. "Just don't leave me out here all alone." He had such a haggard look on his face, LaStanza gave in. Snowood had not only left his western accent at home; he'd left his western clothes, too. He was wearing a regular suit. LaStanza pretended not to notice the fact that he, Jodie and Snowood were all wearing gray suits.

Against his own good sense, LaStanza brought Bunny out of the interview room, took off the cuffs and sat her on the chair Snowood had pulled up next to his desk. Snowood quickly pulled another chair up against Jodie's desk.

LaStanza put a hand up in Bunny's face when she started to talk. He had something to say first.

"You're not a suspect. You're just a witness. I don't have to read you your rights, don't have to get you a fuckin' lawyer, don't have to book you or let you make a phone call. And I can hold you as long is I like.

"Now," he said, settling back in his chair, "tell me what Brooks did to put the fear of the Lord into your black ass."

"You the one who should be afraid," she shot back. "Sam knows all about you and blondie. He's looking for you two."

LaStanza laughed. "We haven't been hard to find."

"He said you were one stupid white boy. Don't have enough sense to forget about two stupid nigger whores."

"Yeah?"

"Yeah!"

"And when did you talk to him?"

She looked away. He kicked her chair so hard, she fell flat on her ass. He could see his partner and Snowood both stand up. LaStanza never blinked. He just kept staring at the whore.

In a low voice, he finally said, "Pick up the fuckin' chair."

Bunny obeyed. But when she sat, she was still defiant,

235

refusing to look at him.

"Sam's a fuckin' coward," LaStanza said. "He picks on women. He ain't about to go face-to-face with the police, and you know it."

"Yeah! You think you bad, huh?" Bunny was looking at him now, her lower lip shaking as she went on. "Sam is bad. Know what he likes to do? He likes to hurt people. He gets off when he hits people. He gets it up when he beats people."

"You finished?" he asked disgustedly.

"Yeah." She folded her arms and leaned back.

"Slapping women around ain't bad. Tying women up and shooting them ain't bad. Bad is facing someone man to man and shooting it out with him eye to eye."

"You oughta know, Wyatt," Snowood injected. He was grinning now.

"Sam gonna kill you," Bunny added, her arms still folded.

"Others have tried before. And they're all dead."

"Yeah?"

"Paul, you still carry that eight-by-ten of the Twenty-two Killer around in your briefcase?"

"As a matter of fact, I do." Snowood jumped up and opened his briefcase, pulling out a large envelope. LaStanza nodded to Bunny when Snowood arrived with the envelope.

Snowood was enjoying this. He pulled out the close-up photo of the Twenty-two Killer's head after LaStanza had blown the cocksucker's brains all over a magnolia tree in Audubon Park.

"Yeah," Snowood drawled, "ole Wyatt here don't miss, does he?"

"Gross!" Bunny snapped, shoving the picture away. In a voice dripping sarcasm, she told LaStanza, "You said others, as in more than one. What happened to the others?"

"Tossed them in the river," he answered dryly.

Snowood was really enjoying this.

236

* * *

Three hours later, LaStanza switched gears. He was tired of butting heads with a hard-headed whore, so he put her back into the interview room for another wait.

Entering with two Coca-Colas, he sat across from her and said, "It's just you and me now. There aren't any people outside anymore. Just you and me, girl." He passed her one of the Cokes.

She took a sip, her shoulders slumping as she looked down at the Coke. He didn't ask any more questions. He just started talking. He talked about himself, about growing up on North Bernadotte Street next to City Park and about his big brother. He told her about the werewolves of City Park and the vampires of the Canal cemeteries.

Then he told her about Vietnam, about the women, the whores that seemed to be everywhere, even in the jungle. He told her about the war, about American boys with balls as big as Southeast Asia, about fire fights he'd witnessed as a combat photographer, about one particular battle where blood clouded the thick tropical air in a fine mist that coated his lens.

He told her about the Michelon Plantation. Not far from Ben Cat in the Iron Triangle, east of Saigon, the Viet Cong had assembled a hundred captured GIs. Lining them up in neat rows next to shallow graves, they put a bullet in the head of each American boy. What he remembered most were the hands. Their hands were tied behind their backs.

"Some of them were still teenagers," he said, "nineteen-year-olds, bound and slaughtered."

She said nothing, but he could tell she was listening as she finished off her Coke.

Then he told her about the Sixth District, about Camp Street skid row bums singing the Keebler Cookie Man song, about an obese woman named Mama Love who used to sit on the St. Charles Streetcar tracks when she got mad and block the streetcars, about the Dryades Street Shootout.

"I was there," she said when he stopped.

"You were?"

"Yeah, I remember all the police, and I saw the dead guys on the sidewalk. Y'all sure blew the shit outta them."

"I was in the store. I almost got the shit blown outta me."

"I was in the crowd that watched y'all."

She didn't look sultry anymore. She didn't even look street tough. Her face looked like that of the young girl she described watching the police process the scene of an ambush that blew three armed robbers to the promised land. She looked tired and small. She looked at him with her purple-brown eyes, now ovaled and big and wet.

He could feel a tingling along the back of his neck. He knew he was close. *If you wait long enough,* he told himself, *if you work at it hard enough, if you persist, it will come together.*

"You want another Coke?" he asked softly.

She shook her head and looked down at his revolver on his hip.

"What kinda gun is that?" she asked, wiping her eyes with her hand.

"A .357 magnum. Smith and Wesson model 66, stainless steel, with a two-and-a-half-inch barrel."

"Sam's guns are both black," she said. "He's got a .38 and a .22."

LaStanza nodded slowly.

"He used the .22 on the girls."

"I know," he said, his heart pounding so hard it rang in his ears.

"He tried to shoot me with the same gun," she said in a voice suddenly deep with emotion. "He just drove by and started shooting at me on my porch. I ran inside, and a bullet just missed me. I still got two bullets in my wall."

When she paused, he picked up the phone and punched out Jodie's extension on the intercom. Jodie answered, and he said, "Bring a tape recorder, tapes and two more Cokes."

"We got him?"

"The show's about to begin."

Jodie brought a recorder, three tapes, three Cokes and a folding chair for herself. He helped her and then popped open a Coke for Bunny and passed it to the whore.

Bunny took a long gulp and shook out her hair.

LaStanza put a tape in the recorder, ran a quick test and then started with, "This is the statement of Violet Clay, also known as Bunny, a twenty-year-old black female, date of birth . . ."

"Now," he said when he was ready, "in your own words, tell us what you know about the murders of Pam Camp and Pam Dillards."

She began in a strong voice, "Sam Brooks did it. He told me and showed me. Sam runs tees and blues and crack cocaine. He killed Fawn 'cause she ripped him off on tees and blues. He told me Slow, that's the other Pam, came with them when Sam grabbed Fawn outta a bar on Prytania Street.

"Fawn was a smart-ass. She a young whore and dopehead that hung around Sam. Slow was a whore, too, but she was really a pussy sucker.

"Sam took their money. He tied them up with shoe laces from their new boots. He laughed about that after. He took them on the levee across the river and shot them in the head. He said he left his shoes in the car so the police couldn't get no shoe prints. It was muddy.

"He came home around daylight and woke me up. He was tired and full a mud. He likes to stay clean, so he cleaned up before going to bed. He told me about the executions of them girls. First, I thought he was joking. But when he looked at me, I went cold.

"He said they begged for their lives before he shot them. He thought that was funny, too. He showed me the gun he used and put some more bullets in it. Then he went to sleep."

Bunny took a deep drag on her Coke before continuing, "Sam is bold. He likes to hurt people. He told me he shot people before. He always carries a gun. He got a black .22 and a black .38.

"A few days after he snuffed those girls, he took me out there one night to show me where he shot them. He took two hundred dollars from my purse and put the same gun against my head and told me he was gonna shoot me, too. But he didn't. He just took my money."

When she stopped, LaStanza started in on the questions, going over every minute detail . He went over everything, particularly about the shoe laces and the stocking feet and as much about the guns as the whore knew. Jodie took notes as the tape recorded the voices. Bunny told them how Brooks was originally from Algiers.

"Where did he take you in the car?"

"To the Lower Coast. To the end of the road by the levee. It was all dark."

When the statement was finished, he asked her about the Batture Again victim. Bunny insisted she never saw the woman before. She said she left Brooks the day after he put the gun against her head. So LaStanza had his partner pull out the pictures of the crime scene and told Bunny about the exact same spot.

"But no drugs?" she asked, examining the pictures.

"No. It was a sex crime."

She studied the pictures, one by one, passing each back to Jodie. Shaking her head, she reiterated how she'd never seen the woman before.

"Well," LaStanza said to his partner, "you start on the warrant. I got something to take care of." He stood up.

Bunny had a question. "That white woman wasn't wearing red drawers, was she?"

LaStanza sat back down. Jodie leaned forward.

240

Bunny went on, " 'Cause Sam's fruit for red panties. He used to have me put them on, and he'd get real hot, tear them off. He used to hurt me then, and I don't hurt easy down there. Then he'd go buy me more to wear."

There was a gleam in Jodie Kintyre's eyes, a sheen, a well-deserved glow on the face of someone who'd just accomplished a feat to be remembered. It was a special moment. He knew he must have a similar look on his face.

"Where are we going?" Bunny asked as they headed down Poydras Street away from Headquarters. It was getting dark already.

"Damn," Bunny said, "I can't believe we been in there all day." She was looking back at the Headquarter's Building. Then she repeated her earlier question, "Where are we going?"

"To your house."

"I don't wanna go there, not till you get him."

"You're gonna pick a few things, and I'm gonna get those bullets out of your wall. Capish?"

"Where am I gonna go?"

"I'm working on that."

Before arriving on Erato Street, LaStanza called for the crime lab and a Sixth District unit for security. The narrow street was especially dark when they arrived. Two of the three street lights on that small block were out. The only illumination came from the headlights of the cars climbing the ramp up to the Mississippi River Bridge at the end of the block.

Bunny's rented house was completely dark. She passed him the keys and watched out for their backs. He handed her his flashlight after fumbling with the keys. Once they were inside and the lights were on, Bunny let out a relieved sigh.

"Take your time," he told her, "pack as much as you need."

241

She headed for her bedroom. He headed straight for the two bullet holes on the front room wall, next to a painting of an emerald lizard on black velvet. They were small-caliber all right. He raised his radio and asked for the crime lab again.

The Sixth District unit arrived first, and LaStanza positioned the two patrolmen out front. The crime lab technician finally arrived fifteen minutes later. LaStanza had the man photograph the exterior of the house and then the front door and then the bullet holes from the open front door and then close-ups of the holes. Then he had them dug out.

One of the bullets had struck a stud and was in bad shape. But the other had gone through the sheet rock and imbedded itself in the sheet rock on the other side of the wall. It was in good shape.

"I need these compared to the bullets from my double 30," he told the technician.

"First thing in the morning," the man said on his way out.

"Thanks."

Bunny called out from the bedroom, "Where am I going? China, I hope."

"I'm working on it."

He looked at his watch. It was seven o'clock. He called Lizette.

"Hey, babe," she answered cheerily.

"Hey, yourself. What are you wearing?"

"Right now?"

"Yeah, I hope it's sexy."

"Where are you?"

"I'm in a house on Erato Street and I need something."

"Want me to talk nasty on the phone?"

"No," he said, "I need to know if that rental property your family's been renovating on Mystery Street is ready to be occupied."

"Two of the apartments are ready," she told him.

"Think I can stash a witness there for a while?"

"Of course."

"Good. I'm gonna need you to meet me with the keys in a little while, okay?"

"Okay, I'll go to the estate and pick them up."

"Thanks, babe."

"By the way, didja eat?"

"No." They hadn't eaten all day!

"Good, I'll bring that, too."

"Bring enough for four."

"Who's the fourth?"

"It's a surprise."

The building at 1414 Mystery Street was nestled on the corner of Maurepas Street, a block from the Fairgrounds Racetrack. It was well lit by the street lamps on the corner. It was a typical mid-city building, stucco painted yellow with a tile roof. A Japanese laundry occupied the first floor with unoccupied offices above. The apartments were in back.

"I'm gonna stay here?" Bunny asked anxiously.

"It don't get any safer than here," he told her.

"You sure?"

He looked back at her and had to smile. "Just keep your ass off the streets and you'll be fine."

LaStanza had made sure they weren't followed, but continued to scan the area while he and his partner and Bunny waited for Lizette.

Jodie read the application for the arrest warrant out loud to him. It sounded fine.

"Who's the duty judge?" he asked.

"LeBeau."

"Good, he'll sign anything. And he don't get pissed off if it's the middle of the night."

Lizette was late. When she pulled up in her burgundy Maserati. she was wearing sunglasses. She rolled down her window and gleeked them and then said, "I hope Chinese is all right?"

Not only had she brought supper; she brought groceries. "Your witness has to eat," she said as LaStanza introduced his wife to Bunny.

Lizette was wearing faded jeans and a matching jacket with a red dress shirt beneath. Her hair was in a ponytail. She left the sunglasses in her car.

"Come on," she said, leading the way. "The best apartment is on the left side."

The apartment was not luxurious, but it was probably better than any place Bunny had ever lived. The off-white sofa looked new, along with everything else, including a brass bed and a complete kitchen where Lizette quickly dispatched their dinner. LaStanza attempted to lend a hand but was nuzzled away by the three women.

He sat with them, but he might as well have not been there. The women tuned him out completely. Jodie was still riding a natural high. She didn't even seem to dislike the whore anymore. Bunny was so relieved she could hardly eat through the perpetual smile on her face. Lizette was at ease, naturally. She was genuinely friendly enough to get along with a street tough like Bunny without even a hint of a glitch.

He had other things to think about anyway. They still had to get the warrant signed and put out an A.P.B. so that some dumb patrolman didn't stumble on Sam Brooks and get a rude surprise.

For a minute, near the end of the meal, he gave himself the pleasure of reliving that scintillating moment when it all came together, when Bunny had said, "He used the .22 on the girls."

244

Sixteen
South Saratoga

There was a note from Lieutenant Mason on LaStanza's desk the next afternoon. It read, "No shit, Sherlock! The fuckin' bullets match!"

He knew that. He'd called the crime lab first thing that morning. Still groggy from the previous late night, he couldn't wait. He'd punched out the numbers to the crime lab on his bedroom phone and waited with a sleeper's headache pounding in his temples. He didn't have to ask the firearms expert to repeat the results a second time. He just rolled over and went back to sleep.

LaStanza placed Mason's note in his case file before putting on a fresh pot of coffee. Kicking his penny loafers up on his desk, he started planning the evening's work. First, he'd call Bunny. He promised to keep in touch. Then he'd load his partner in the Maserati and hit the Sixth District. He planned to search for Sam Brooks in an orderly manner after he'd paid his respects at the Sixth District station. As the coffee brewed, he closed his eyes and waited for his partner.

Taking the Maserati was a mistake. Arriving at the Sixth District station when the watches were changing was another mistake. Dressing in the new charcoal gray suit, red silk tie and button collar, blue dress shirt Lizette had laid out for him was also a mistake. But his biggest mistake was taking Jodie with him. With her hair fluffed out and her face made up, she easily turned the head of every patrolman entering and leaving the station house. The tan business suit she was wearing did not help. The top was loose fitting enough; it even dropped over her waist, but the skirt was a little too slim. The topper was her new reddish brown lipstick. On the way, she had told him how Lizette had suggested she switch to a darker hue.

Catcalls followed LaStanza into the only police station in New Orleans with burglars bars and metal-grated doors.

The ironwork security and blacked-out windows were in place in the event the neighbors finally got pissed off enough to run the police up the street.

At least Stan Smith wasn't on duty. It was hard enough asking the latest captain of a lost district for the help of the uniforms, without getting needled by a lunatic ex-partner. The captain of the Sixth was fighting a horrible head cold as well as an infestation of inquiring sergeants asking inane question after inane question. He promised to get the word out on Sam Brooks. He said he would get their snitches working on it right away.

LaStanza dropped by the roll call room on his way out and put a fresh copy of the wanted flyer on Brooks in the message book so that it could be read at each roll call. He put a special notation on it with his name. The men who still remembered him, he hoped, would take notice.

On his way back out, he marveled at how many of the incoming patrolmen he did not know. He felt like a stranger in a station house that had been home for him for over six years.

Jodie was standing across Felicity Street when he exited. She wasn't surrounded by uniforms anymore. She was surrounded by kids. About twenty black faces were staring at her from every possible angle. She didn't seem to notice the boys studying her legs. She was talking to a couple pre-teen girls when he approached. She was telling them what it was like being a policewoman. He stayed in the background and let her finish. Jodie passed out business cards before leaving.

The south side of Saratoga Street was even more run-down than Erato or Coliseum or even Camp Street, and Camp Street and skid row went together like red beans and rice. It looked more like a garbage dump than a thorough-fare. Cardboard boxes lined the gutters between the usual amount of abandoned vehicles, discarded stoves and sofas, automobile tires, twisted shopping carts and disemboweled television sets.

The address where Sam Brooks used to live, in the twelve hundred block, was between Clio and Erato. It took LaStanza a couple seconds to figure out they'd found the place, because all that was left was a burned hulk of charred timbers.

Jodie checked the address again on the computer printout sheet as the Maserati continued on. "That should be it," she confirmed as they crossed Erato. Near Thalia, LaStanza saw someone he recognized.

He rolled down his window and called out, "Say, Renee, what's happening?"

A tall black girl in a purple flower dress stepped away from the usual entourage of people meandering on the side-walk and leaned over for a closer look at the Maserati. Her eyes lit up a second later, and she began to laugh her way over to the car.

Renee Unzaga was Latino, a black Hispanic, with curly red hair, gray eyes and a large, sensuous mouth made for yelling at people and for whoring. Still good-looking after all her years on the street, Renee was the unofficial madam of South Saratoga Street. Actually, she was a pimp. Her street name was The Snake.

"Man, oh, man," she said, leaning her hip against the left front fender of LaStanza's car. "I thought I seen everything!"

"You like my car?" he asked in mock surprise.

"No. It ain't red. A car like this should be red." Renee leaned into the driver's window and took a look at Jodie.

"Who are you?" she asked.

"I'm a detective," Jodie answered in an even voice. She was getting good at that, replying without emotion.

Renee shrugged and looked back at LaStanza and said, "She don't look like no cop."

"Yeah?"

"Women cops are fat."

LaStanza grinned and replied, "She's wearing a girdle."

He felt Jodie give a yank on the back of his hair.

"So," Renee said, "what the hell are you doin' around here?"

"Looking for a scumbag named Sam Brooks."

Renee's face did not react. She just nodded slowly and said, "He don't have many friends around here."

"Know where he's staying?"

"He used to stay on the other side of Erato." She nodded back down Saratoga. "It's burned down now."

"We know."

"I'll keep my eye out." Renee winked at him and licked her large lips with a tongue that actually looked pointed. "You know, you may wanna check on a couple live up Saratoga just this side of Jackson. Lee Diamond, he stays in the front apartment, big white building with green trim, bent-up magnolia tree in front. Lee's girlfriend named Sandy Courane. She a whore, too. Sandy knows Brooks."

Renee looked over her shoulder back at the street people sitting on the front stoops of the worn buildings. When she looked back at LaStanza, her face was masked in a big smile.

"I'm gonna tell them how I just paid you off," she said. Grinning like a pit viper, she let her left hand fall into the car for a moment as if she were giving him something.

LaStanza passed her one of his business cards and said, "Find Brooks and I'll pay you even more."

"He a bad dude, you know," Renee said.

LaStanza let his eyes widen.

"I know," she said, "you a pretty bad little bastard, too."

She looked over at Jodie again and said, "He shoot anybody lately?"

"No."

Patting LaStanza's arm, the madam of South Saratoga added, "I sure would like to see you and Sam tangle." And with that she walked away, her thin hips rolling slowly back and forth as she moved.

LaStanza started to explain to Jodie about how he'd met The Snake years ago when one of Renee's whores had been beaten badly by a Wyoming cowboy, but Jodie wasn't listening.

"Lee Diamond and Sandy Courane," Jodie said, examining the notes she'd taken when Renee was leaning in the window. "Those names are awfully familiar."

"Yeah?"

"Yeah. I just can't remember."

"Maybe it'll come to you."

The Maserati crossed Josephine and closed in on Jackson. Renee hadn't lied about the house. It was right where she described, bent magnolia and all. It was two doors from the intersection. They turned the corner and parked on Jackson Avenue.

"She said it was the front apartment, right?"

"Right," Jodie confirmed as they approached the house. There was a hint of nervousness in her voice. He switched his portable radio to his left hand and kept his right hand ready for a quick draw.

There was no answer at the front door. The old woman who answered the side door claimed to be the owner of the house. She had salt-and-pepper hair and large dark brown rings around her eyes. She said the front apartment was vacant, been vacant for months. She never heard of Lee Diamond or Sandy Courane. They tried the addresses on either side and came up with the same results.

"Those names are familiar," Jodie repeated herself as they turned the corner back on Jackson to find the Maserati gone.

LaStanza froze. Jodie kept walking until she noticed her partner wasn't with her. She looked back at him and then at the street, and it came to her. She took a step back, as if the car had just been zapped by a vanishing ray as she was about to get in.

Slowly, LaStanza looked around, in case his mind was playing with him and he'd actually parked his car at a different spot along the avenue. But there was no Maserati on the street.

Swallowing hard, he lifted his radio and said hoarsely, "3124—Headquarters."

"Go ahead 3124."

"We're gonna need a Sixth District unit at Jackson and Saratoga."

"You need back-up?"

"Negative. We need one for a report." That was all he could manage to say. He passed his radio to his partner and then sat down on the curb. The sun was setting, sending dark shadows into the street. Across Jackson Avenue, several men standing outside the front of a neighborhood bar were watching them. A large yellow dog came along and sat

250

next to LaStanza with an innocent look on its goofy face that seemed to ask, "Okay, I give up, what's happening?"

"Think I should ask if they saw anything?" Jodie pointed to the men across the street.

"No."

"You want me to canvass over here?"

"No!" he answered disgustedly and added, "I can't believe how stupid I am."

Jesus, he was *never* gonna live this down. He could hear it already. Snowood was gonna bust a gut laughing so hard. Fel Jones would howl at a fellow Sixth Districter, getting nailed on his own turf. And Stan Smith, LaStanza didn't even want to think of what that fool would do. It made his stomach churn and scream at him, "Moron! Dumb Wop!" Only a tourist would be dumb enough to get clipped like that. What a fuckin' idiot, he told himself over and over again.

When the Sixth District unit arrived and two young patrolmen he'd never seen climbed out, LaStanza stood up and told them. He tried his best to sound calm and unaffected, as if he were just reporting an ordinary theft. The patrolmen listened to what he said and then looked at one another and started laughing, right in LaStanza's face.

For the next ten minutes, he felt as if he were being personally violated, right on Jackson Avenue, in front of God and the whole goddam world. He was forced to describe his midnight blue, Biturbo 425I with its sunroof, rosewood dash and Swiss clock, with its soft leather seats and digital stereo, to a pair of patrolmen who thought everything he said was unbearably funny. He felt like shit because they were right.

"You want us to take you to the Bureau?" one of the patrolmen asked when their report was finished.

Through gritted teeth, LaStanza said yes and climbed into the backseat of the unit with his partner. The patrolmen even thought the red lights they caught were funny.

Lizette did her best not to laugh.

"Actually," she said, "your new one will be here in forty-eight hours. I'll make the call in the morning."

"Huh?"

He'd just popped the top off a cold Abita. He was standing next to his kitchen counter, still feeling like a dumb fuck.

"What are you talking about?" he asked his wife.

Lizette shook out her wet hair and tucked her hands into the pockets of the short silk robe she was wearing.

"I ordered you a new Maserati when you started taking yours to the projects. It's identical. Except it's charcoal gray. And I had them put in an enhanced stereo, since you liked the stereo so much."

He couldn't believe his ears. "Since he'd been taking his to the projects"? She actually said that. His face must have looked awfully strange because Lizette stopped and asked, "Are you all right?"

"We got any arsenic?"

It bothered him even if it didn't bother her. It bothered him because some sneak thief bastard was driving his car, listening to his tapes on his stereo, probably using his hairbrush right now. It bothered him because of the money, too.

Lizette told him not to worry, reminding him he had a lot of getting used to about having money. How much money? He didn't know and didn't want to know. When Lizette had started telling him just how much she was worth, shortly before their wedding, he'd listened to her name banks in Luxembourg and Monte Carlo. He'd stopped her when she started in on the Swiss Banks.

She called it "old world" money, very old money that had been in the Louvier family since the French kings that preceded the Bourbon kings. The Louviers were bankers to bankers, and still were. The trust funds were set up for generations and generations to come. She was right. He had a lot of getting used to about money.

When he finished the beer, he poured himself a scotch and thought about how was he gonna get it the next day. After a second scotch, he started to feel angry again but not at himself. He started thinking about what he'd do if he ever found the car.

Whoever stole his car had better leave town. Otherwise, LaStanza was sure he'd be in front of another grand jury.

God, was he gonna get reamed by the fellas!

Jodie picked LaStanza up in the Ford the following afternoon. She was wearing a yellow business suit. He was in jeans, a black tee shirt and a dark blue work shirt hanging over his magnum, the speed loaders clipped to his belt.

"Guess I better change," she said as he climbed in without even greeting her. On the way to her place, she passed him a copy of a daily report and said, "I told you those names were familiar. I went by the office and picked this up. I just read it the other day."

The daily was from the other homicide platoon. It involved a murder/suicide. The victim was listed as Sandy Courane. The perpetrator was Lee Diamond. It had happened four days earlier in the Magnolia Housing Project. According to the report, they'd had a fight. Some fight.

LaStanza glanced down until he found what he was looking for. Diamond had used a .45 Smith and Wesson. It had been recovered at the scene. The only witness was a seventy-year-old neighbor who lived across the hall.

He didn't go in Jodie's apartment, preferring to keep the

253

interior of his partner's life an unknown quantity. "Put on something dark," was all he told her.

She came out in black jeans, a gray tee shirt and a dark green dress shirt, unbuttoned just like his. "Dark enough," she said icily, as she climbed in.

"Yeah."

The Ford lurched forward, and he knew she would give it to him before they hit Magazine Street. She did. "Don't take it out on me, mister," she began. He let her ventilate. He deserved it. He felt like getting it. But when she turned toward the office, he cut her off.

"Don't go to the office," he said.

She shot him a hard look. "Know what's waiting for you there, don't you?"

He could imagine.

She let out a frustrated sigh and told him. "Paul and Fel already left a little model sports car on your desk."

He didn't respond.

"Even Mark's laying in the gap for you."

He nodded.

"You're gonna have to face them sooner or later."

"What are you, my mother?"

Boy, was that the wrong thing to say. She jammed the brakes and climbed out, stormed around to his side and told him, "You drive!"

At least calling her a mother accomplished one thing. She quit talking to him. She just sat there with her arms folded and her teeth gritted as he began to cruise the entire Sixth District area.

They passed back and forth, from the St. Thomas Project through the Melpomene to the Calliope to the Magnolia and all the lovely neighborhoods in between. But there was no sign of Sam Brooks or his brown Oldsmobile.

When it was getting time to eat, Paul called them on the radio and asked if they wanted to meet. LaStanza told him no. A minute later Mark offered and got the same response. When Fel Jones called, LaStanza caught a gleam of a smile on the corner of his partner's lips. She was itching.

He picked up his radio and answered Fel. "Sure, we'll meet you. But no fried chicken or barbecue."

"How 'bout pizza?" Fel responded.

"New York?"

"10-4."

Jodie was definitely smiling now. He turned the Ford around and headed uptown to a narrow place on Magazine called New York Pizza. It used to be a trucker's grill, back in the days when trucks were allowed on Magazine. Now it popped thick-crusted pizzas from its two ovens. The pizzas were pretty good. What LaStanza liked most about the place was the smattering of Yankees paraphernalia on the walls, from autographed pictures of Yogi Berra to a Mickey Mantle jersey to a scorecard in Casey Stengal's handwriting.

Jodie was almost bouncing in anticipation. She was going to enjoy this, and somehow, he wanted her to enjoy it. He'd been a real shit.

They were waiting inside for him. Paul and Fel were wearing identical red baseball caps with little sports cars glued to the bills. Mark presented LaStanza with a carton of milk with a picture of a Maserati pasted over a picture of a missing child.

They saved the best for last. Mark told him how Lieutenant Mason had just established a new tradition. It was called "loser of the month."

"Guess who won?"

The next day, LaStanza and Jodie worked the day shift, figuring Brooks had to sleep sometime. But they came up empty again.

"Maybe he left town," Jodie speculated.

"Who fuckin' knows?"

It was a hot day, a boiling day, a goddam sweltering, semitropical, typically humid New Orleans summer day with no breeze and an angry sun raining down on them like a heat lamp on steroids.

"Jesus," Jodie moaned, pulling her sticky shirt away from her wet neck, "no more days, okay?"

He nodded wearily. A minute later he said, "Jesus, I just hope the son-of-a-bitch doesn't swap cars on us."

They knocked off early.

LaStanza found Lizette sitting in a lawn chair out back next to the Jacuzzi. She was in a garden dress, a thin, white cotton dress with nothing underneath. She looked almost cool beneath the overhang. She was sipping iced tea and reading a book called *The Wandering Daughter*.

She looked up and smiled when he opened the french doors. She leaned back and stretched. The full shape of her breasts pressed against the buttons on the front of her dress.

He moved behind her and began to rub her neck.

"Ohh, that feels good." She craned her head forward and closed the book.

"Book any good?" he asked.

"It's very good. It's a mystery. Set in New Orleans. You should read it."

"As if I don't have enough mysteries of my own."

She rolled her shoulders beneath his touch and then leaned back, her eyes closed, her face masked in pleasure.

"What happened to your thesis?" he asked.

"Finished it last week."

"Oh."

She smiled, her eyes still shut.

"I graduate in two weeks, mister. Then we're gonna spend some time together. Capish?" She peeked up at him and winked.

256

"Capish," he said.

All he had to do was catch Brooks in two weeks.

"You hungry?" she asked.

"Yeah. Get dressed. I'm taking you out, young lady."

She liked that.

He took a shower first to wash away the sweat and dirt of a frustrating summer day.

"I hope you're hungry," LaStanza told his wife a half hour later as they pulled up in front of Erede's Italian Restaurant on Canal Street, just below the cemeteries.

"As a matter of fact, I am," Lizette said as she climbed out of the passenger door of the burgundy Maserati. He'd made sure he parked directly in front of the restaurant's picture window, so he could keep an eye on the Maserati.

As soon as they entered the front door, they were approached by a large woman in an apron. Her arms open wide, the gray-haired woman bellowed, "Dino! *Caro mia!*"

It was Signora Erede in all of her overweight sweetness. She gave him a bear hug and rubbed her cheek against his face. Pulling back in embarrassment, the woman apologized for bowling him over and then asked, "How's your mom and 'em?"

"Fine."

The woman's beaming face revealed just how happy she was to see him. Looking at Lizette, the signora took a hesitant step back and asked, "And who's this?"

"This is my wife, Lizette." Dino grabbed Lizette's hand. Nodding forward, he said, "And this is Signora Erede."

"*Si*, I'm Dino's other mother." With her hands on her hips, Erede appraised Lizette up and down and then concluded, "Oh, *bella!* She's darling, Dino. You sure gonna have beautiful babies."

Erede reached over and patted Lizette gently on the

257

stomach and said, "You're not a mama yet, huh?"

"No." Lizette linked her arms around Dino's right arm and added, "Not yet."

"Now," Signora Erede said, ushering them toward the rear, "I have a special table . . ."

"We'd rather sit up here," Dino said as he pulled a chair out for Lizette.

"All right. All right. *Testa dura!*" the old woman teased. "You sit right here and I'll bring you something special."

He had a clear view of the Maserati.

"What's *'testa dura'* mean?" Lizette asked after the woman departed.

"Hard head."

"She knows you." Lizette grinned. She had let her hair hang loose and free and had thrown on one of his dress shirts over blue jeans. There was hardly a hint of makeup on her face, but she looked lovely, especially under the amber lights of the old-style family restaurant.

Dino liked this place a lot. When he was a boy, it had been almost a part of his house, back when the Eredes lived down the street from his parents' house, before the Eredes moved to a house uptown. Signora Erede had no children. The LaStanza boys were her children, especially Joe. Dino's older brother had not only been his mother's favorite, he'd been everyone's favorite, including Dino's.

Red checkered tablecloths covered the small, round tables. There was a bar, separated from the dining area by a brick wall topped with latticework. Dino's father spent many a night at that particular bar. Lizette's gold-brown eyes shined like topaz in the yellow light.

They dined on tortellini, followed by cheese lasagna, beef ravioli and deep red Valpolicella vino from the Bolla vineyards outside Verona. Signora Erede left them alone, although he saw the woman peeking at him from behind the latticework. Each time, she smiled a warm smile that told him again how much it meant to her to see him.

Signora Erede tried to push dessert on them.

"Oh, no, we're stuffed," he complained.

"It was delicious," Lizette said.

Then Erede refused to let him pay.

"I'll just leave it for the waitress."

Erede scooped up the forty dollars and returned with his change. He asked if she would sit with them over coffee, and the woman's eyes lit up. Sitting like a new customer, she called to the waitress to bring three cappuccinos.

She became quiet, sitting across from them at the small table, a perpetual smile plastered to her lined face. Then, in a low voice, she began to tell Lizette stories of the LaStanza boys. She told the story of how Dino became locked in Odd Fellow's Rest Cemetery after midnight and about the time Dino ran away from home, only to be found sleeping in a closet.

Before they left, the signora hugged Lizette and then hugged Dino especially hard. "Come back and see me sometime, *Caro mia,*" she added as they left.

"What happened to her husband?" Lizette asked as soon as they were out of earshot.

"Cancer."

"Oh."

At least the Maserati was still there. Lizette became especially quiet on the way home. By the time they pulled up at the mansion, she had a look on her face that he had to investigate.

"What is it?"

She waited until they were inside. In their kitchen, as she prepared hot chocolate, with him leaning against the counter, she said, "You know, I hate this part worst of all."

He knew what she meant.

"Every time you get close to catching a killer, there's always a wait, and it gets to me." Her voice was strained. "I wish you would just get it over with."

"I'm working on it."

He reached over and ran his hand down her back to her waist and left it there. She turned her golden eyes to him and said, "I'm not really brave, you know."

That night he dreamed of the batture once again, of a midnight fog that covered the land like a veil of red death. There were bodies on the batture. Scarlet stained the grassy levee along the lower coast of a slumbering city. He dreamed of an ebony clock that went out and flames like a thief in the night and of darkness and decay. He dreamed of the batture once again. Fog covered the land like a veil.

Seventeen
Simon Bolivar Avenue

A brown Oldsmobile was parked in the thirteen hundred block of Simon Bolivar Avenue, directly across from the Melpomene Housing Project high rise. LaStanza slowed the Ford as they passed.

"That's it!" Jodie snapped excitedly as both recognized the license plate number.

LaStanza nodded and continued on before making a U-turn through the neutral ground to double back. Jodie called Mark on the radio right away with the news. As their sergeant acknowledged the transmission, his own voice rising with excitement, Paul Snowood and Felicity Jones came on the air to say they were en route.

LaStanza found a spot in the fourteen hundred block and parked behind the Oldsmobile. He killed the engine, turned off the lights and rolled his window down the rest of the way and waited. Jodie sank as far down in the seat as she could and called in a Code 5 with Headquarters, alerting them to the stakeout. When she finished, she put the radio in her lap and unsnapped the hammer snap on her shoulder holster, withdrawing her nickel-plated Smith and Wesson .357.

Jodie squirmed in the seat, rubbing her back with her free hand.

"You okay?" he asked.

"This goddam shoulder rig kills my back."

"Oh." It took her long enough to find out.

LaStanza's magnum was already in his hand, resting against the side of his right leg.

"You put those magnum loads back in?" she asked in a hoarse whisper.

"Abso-fuckin'-lutely."

It was against departmental regulations to have magnum rounds in your gun. Only .38 ammo was authorized. With a hot load, you might miss and kill a pain-in-the-ass innocent bystander or two. LaStanza didn't worry about regulations. He never missed. Anyway, if he shot one more person, he'd be a gelding.

"Well," she said a minute later, "you were right about Simon Bolivar."

He nodded slightly but kept his eyes trained on the Oldsmobile and the area surrounding the parked car. He felt no satisfaction in coming up with the latest lead, even if it was the one that finally worked. He was too focused on the job at hand to linger on the fact that he had found something in the police computer that pointed them in the right direction. He had found that Sandy Courane had been arrested three times in the thirteen hundred block of Simon Bolivar for turning tricks. Sometimes, a little luck went a long way.

Nine minutes later, Mark's white Ford pulled up across Simon Bolivar, stopping directly in front of the Melpomene high rise.

"I see it," the sergeant grunted on the radio.

A minute later, Snowood and Fel drove slowly past LaStanza's position before settling in a spot in the twelve hundred block, on the other side of the Oldsmobile.

Glancing at his watch, LaStanza noted it was exactly eleven P.M. Traffic was still heavy on Simon Bolivar. Pedestrian traffic wasn't as heavy on their side of the street. Outside the high rise, where Mark was parked, there were enough people to call an election.

Eight long minutes later, Mark came back on the air.

"Looks like there's an abandoned car two cars behind the Olds. See it?"

LaStanza leaned out his window to take a look. There was a black Pontiac Bonneville, about a '68 or '69 model, parked behind the Pinto parked behind the Olds. He could see its back window was gone as were both tires on the driver's side, the street side of the car.

"Cover me," he told his partner as he started to get out. Hesitating a moment, he looked back at her and added, "Don't just keep an eye on me. Capish? Keep an eye around here. Don't let anyone sneak up on you."

Her cat eyes were glued to his, as if she was about to say goodbye. She blinked and let a slight smile crawl across her nervous lips. He nodded, turned and climbed out.

With is radio in his left hand and his magnum held against his right thigh, LaStanza moved steadily along the parked cars, crossing the narrow expanse of Thalia Street to the Bonneville. Shards of broken glass surrounded the car, along with shattered wine bottles, twisted beer cans and a blackened banana peel.

The windshield was the only glass left on the car, and it had several long splits across it. Pausing momentarily to make certain nothing alive was inside the car, LaStanza noticed more refuse littering the seats.

He opened the rear door. It popped on rusty hinges. He quickly slipped into the backseat, closing the door behind him. He rested the back of his head against the door he'd just entered and sprawled out across the floorboard. His vision was limited to the sidewalk side of the car. He called Mark and told him.

"10-4," his sergeant responded, "I'll let you know if anyone approaches."

"10-4."

Damn, he had to readjust himself three times immediately to remove a Coke can, an ashtray and the base of a desk lamp from under his backside. *Damn again,* he thought, settling back on the sticky floor. He'd just given Jodie a speech about partners not separating, and look where he was.

"Never split up," he'd told her earlier, as they cruised. "Whatever happens to your partner, better happen to you."

She had agreed. Except now she was a half block away.

Sucking in a deep breath, he was nearly gagged by the stink inside the car. He didn't even want to know what it was. It smelled too bad.

He cracked open the door on the street side to let in more air and to leave him a quick exit when the time came. Only it didn't come. It just got hotter and stickier in the confines of the dead Pontiac. The wait was gruelling. Besides the stench and the filth, the car was an oven, a sweltering steamer, a pit where no air entered. It plastered his tee shirt against his chest and sent rivulets of sweat down his back and wrinkled his hands into the hands of an old man. He thanked God he wore jeans. He thanked God even more that he had rubber grips on his revolver.

With his radio turned down low and pressed against his left ear, he waited. Cars zoomed by outside, as if in another world. Occasionally a pedestrian would stroll by, but no one even looked in at him; and Mark never called, so there was no danger and no Brooks.

The minutes stretched by like taffy dripping from a Salvador Dali clock. Blinking sweat from his overheated eyes, La-Stanza concentrated with all his might on what he could see outside and hear on the radio cradled in his damp hand.

Then the word "gelding" crept into his mind, and he flushed it away quickly. Readjusting himself, he glanced at his watch. It was now five minutes until one in the morning. He sucked in another breath of superheated air and reminded himself of the old Sicilian saying his father had put on him when he was pursuing the Twenty-two Killer.

"Ice in the veins," he told himself over and over again and tried his best to control his breathing. There was no way to control his racing heart. And the minutes dragged on.

When Mark's voice came on the radio, he nearly hit the roof of the Bonneville.

"I think that's him," Mark whispered over the air.

LaStanza held his breath and waited for the longest seconds of his life to pass.

Come on!

"Okay," Mark said again, this time a little louder, "we got Brooks coming out of the house right next to his car. He's in a white shirt and dark pants, and he's moving to his car now."

LaStanza listened for footsteps. A car passed so close it rocked the Bonneville. His heart pounding hard, his face reddening in anticipation, he held back and waited for Mark. *Come on, you son-of-a-bitch,* he was thinking, his teeth grinding so hard his jaw ached.

Then he heard it.

"NOW!"

LaStanza moved quickly and silently. Rising and opening the door at the same time, he had one foot on the pavement as he caught sight of Brooks climbing into the driver's seat of the Oldsmobile.

Before Brooks could close the door, LaStanza was on him, jamming the muzzle of his .357 magnum against the man's jugular vein and growling, "Freeze!"

The man's eyes bulged at him as he tried to pull away.

LaStanza cocked the magnum and screamed, "POLICE!"

Brooks froze.

"Hands against the windshield! NOW!"

The man reached forward slowly and placed his palms against the windshield. His eyes were riveted to LaStanza's in a lingering, unblinking stare. There was fear in those eyes. LaStanza knew, for certain, that there was blood in his own eyes. He heard Jodie running up behind him. He also heard screeching tires and the sudden blare of a siren and whooper as the other two police cars tore around a mad dash.

"Open your mouth!" LaStanza told Brooks.

The man hesitated.

"OPEN YOUR FUCKIN' MOUTH!"

Brooks obliged, and LaStanza shoved the magnum into the open mouth.

"Now close it!"

Brooks' lips sealed around the muzzle of LaStanza's gun.

"Now, follow me out the car!" LaStanza inched backward with the man following the magnum.

Jodie was in perfect position. She opened the door, reached in and slapped a cuff on Brooks' left wrist. Then, as the man slowly exited the car, she pulled the arms behind him and cuffed the right wrist.

Only then did LaStanza tell Brooks to open his mouth so that the magnum could be withdrawn. Jodie shoved Brooks around the open door to the hood of the Olds and laid him facedown on the hood. She began to search him as Mark's car screeched to a halt behind them at the same time Snowood's car slid up from the wrong way on Simon Bolivar.

Jodie found a .38 tucked in the waistband of Brooks' pants. Jerking it out, she passed it to LaStanza, who tucked it into his back pocket.

LaStanza wiped the muzzle of his own gun on the back of Brooks' shirt before reholstering it. Then he leaned forward and yanked at the hair on the back of the man's head and began reciting the ritualistic dogma of police work.

"All right, Fuck Head, you have the right to remain silent . . ."

His heart was still pounding, and he knew that the blood in his veins was anything but ice. A crowd quickly collected around them. He could hear Snowood calling for a marked unit. The street lights seemed to brighten in the excitement. LaStanza looked at his watch and saw it was two in the morning of a simmering summer morning in the big city, with kids edging forward to watch grown men with guns and radios, and a blond woman with her own gun and radio, holding a killer against the hood of a brown Oldsmobile.

266

Mark began barking orders. He told Snowood to jot down a description of Brooks' house for a search warrant. He assigned Jodie to search the Oldsmobile.

"I'll sit tight with Jodie," he told LaStanza. "Soon as you get the search warrant, send Snowood back here and we'll search the house."

Two Sixth District units came flying up, blue lights splattering across the dark night, sirens wailing like banshees. LaStanza and Snowood each grabbed an arm and led Sam Brooks from the Oldsmobile to Snowood's Ford. Brooks was so big, he even towered over Snowood.

Glancing back, LaStanza caught Jodie's eye and winked at her. She smiled back and said, "Fuckin'-A!"

"What about me?" LaStanza heard Fel Jones ask Mark.

"Talk to these people," Mark said, waving his hand at the gathering crowd.

Brooks wouldn't talk to LaStanza. He wouldn't talk to Snowood. Seated in the chair next to LaStanza's desk, he set his square jaw and rolled his eyes away from their peering stares. He was light skinned all right, with a wide face, a flat nose and big lips. His face looked extra large, especially with the receding front hairline.

He surprised LaStanza a minute later when he said, "I'll talk to Blondie."

LaStanza's eyebrows rose.

"Yeah, she's got a nice ass." Brooks lowered his voice in adding, "I seen her around. With you."

LaStanza had never hit a man in handcuffs before. So he put Brooks in an interview room before he broke that tradition.

"Yeah, Blondie's just my style," Brooks said defiantly as they closed the door on him. His evil smile was dotted by a gold front tooth, just as Abby Marshall had described.

Snowood was already busy cutting the search warrant for

Brooks' house. LaStanza mixed up a fresh pot of coffee. Then he called Lizette.

It was a quarter until three in the morning, and she was asleep. "Yeah," she said in a groggy voice.

"It's over. We got him."

"Oh!" Her voice rose. "Good. I'm glad you called."

"Now go back to sleep."

"Wait. What time is it?"

He told her as he kicked his feet up on his desk.

"Everybody okay?" she asked.

"Sure. Mark and Jodie are searching his car. Paul's typing a search warrant and I've got my feet up on the desk."

"What about Fel?"

"He's talking to his brothers."

He could hear Lizette yawning. When she finished, she had another question, "Was Brooks a wimp?"

"Naw. He just french kissed my magnum."

"Dino, you didn't stick your gun in somebody's mouth again." She sounded like mother superior.

"Sure did."

She yawned again.

"Guess what he wants?"

"Huh?"

"He wants to talk to Jodie."

Lizette let out a hollow, "Wow!"

He called Bunny next. She was harder to wake up but became so excited he had a hard time getting her off the phone.

He wrote a note to himself to call the Camp family in the morning and the Dillards family, too, even if they didn't give a fuck about their daughter. Then he'd call Mrs. Roberts on Constance Street. Tomorrow, he'd put in a call to Hot Coffee, Mississippi, and talk to Cherry. He'd also call Los Angeles for Abby. He'd leave Marid Ahbhu, the French-Algerian, to Jodie.

When he pulled his feet off the desk, a piece of paper followed and fell to the floor. It was another phone message from

Mr. Clark of the Lower Coast. LaStanza picked up his receiver to call the old fool.

Jodie entered at that moment, and he hung up before dialing. Covered in sweat, her hair partially matted against her head, she certainly did not look fresh and crisp anymore. She was smiling like a Cheshire cat.

She dropped her briefcase on her desk and held up a plastic bag with something in it. He leaned over and looked. It was a button. His eyes lit up.

She was nodding. "It's the one from Margaret Leake's skirt."

It looked like it to LaStanza.

"I already went by the lab. It's *identical,*" Jodie said.

"Where'd you find it?" He sat back down.

"Under the front seat. And that ain't all. We found blood in the backseat and the trunk."

He jumped up and almost hugged her.

"That's fuckin' *great!*" God, he wanted to slap her on the back. He settled for slapping the top of his desk.

Jodie was rolling, too. He knew he had to bring her down fast.

"Sit down," he told her.

"Huh?"

"Brooks wants to talk to *you.*"

She sat down.

"I got some suggestions," he told her. "But this one's yours, padna. He's all yours."

LaStanza let it sink in a couple seconds before continuing. "You can try the direct approach. 'I know you did it. You know you did it. You wanna lie? Go ahead.' Or you can try pride. 'Hey, that was the hardest murder to solve. You're smart.' Or you can tell him he made a big mistake and then don't tell him what it was. Let him sweat. Or you can tell him to be a man and face up to it. Or you might wanna walk in and sit down, cross your arms and just stare at him and then say, 'Well?'"

Jodie liked that one.

"Okay," LaStanza was far from finished, "if he stares you back in the eye, he's not afraid, but don't let that put you off. If he crosses his arms, that's a defensive move. If he lowers his head, he's falling."

Jodie was taking notes now.

"Remember," he said, trying to slow down, "take a separate confession for each murder."

Then he reached into his briefcase and pulled out his new tape recorder and handed her three cassettes. "You need anything else," he added, "call me on the intercom."

"Anything else I need to know?" she asked, her face masked in nervous confusion.

"Yeah," he said with a smile, "go get him, partner."

There was no need to tell her how important the confessions were. She had to know.

Rising, he told her, "Keep him cuffed. Behind his back. And keep your gun on your hip. If he starts anything, shoot him in the head. Twice. Fucker's already killed three women. You hear me?"

"Yeah."

She paused just outside the door and closed her eyes. He let her collect her thoughts. Then she went in. He leaned against the door and listened. He heard a chair moving and then silence for a long time until, finally, Jodie said, "Well?"

Brooks' reply was too muffled to hear. But the voices continued, so LaStanza moved to the coffeepot and poured a cup into the FUCK THIS SHIT mug before returning to his desk.

He remembered his first whodunit, how the Slasher would only talk to him and not Mark. He remembered how he had felt facing the monster one on one and taking the confessions of probably the most important murder case he would ever handle. He'd been a rookie dick then, just like Jodie. She would be all right.

He kicked his feet up on his desk and tried to relax his mind. It was then he noticed Snowood was gone, probably en route to the judge's to get the warrant signed. LaStanza was alone in the wide squad room. He took a sip of coffee, cradled the mug between his hands resting in his lap and closed his eyes.

He let his mind roam back to the batture, to the water and the levee, to a tranquil scene of Acadian girls who looked like Lizette. Then he envisioned the bodies. He wanted to think of the bodies, of the Pam known as Slow and her new black boots, of the Pam known as Fawn and the five-point star on her gold tooth and of Margaret Leake and her torn mauve skirt. He wanted to recall every detail, the mud, the heat, the strains of Reverend Stokes' deep voice echoing "Amazing Grace" through the projects.

Opening his eyes, he put the mug on his desk and grabbed his pen and wrote himself a note. Usually a homicide man wasn't as concerned with "why" as much as "who," "what," "when," "where" and especially "how." "Why" was what sold mysteries to civilians who never saw a dead body that wasn't in a casket. But now, now that it was nearly over, he wanted to know why, why that spot.

When the phone rang three quarters of an hour after Jodie went into the interview room, LaStanza answered quickly. It was Mark. He was calling from the killer's house.

"Guess what I found?" the sergeant quipped.

"Surprise me."

"A Beretta .22 caliber, Model 21, blue steel with black plastic grip."

"That's got to be it," LaStanza said.

"Let's hope so." Mark let out a sigh before adding, "We also found a shit load of pictures of girls from magazines."

"Porno?"

"Some. But most have undergarments on. Mostly red."

"Red panties?" LaStanza sat up.

"Yep."

"Take them."

"I already have."

Mark told him they'd be finished shortly and then hung up.

Red. Red panties. How had Bunny put it? "Sam's fruit for red panties." Sam used to have her put on red panties, and he'd get hot, tear them off and hurt her. Margaret Leake wore red panties on the night she died. Her killer ripped them. Jesus! It was all fitting together like a fuckin' jigsaw puzzle.

LaStanza picked up the phone and called the Fourth District. When a patrolman named Curtis answered, he asked if Kelly was working that night.

"No, he's off."

"Look, I need his home number. This is LaStanza. Homicide."

"Sure. Is it important?"

"Everything I do is important," LaStanza said and started laughing right away. "I'm just kiddin' ya. It's not important. I'd just like to talk to him. Okay?"

"Sure."

Kelly must have been in a dead sleep. His phone rang ten times before he answered.

"What ya doing?" LaStanza asked.

"Sleeping."

"You wanna meet the Batture Murderer?"

"You kiddin' me?"

LaStanza could see the man sit up in bed.

"Nope. He's right up here in the office. Take your time and come on over and I'll introduce you."

"YEAH!"

Then LaStanza called Mr. Clark. The old man sounded as if he was already awake.

"Glad you called," Clark said, clearing his throat. "I got an idea. This may sound screwy."

Oh, no!

"Ever hear of Che Guevara?"

LaStanza put a hand over the receiver so that the old man couldn't hear him laughing.

"Are you laughing at me?" the man said.

A hand over the receiver didn't work.

"Mr. Clark," LaStanza explained, "we caught the killer. He's sitting twenty feet from me right now. It's all over."

"Was he Cuban?" The old man was in a foul mood now.

"No, we think he's Venusian."

"What's that?"

LaStanza bit his lip so that he wouldn't laugh again. "It's kinda complicated," he told the old man. "Look it up. It's in the dictionary." He spelled the word for Clark.

"Venusian," Clark repeated before hanging up.

LaStanza stared at the receiver as a dial tone replaced the angry voice. Then he shouted, "It means the mother-fucker is from Venus! That's right. The fuckin' planet!"

He fought the urge and hung up the receiver without slamming it. He looked at the clock on the wall. It was after four now.

Stretching and rolling his neck around in a slow circle, he caught sight of an envelope in his IN tray. He picked up the envelope and pulled out the sheet within. Leaning back in his chair, he read the contents again, aloud, to the empty room. It was a note sent to him by Stan Smith.

"This has been posted in the Sixth District Hall of Shame."
There once was a fancy dress cop
Who forgot that he was a wop
He parked his Italian sports car
Near a Jackson Avenue bar
AND THE NIGGERS STOLE IT!

Stan was such a fuckin' asshole, but LaStanza figured he deserved that note. Abso-fuckin'-lutely.

Kelly entered as he was going for a refill of coffee. Eager and excited, the tall patrolman looked even younger in a muscle shirt and blue jeans. Son-of-a-gun had a better build on him than most of the New Orleans Saints; then again, so did most people.

273

Wide eyed and eager, Kelly wanted to know the whole story. LaStanza raised a hand in protest and passed Kelly the dailies.

"Read these first."

As Kelly was reading, Bob Kay waltzed into the squad room. Wearing a sweaty gray jogging suit with an N.O.P.D. gym logo on its front, Kay sported a fresh crew cut. The man's glasses were secured to his oval head by a wide red, elastic band that made him look more like a Cherokee than a police lieutenant.

Nodding as he arrived at LaStanza's desk, Kay caught his breath before stating, "Word's out that you got a triple murderer up here."

"Where'd you hear that?"

"Police garage," Kay panted, winking at the same time. "It's the talk of the town."

"We got the Batture Killer."

"Who?"

"The whores on the levee," LaStanza gave him a hint.

"Oh, yeah." Kay looked around the empty room.

"My partner's interviewing him in there." LaStanza pointed to the small interview room door.

"Kintyre?"

"Yep."

"Outstanding!" When the big man smiled, his entire face broke open. He always liked Jodie. He was nodding again as he added, "She'll break it off in his ass."

With that last remark, Kay turned to leave, but only after patting Kelly on the shoulder and winking again at LaStanza and leaving them with a goodbye, "Brother."

LaStanza wondered when the man ever slept.

Kelly was still reading a minute later when another lieutenant entered the squad room. This time it was William Fredericks, commander of Burglary. Almost as tall as Kay, Fredericks was much older but just as friendly. He was a contemporary of LaStanza's father, in fact, actually partnered with the old man back in the good-ole-bad-ole days. Fredericks wore bifocals and a gray toupee atop his bald head. That morning, he had a Rip Van Winkle look on his face as if he'd just been yanked out of a hundred-year sleep.

Acknowledging Kelly's presence, Fredericks greeted LaStanza with a, "Hello, son. I understand you have Sam Brooks up here."

Jesus, the fucking *Picayune* wouldn't be out for hours, but every cop in town already knew.

"Sure do."

"I don't know how much you know about Brooks, but he's been my main snitch—" Fredericks paused for emphasis before continuing, "for quite a while."

LaStanza felt his eyes kick into Sicilian. They narrowed and did not blink. In the back of his mind a flag was waving. No wonder Brooks never did any time.

Fredericks got straight to the point. "Can you cut him some slack?"

LaStanza almost laughed in the man's face. Shaking his head slowly, he answered, "Not really, Will. We're talking about murder." He was trying to be nice, but his heart wasn't in it.

Fredericks tried a fatherly smile and said, "I know you can't just let him go, but can you give him any kinda break?"

"Not a fuckin' inch."

LaStanza's voice must have been a little too sharp. He saw the lieutenant recoil a bit before reaching for the nearest chair to pull up next to LaStanza's desk.

Fredericks kept his voice low and soft as he said, "Aren't we talking about two nigger whores?"

"And a white woman, not that it makes a fuckin' difference."

"I didn't know that." It made a difference to Fredericks.

LaStanza felt his stomach twitching. The flag was waving madly now, and he figured it out, suddenly.

"You knew about the two whores, didn't you?" LaStanza asked his father's old partner.

275

Fredericks didn't answer. He didn't have to. It was in his eyes. The bastard.

LaStanza leaned toward the lieutenant. He tried to keep his voice under control when he said, "Why didn't you just come and tell me?"

Fredericks didn't answer. He leaned back and looked at LaStanza as if someone had just spit in his face. The old man blinked twice and started to speak. "Son —"

LaStanza sawed him off with, "Don't call me 'son.' "

Fredericks got hot. Huffing, he started up again with, "Your father and I —"

"I'm gonna say this one time," LaStanza snarled, his fingers digging into the arms of his beat-up chair. "Get the fuck away from me!"

Eighteen
Hollywood Walk

Mark arrived just as Jodie opened the door and came out of the interview room with Brooks. They both looked a mess. Jodie's makeup had worn off. Her eyes looked puffy. Her hair looked matted and tired.

Brooks looked as if he'd just been in a brain torture chamber. His hair was sticking straight out. His eyes looked red and sunken, and he was bouncing in place, his large arms still manacled behind with Jodie's handcuffs.

"He's got to go to the bathroom," Jodie announced the obvious.

Kelly took Brooks to the men's room. Jodie, as soon as she noticed Kelly, stepped back in embarrassment, smiling faintly and running a hesitant hand down the sides of her hair.

When Kelly and Brooks were out of earshot, LaStanza and Mark started talking at the same time, but Jodie shook them off, declaring she had to go to the ladies' room.

"I'll be back in a second."

Mark put the paper bags he was carrying on LaStanza's desk and excused himself. He had to go, too.

"What's in here?" LaStanza called out behind the retreating sergeant, a hand over the bags.

"Just wait a minute!"

Mark looked worse than any of them, now that LaStanza noticed. He looked like an unmade bed most of the time anyway, but that evening he looked like a skid row mattress. The only way to describe the state of Mark's hair was . . . Harpo Marx. His clothes looked like a dump site.

Jodie rushed back in before any of the others. She looked weary, and her voice was a touch on the hoarse side; but there was no hiding her glee.

"I got an inculpatory on the double 30," she said, looking into LaStanza's eyes, a wide smile on her face. "But he won't bone up to the Batture Again."

She looked back over her shoulder to make sure they were still alone before adding, "I think he's ashamed of that one."

"Good. You're gonna work on it, right?"

She turned back with an, "Of course."

"You need anything in there?"

"No." Her brow furrowed as she asked, "How did Kelly get here?"

"I called him."

"Thanks." She put a hand on her hip and gave him a good stare.

Jesus, he hadn't thought. He shrugged and half smiled and said, "Better worry about Brooks."

"I got him," she explained, her voice dropping an octave.

"You got him by the balls," LaStanza said. "Typical fuckin' criminal idiot. Confesses to a crime that'll send him to the chair but not to a sex crime."

In Louisiana, if you murdered more than one person at the same time, it was first-degree murder, and therefore a capital crime, qualifying for the ultimate prize, the electric chair. Kill someone above the age of twelve, who wasn't a policeman or fireman engaged in their lawful duties, and it was not a capital case. It was second-degree murder.

The only way to pin a first-degree murder rap on Brooks for the Batture Again would be to prove he had specific intent to kill or inflict great bodily harm and was engaged in the perpetration of one of several qualifying felonies: aggravated kidnapping, aggravated escape, aggravated arson, aggravated rape, aggravated burglary, armed robbery, or simple robbery.

LaStanza wanted that. He wanted it all. Reaching into his briefcase, he withdrew the plastic bag containing the button Jodie had found in the Oldsmobile. He had an idea.

"If he stays cagy, call me in and I'll show him this and then walk out."

"Then I'll hit him with it, right?"

"Right between the eyes."

Kelly came back in with Brooks, followed by Mark, who still looked like the walking dead. Jodie asked Kelly to put Brooks back in the interview room. When the killer was behind the closed door, Jodie and LaStanza asked Mark for the scoop on the apartment search.

LaStanza liked the pictures of the women in red drawers best of all. They were cut out of magazines. Jodie glanced at them before turning her attention to the .22 Beretta.

"Firearms man'll be in at five," Mark explained, fighting back a yawn, "and we'll compare it ASAP."

"Good."

Jodie took in a deep breath and started back for the interview room.

"Wait up," LaStanza said, showing her a picture of a blond-haired girl in a red and black bra and matching panties.

"See the edge?" He pointed the bottom end of the picture at her. There were teeth marks along the bottom of the page, as if someone had gnawed on it.

"Yuk," Jodie said in a near whisper.

"Interesting," LaStanza said. "I bet those dried marks on some of the others is semen."

"ECK!" Jodie said.

Mark headed back to the bathroom to wash his hands again. LaStanza joined him, but only after reminding Jodie to buzz when she needed him to enter with the button.

Kelly was at the coffee table when they returned. LaStanza

279

went to his desk and dialed directory assistance to get George Lynn's home phone number. Lynn woke after the ninth ring.

"It's me, LaStanza."

"Huh?"

"You wanna scoop the TV stations?"

"Oh, yeah."

"We got the Batture Killer here at the office. Get a cameraman ready. When we're ready for the Hollywood Walk, I'll call you back, and you can get it all. I'll even type up a memo for you on it."

"Sure. Yeah. Thanks!"

"Anytime."

Snowood and Fel entered at that point, looking as if they had been trudging through a swamp. Fel looked up at the clock and moaned, "Look at the time. And I had a date!"

Snowood, brown saliva dripping from the corners of his mouth, gave LaStanza a long, disgusted look. He spit a huge wad of crappy tobacco into the wastebasket next to LaStanza's desk. Wiping the residue of brown shit from his moustache on the sleeve of his shirt, Snowood cleared his throat and then drawled, "I'm real disappointed in you, Wyatt."

LaStanza grinned up at the man, knowing an explanation would follow. Snowood did not let him down.

"You catch a triple murderer. With a gun on him. And you don't shoot him. Mighty disappointing."

"I'm leaving," Fel said as he wheeled and walked out.

"Yeah," Snowood drawled again, "I think I'll mosey on outta here, too. I'll bet Bill Hickock and Wyatt Earp are both spinnin' in their graves tonight." The man in the soiled cowpoke outfit turned and moseyed out of the squad room, leaving tiny drops of brown in his wake.

At five, Mark headed for the crime lab with the Beretta. LaStanza passed him the .38 they'd taken off Brooks to compare against the pellets from any unsolved murders.

Jodie buzzed LaStanza on the intercom ten minutes later. He scooped up the plastic bag and headed for the interview room.

Jodie was standing and stretching and didn't even look at LaStanza. Brooks was seated in the room's uncomfortable folding chair. He was leaning forward, as a man who was used to wearing handcuffs would do to relieve the pressure on his wrists. Brooks glared at LaStanza, his nostrils flaring.

"He bone up to Batture Again?" LaStanza asked.

"Nope."

"Guess he don't have the balls to admit that one."

Brooks puffed his chest out in defiance but said nothing.

LaStanza had the bag behind his back. He pulled it around and showed it to Jodie. Grinning, he said, "This button you found in good ole Sammy's car, it's identical to the button missing from Margaret Leake's skirt. And the blood in the trunk matched, too. You can tell him we're booking him with her murder anyway. We don't need a confession. Let him explain to the jury how her button and blood got in his trunk."

Leaning over, he whispered in his partner's ear, "Remember the red panties."

Jodie nodded.

"And then," LaStanza added in an even quieter whisper, "break it off in his ass."

Then he walked out.

He went straight for the coffee table and fixed up another pot. He was beginning to feel the exhaustion, but fought it. He made this batch of coffee extra strong. Then he joined Kelly at his desk and waited.

He was listening to his own breathing when Mark came clattering in, dragging his feet like a little boy. Mark looked even worse. He barely made it to Jodie's chair before falling into it. Focusing a pair of bloodshot eyes on LaStanza, Mark said, "Bingo. The Beretta's your murder weapon, all right."

LaStanza was too tired to applaud. He just nodded and waited. He kicked his feet up on his desk. Kelly followed suit.

Mark did the same on Jodie's desk.

When Jodie finally came out, sunlight was creeping into the squad room. Kelly was sleeping. Mark was snoring so loud, he'd prevented LaStanza from dozing off. Jodie stepped up briskly, tapped her partner on the shoulder and handed him three cassettes and a host of Miranda Rights forms.

He looked up at her. She was beaming.

"He didn't want to be listed as a sex criminal," she said.

"Inculpatory?"

"Confessed to it all," she said.

He could see she was too excited to sit.

"Says he was all fucked up when he picked up Margaret Leake. She was walking down Prytania. She said she needed a ride. He figured what she needed was a man."

Jodie started for the coffeepot.

"Then what'd he say?" LaStanza was standing now and trying to stretch.

"He took her to the warehouse district and did her there. Says he can't remember how it happened. He blanked out. She just died. He put her in the trunk and took her to the Lower Coast."

"Blanked out?"

"He said he saw red."

LaStanza joined his partner next to the coffee table.

"I asked about the red panties, and he wouldn't admit it, even when I told him I always wear red panties. He started sweating and breathing hard, but he wouldn't admit it."

"Told him you had red ones on?" LaStanza liked that touch.

"Yep. He looked like I poured itching powder on him."

"Did he tell you why he chose that spot on the batture?"

"No."

The coffee was burnt, so they left it. Before returning to the interview room, LaStanza grabbed the eighteen-inch ruler from his desk and then called Lynn and told the reporter to be along Hollywood Walk in a half hour.

Brooks was standing in the corner of the room and immediately complained about the cuffs.

"They're too tight, man!"

LaStanza checked them. "They're not too tight," he said, "quit twisting your hands around."

He lifted Brooks' left foot, untied the man's shoe and pulled it off. Then he withdrew the ruler from his back pocket and measured the foot. Twelve inches exactly. He smiled to himself.

Brooks was giving LaStanza the hard stare now. Real tough-guy look.

"You think you smart putting that gun in my mouth. I'd like to get you one on one, alone."

"Yeah? Well, you're gonna be a little tied up for a while." LaStanza didn't return the hard stare. He had something else on his mind.

He looked at his partner and said, "Did you tell him how he had us?"

Jodie played along and shrugged.

"Did you tell him that we couldn't figure out why he picked that spot on the batture?"

He looked back at Brooks, who took the opportunity to say, "It was the end of the road, man. Get it?"

Mark was awake now, standing with Kelly and several other dicks and a couple patrolmen who came in to take a look at the newest exhibit in the New Orleans criminal zoo.

Jodie led the way into the squad room, followed by Brooks and LaStanza. Mark caught LaStanza's eye and pointed to Mason's office.

"He wants to see you."

LaStanza left Jodie with the ever-growing entourage. He found Mason on the phone. The lieutenant was laughing through a gray cloud. When LaStanza entered, Mason pointed to the chair in front of his desk and then handed the phone to him and said, "It's your wife."

Lizette was still laughing on the other end.

"Hello," he said.

She quieted enough to say, "Hey, babe."

"So, what's so funny?" he asked, watching Mason remove his blue blazer and hang it behind the door.

"Your lieutenant was just telling me you still have two weeks of vacation time on the books." Her voice had a mischievous tone to it.

"Yeah?"

"Yeah. And right after my graduation, we're gonna use them up, okay?"

"Okay." A second later, he asked, "Where're we going?"

"It's a surprise."

She was having such a good time with this, he hated to hang up.

"Um," he said.

She took the hint.

"You're kinda busy right now, huh?" She was having fun, putting him on.

"I only got a triple murderer to book. That's all."

"Then, I'll catch you later, hot shot."

"Yeah, bye."

"Ciao."

Mason was still chuckling, so LaStanza asked what was so funny.

"We were just laughing about how you got that Maserati stolen."

The men in Homicide called it Hollywood Walk, that short piece of White Street between Police Headquarters and Central Lockup, where prisoners were walked out in the open for the cameras. It was a location featured on the evening news nearly every day and on the front page of the Metro Section of the *Picayune,* just as often.

It was full daylight when LaStanza and Jodie escorted Brooks out of Headquarters. Kelly was right behind LaStanza, at the detectives' invitation. Lynn was waiting with a photographer. LaStanza eased to the rear, just as the cameraman stepped forward. When the strobe flashed, LaStanza was behind Brooks, completely out of sight.

"Thanks," Lynn said as LaStanza handed his old classmate the memo.

Jodie waited until they were out of earshot before asking, "Were you hiding?"

"I've been in the paper enough," he told her.

"Thanks," she said sarcastically.

"You're welcome. I even spelled your name right in the note."

"Thanks a whole lot."

Jodie would be the featured player in that photo, funky hair and all, her and the wide, ugly face of Sam Brooks.

"Spell my name right?" Brooks asked in an angry voice.

"Sure. Sam Mook Brooks."

"When I get out, I'm gonna get you!" Brooks craned his neck back at LaStanza and said, "You know that. I'm gonna kill you!"

LaStanza had to laugh. "You're gonna have to take a number and stand in line." Then he shoved Brooks through the front door of Central Lockup.

The Bureau was crowded with the rank and file when they returned. Jodie hesitated as she entered. LaStanza grabbed her arm and pulled her into the nearest interview room. She looked worn but was still on a natural high.

"What is it?" she asked.

"I just wanted to tell you," he said, "that getting those confessions was good work. Good police work." He quickly corrected himself, "No, it was good *detective* work."

She bounced on the balls of her feet, her face masked in a wide smile, her eyes shining back at him. She leaned forward, and he thought she was going to hug him.

He reached over and landed a light punch on her left shoulder. "Come on, partner, let's go celebrate."

He opened the door but paused a moment. Looking back at Jodie, he had to say it, just one more time: "Remember, in Homicide, you're only as good as your last case."